MW01043364

The
Oracle
of Y'alan

By A. A. Powley

Cover Design/Artwork by Susi Galloway

Order this book online at www.trafford.com/07-1994
or email orders@trafford.com

Most Trafford titles are also available at major online book retailers.

Note for Librarians: A cataloguing record for this book is available from Library
and Archives Canada at www.collectionscanada.ca/amicus/index-e.html

Printed in Victoria, BC, Canada.

ISBN: 978-1-4251-4659-7

*We at Trafford believe that it is the responsibility of us all, as both individuals
and corporations, to make choices that are environmentally and socially sound.
You, in turn, are supporting this responsible conduct each time you purchase a
Trafford book, or make use of our publishing services. To find out how you are
helping, please visit www.trafford.com/responsiblepublishing.html*

*Our mission is to efficiently provide the world's finest, most comprehensive
book publishing service, enabling every author to experience success.
To find out how to publish your book, your way, and have it available
worldwide, visit us online at www.trafford.com/10510*

 www.trafford.com

North America & international
toll-free: 1 888 232 4444 (USA & Canada)
phone: 250 383 6864 ♦ fax: 250 383 6804 ♦ email: info@trafford.com

The United Kingdom & Europe
phone: +44 (0)1865 722 113 ♦ local rate: 0845 230 9601
facsimile: +44 (0)1865 722 868 ♦ email: info.uk@trafford.com

10 9 8 7 6 5 4

To my sister, the comma master.

Prologue

(7000 years ago…)

"It's HOT!" the little girl complained. Her sleeveless powder-blue sundress clung to her body. The field of spindly grapevines offered no protection from the blazing noonday sun. On the horizon to the east, a crystal blue streak of ocean separated the earth and the sky.

"You've got that right," Vaughn replied, wiping his brow, "I'm drenched." The humidity was unbearable. His white robe was soaked, a by-product of his morning toils. He and his niece had spent their morning picking grapes and now had two overflowing baskets to show for their efforts.

"You can fix it, can't you, Uncle?"

Vaughn smiled. Drawing moisture out of one's clothes was an old trick, one that most novices mastered before even entering the academy. It was second nature to anyone who worked long hours outdoors in this humid climate or to anyone who did a lot of laundry.

"Very well," Vaughn replied. With a slight flourish of his hand, the air stirred with a cooling breeze. Droplets formed on the surface of their robes as moisture was wicked away from their skin and quickly evaporated, drying their drenched clothes. A brief mist formed around them, taming the blistering heat.

The little girl giggled with appreciation.

"Come, we should be getting back," said Vaughn.

"Already?" she protested.

"I'm afraid so, Princess. Come."

They each lifted a basket and headed south towards the Travel Arch. This branch of the Arch system was newly constructed. The Arches had once been the private domain of the government, and had linked only the farthest reaches of the empire, allowing citizens to travel instantaneously to their destinations. Now, the wealthy and the privileged were free to construct private Arches, such as the one connecting the island they were on to the capital. Even with these new gates, the capital city of Baurum'tatus remained the central hub of their rapidly growing society.

Vaughn looked down from the orchard hill and across the Straight of Opa toward the distant metropolis they called home. Baurum'tatus's white walls gleamed in the sun, a majestic home to humanity's greatest civilization. The image never ceased to inspire pride and fidelity in him.

Across the field, the Arch flashed suddenly, marking the transit of three Peacekeepers. Vaughn noticed they were wearing green and platinum robes with black trim, identifying them as part of the elite Royal Guard, solely responsible to the High Council.

Vaughn couldn't identify the approaching men in the glaring sunlight, but he wasn't alarmed. Keeping track of time was not his strong suit. Most likely he had missed an appointment and was being sent a reminder, or so he hoped. Royal Guardsmen weren't lightly used as messengers. *Best to play along.* He waved at them as they drew near.

"I'm sorry, my friend."

Vaughn recognized the voice before the face.

"I have orders from the council to place you and your colleague, Rolimus, under arrest," continued Leo. His two companions stopped behind him, waiting for instructions.

"What?" Vaughn was shocked. The indignity was unbearable. Never before had any sitting chancellor been accosted this way. "What's the meaning of this?"

"Chancellor, the Oracle is missing. The council demands an explanation! You are to return at once and stand before the Council or..."

At that moment a thin red line streaked into the heavens from the city below, distracting them. It winked out a moment later, leaving a shimmering stretch of warped space to mark its passing, just before an enormous crimson wave blazed into the sky, consuming the city beneath. It took seconds for the sound and shock waves to reach them. The earth quaked beneath their feet, knocking them all to the ground.

"Uncle!"

Quickly, Vaughn grabbed the dark-haired child and held her close, shielding her eyes from the destruction.

"Sir!" One of the Peacekeepers gestured towards the Travel Arch as it erupted in a conflagration of blue and purple flames, sending huge chunks of marble high into the scarlet sky.

"Those fools!" Vaughn cried. "What have they done?"

The land shook again as if in reply. A great rumbling came from the east as the city's remains, the jewel of their civilization, disappeared beneath the waves. Vaughn watched in horror as the crystal-blue water filling the straight between them and the city reached for the sky, forming a massive liquid wall rushing towards them. Transfixed, they stood watching as it slammed into the hill directly before them with a deafening roar. Water engulfed the hillside and streamed across the vineyard, sweeping away everything in its path.

Chapter 1

That Time Again

(The not too distant future…)

The crowd cheered as the gates opened and the turnstiles chimed in tune with patrons pushing their way past them onto the fairgrounds. The midway was a chaotic ballet of ice cream vendors, thrill seekers and carnies, eager to aid fairgoers in spending their hard-earned money on rides and fuzzy stuffed animal prizes of all sorts. Screams of terror and delight echoed from the Drop of Doom, and the lights from the Tilt-a-Whirl splashed across anxious faces waiting in line. The air was alive with fun and excitement.

Nigel sighed to himself as we walked the last few steps towards his assigned station, wondering what overactive revelries would occur this season. Every year a different theme was given to the London fair. This year it was *Ancient Treasures*, or as some of the younger folks were calling it, the 'Phat Lewt Fair'. It promised to be a luxury-item bonanza with displays ranging from plush antique furniture and vintage cars, to shining suits of armor and exquisite gems and jewels. Many of the country's most extensive private collections were on display this year, some for the first time ever.

With the abundance of precious possessions on display, security was a heightened concern at this year's fair. Nigel Coleman, a 37 year veteran of the London Sportex and Agricom facilities, arrived early for his night shift, as usual. His job had seen him through two divorces, three dogs, four children (none of whom remained in his custody), and was probably the only thing keeping him going. All of which suited Nigel just fine. His partner, Frank, the youngest on the team, was relatively new to the security scene. Nigel had taken him under his wing early, educating him in the nightly routine of coffee and donuts between rounds, and showing him when and where to take those much needed catnaps.

Nigel's uniform and boots were pressed and polished and his graying hair was neatly trimmed. The fair's opening day had seen record crowds, which were expected to continue into the night. Determined to see the event continue without a hitch, Nigel began his nightly grind by starting a fresh pot of coffee. Over the years, coffee making had become more than a passing hobby for him. His lunchbox doubled as a mobile canteen with at least a dozen different bean varieties crammed into it. As he entered the staff's small break room he noticed a large stack of chocolate custard donuts sitting on the table, enough for everyone on the night shift twice over.

Certainly nothing to complain about here. Nigel helped himself to a pastry.

Munching merrily, he picked up the coffee pot and held it close to his nose to get an idea of the contents.

"Barbarians," he muttered, lowering the pot quickly to pour its rancid contents down the drain. Only after giving the pot a proper cleaning would he allow a new batch to be started.

The distinctive clomp of safety boots echoing from the hall caught Nigel's attention. He looked up from rinsing the coffee pot and spied his supervisor, Colin, walking towards him.

Colin Thatcher had worked at the museum even longer than Nigel, and over the years they had shared many a pint.

That, and the fact they saw eye to eye on so many security issues, had allowed them to become close friends as well as co-workers. Colin's short legs were almost entirely hidden by his squat stature and burgeoning belly. His long white mustache carried on well past his chin and down his neck framing his tiny mouth, giving him a jovial appearance that contrasted sharply with his gruff voice.

"Coleman, a word please."

"Everything all right, Colin?" asked Nigel. He was sure it was nothing. A few exhibitors were probably making late night touch-ups to their displays or something.

"There have been a few last minute changes," said Colin, eying the plate of donuts. "Some special security chaps have been brought in to keep tabs on the Haldwell exhibit. Seems they have a lot of precious gems on display for the fair this year. Obviously they're a tad off their trolleys to think extra security is needed, but the proprietor is insistent and is paying extra for them to be here."

"Really?" replied Nigel warily. It was extremely unusual for outside security to be working at the fair grounds. "Daft old codger. I wonder why Haldwell even bothered displaying those gems if he's going to make all this fuss." At least this explained the extra donuts. Aside from a few incidents at the gift shop, Nigel couldn't remember there ever being a serious security breach in the complex, and certainly not on his shift.

"From what I've heard," said Colin, "he's getting on in years and becoming a bit paranoid. Maybe he's worried some family members won't wait for him to die to get their inheritance, but will opt to try nicking them instead. Damn insulting is what it is. It's ridiculous to think that after forty years in the security business I haven't learned how to protect a few shiny baubles." Colin's eyebrows furrowed as he spoke and he helped himself to a donut. His daily schedule was sacrosanct and he despised outsiders looking over his shoulder.

"Be sure to tell Frank, about our associates. Remember, they're trained professionals and are here to help us, no matter how much we don't need them. And try not to get in their way. You wouldn't believe the ruckus they caused covering the exhibit room in some special protective coating last night. Ruddy wallpaper if you ask me. The one in charge, Mark, seems rather spirited, with a chip on his shoulder to boot; you know the type. Do us all a favor and try not to test his patience. From what I understand, they'll be here until the fair is over."

"You know I'm easy, Colin," Nigel said, drying the coffee pot. "Best of the British to them."

"Right, get it sorted then." Colin turned to leave. "I'm off for a kip."

Ah... management at its best, Nigel thought. *Yes, it was going to be a good night.* Nigel chewed thoughtfully on a bite of pastry.

***

"Do you sense them yet?" Mark paced anxiously. His blond hair flitted in rhythm with his steps. "It's been almost a week and still nothing."

The fair had almost run its course. Today had been another waste. With night approaching, their time was running out. Tomorrow would be the final day of the exhibition. Mark's wiry frame tensed as he circled in front of an equally blonde girl sitting cross-legged on the floor. The dull black uniform he wore gave him a maturity his youthful features lacked. Devoid of color, the uniform, with its glossy black squiggles around the cuffs and collar of the coat and pants, made a stark contrast to his pale skin and blond hair. On his left breast a small logo with the words 'Terra Protectra' were embroidered with silver thread. His blue eyes bore into the floor as if trying to summon the people he was waiting for from the tiles beneath his feet.

A knowing smile sprang to Maude's lips, "They will come. Leo is certain of it."

"How can you be so certain?" asked Mark.

The room was bare except for a small Jaipur throw-rug on which the young woman was seated. The rug's swirling gold threads and red background stood out vividly in the stark room. The white walls and floor seemed to run together under the dim fluorescent lighting. No table or chairs cluttered the space. A small shelf was built into the far wall.

Maude's fatigue was obvious. Dark crescents swelled beneath her closed eyes as she concentrated. Except for the treasures they were protecting, the area around them was fantastically devoid of anything remotely magical. Trying to detect any magical activity was challenging at the best of times. Keeping a continual surveillance over the entire fairgrounds was beyond exhausting, and worse, boring. Constantly focusing on nothing was frustrating, making the hours creep by with no end in sight.

Silently, Mark cursed Leo for not allowing them to bring an automated sentry. Terra Protectra relied on them the world over to compensate for their lack of manpower. Still, Leo had been insistent. "This mission is too important to leave to a machine," he had said, "and besides, I want to see what Maude can do." The whole conversation had left a bad taste in Mark's mouth, but Leo was the boss.

The uniform he wore was identical to that of his twin, though its masculine tailoring was completely unflattering to her feminine figure, hiding her physique and making her appear older than she really was. In fact, dressed as they were, a passerby would be hard pressed to tell the twins apart.

"You should rest, Mark. It won't do us any good if you're already worn-out when they show up. We'll need your strength when they arrive." She scrunched her brown eyes tightly closed to regain her concentration. "Perhaps, they aren't using magic to get here."

"Hmm…" A scowl creased Mark's face as he ceased pacing and glanced at his sister. *That was a possibility but…* "Perhaps, but they'll certainly use it to gain entry into the main auditorium and find the gems." His patience was thinning by the second. "We must be on guard. There won't be much warning if that's the case."

The constant waiting frustrated him immensely. This sting operation had not gone as planned, and the lure of the exhibited gems was now in question. For over a week they had been waiting for their prey to make a move. Waiting, waiting… and waiting. This place was driving him nuts! The museum staff was equally annoying. Did these guards actually believe they were protecting anything? *Certainly not their waistlines!* he thought.

The click of his boots echoed rhythmically in the little room as he resumed pacing the length of the floor. Unconsciously he flexed his fingers, feeling his knuckles rub against the Misorbium reinforcements in his gloves. They resembled fingerless driving gloves except for the bulbous reinforced knuckles that would have made any seasoned thug nervous. The gloves were the only weapons they carried and needed. Mark wasn't sure how Misorbium was discovered, but its ability to enhance his gift of absorbing mana was unquestioned. With its aid he could strip his foes of their magic rendering them defenseless or incapacitated. Officers in Terra Protectra relied on Misorbium to defend themselves against the rogue wizards they pursued.

They must come. Surely they can't resist the bait we've offered.
He let his mind wander for a brief moment. The thought of
saying the final words these rogue wizards would ever hear made
him feel warm and fuzzy inside. A small smile crept across his
lips. *We'll capture them and I'll prove my worth to Leo.* He'd worked
hard to earn the man's trust, and he'd make sure Leo wasn't sorry
for bestowing this assignment to him.

A soft voice cut into his thoughts, "Mark, they're here."
Maude reached down to steady herself as the shock washed over
her.

"Monitor them as they enter, Maude," said Mark, snapping
into action, adrenalin abolishing his weariness. "And proceed to
the display room where we'll capture them as planned. I'll inform
the men and contact Leo to tell him we've made contact with the
enemy. He'll want to know that everything is going as planned,
and I'll reassure him that we shouldn't need his assistance."
Excitement sparked through each step as he headed for the door.
His time had come. Leo would be gratified for entrusting this
task to him.

***

"As you wish," Maude confirmed, but Mark had already
disappeared through the door.

Strange, she thought. She should have been able to sense
their approach long before they reached the main pavilion. There
was no mistaking the blazing imprints of the intruders that were
streaking through her head yet they appeared so suddenly right in
our midst. Could they know a way to shield themselves from her
probes or were they simply saving their mana for later use? The
thought sent a shiver down her back. Would they really be able to
catch them? For all Mark's bravado, she still had doubts. Should

she warn him? With a mental sigh, Maude quickly rolled up her carpet, tucked it under one arm, and ran to catch Mark who was already halfway down the hallway. *Someone is eager tonight,* she mused.

Chapter 2

Unexpected Adventures

Murky waters lapped the banks along the Thames River path. Near the university, an elderly man walked with a lovely young aide at his side. He coughed as he slowly shuffled his feet, his wispy white hair tousled by the evening breeze. One hand clutched a gentleman's walking stick and the other was firmly wrapped around his companion. Old age seemed to command his every gesture, no matter how hard he tried to conceal it, everyone who saw him recognized it instantly. His grayish brown wool overcoat was done up to the last button, covering most of his wrinkled face. Dark wool pants and shoes sheltered his legs and feet from the brisk autumn weather.

"Is there really time to be picky?" asked his companion as a gust of wind blew the old man's coat open at the neck. They stopped briefly while she fixed his collar, never loosening her grip on him with her other arm.

As they resumed walking, his companion spied a small white dog making its way down the path, pausing to sniff the grass every now and then. The ruffled white fur on its legs and belly was gray with dirt and debris collected from its adventures. It stopped in front of the pair and barked playfully until a sharp look from the old man sent it scurrying away.

"Patience, Princess," he said looking up at her face with a sly wink, "I'm not that old, am I?" His wink spread into an infectious grin. A child of four or five would be hard pressed to look more mischievous.

The corners of her mouth tightened in silent exasperation. She adjusted the collar of her own overcoat with her free hand and let her gaze stretch across the river. It was almost fully dark now. Streetlights were popping on, creating pockets of illumination in the darkness. Lights from various buildings across the river reflected in the water. She found the smell of the riverside gardens refreshing. Their scent was clean and made her regret the dirty business at hand even more.

"I suppose you move quite well for someone over 7,000 years old." A small smile escaped her lips. "Vaughn, I'm just worried that your mind may not be holding up as well as your body.

"Nonsense, Alana. I'm as fit and alert as a man barely half my age! I… "

"Indeed… You're certainly very spry, if you happen to be a mountain, or even a glacier," Alana finished for him.

"Oh," Vaughn sighed. She was right of course. His mind raced back to the first time they had done this. *How many times was it now? Far too many to count.*

"You'll be performing this yourself soon as well, I assume." Vaughn let an eye linger on Alana's face for a moment. Her cheeks were still smooth and rosy; her hands still soft to the touch. Her long dark hair was up today, partly because of the wind and partly to make her look the part of his attendant. There were no visible signs yet but they would come soon. She wasn't much younger than he was - even though she was his niece. He dropped his gaze to the ground and forcefully suppressed the unpleasant memories that arose whenever he allowed himself to consider his age and how he had achieved it. There was no point dwelling on the past, on the sacrifices that had been made. The present needed his full attention.

"It'll be a while yet before I require it. Unlike others, I've learned some restraint over the years," Alana said as she brushed a stray strand of hair out of her eyes. "I've learned to conserve my energies."

"Restraint? Hmmmph," retorted Vaughn. "I've noticed you've gotten quite proficient at getting our fellow fugitives to do your bidding." He smirked and gave her arm a little squeeze. "My tasks simply require a more hands on approach."

Alana laughed at this. "They seem eager enough to please, and capable too. I suppose if you could you'd be raiding the fair grounds yourself tonight? Simply, to show them 'how it's done' of course."

They stopped walking and Vaughn's brow creased in frustration. "I should be there. If they really are the gems we need… after all the years they've been hidden, why would someone display them now? Old people don't like strangers playing with their prized possessions, and the wealth these gems would represent to normal people is enormous. The possibility of it being a trap is very real. We shouldn't have let them go alone. If only I was… stronger…"

Thoughts of the others hung in the air between them. After a moment, of strained silence they resumed walking.

"Perhaps we need to hurry after all," suggested Alana.

"They'll be fine," Vaughn seemed to straighten as he spoke. "As long as they don't get too cocky, they'll be just fine," he added, not quite sure who he was trying to convince. He shook his head, firmly fixing his mind once again on the task at hand.

"And if they should be captured?" Alana asked.

"They know how to handle themselves." Vaughn exhaled slowly, not wanting to entertain the idea. "Together they're more than a match for those Terra Protectra goodie goodies."

Neither of them seemed eager to carry on the conversation as the trail lights labored to push back the inky darkness around them, intermittently marking the path before them. As if on queue, the wind picked up and whisked a few more leaves from their treetop homes to the ground below.

A young boy ran down the path towards them. He looked at most twelve, maybe thirteen, to Vaughn's tired eyes. He was wearing ripped blue jeans and a dark green T-shirt with a bright yellow stripe on one side. His sneakers squeaked with each footfall. *Just what the doctor ordered,* Vaughn thought. He could feel Alana's arm tensing around him. She too sensed that they had finally found what they were seeking.

"Excuse me, has a white Maltese dog come by here?" the boy asked, fighting for his next breath. "My mum is going to kill me for letting him get away."

Vaughn smiled and beckoned the boy closer. "Actually, my dear boy, I do believe I've seen him. Would you care to walk with us for a bit? I'm sure your dog will turn up if we look for him together."

"Really? You've seen Scooter!" the boy exclaimed. "I've been looking everywhere for him."

"Indeed," replied Vaughn playfully. "And what might your name be, young sir?"

"Ethan. Ethan Thatcher."

"Well, Ethan, shall we go find dear Scooter together?"

***

Three silhouettes, trying hard not to disturb the natural pattern of the night, crept along the roof of the auditorium. Neon lights glared at them from the midway, illuminating the rooftop with a dance of bright colors mixed with the fading rays of sunset.

The trio hunkered down close to an electrical box beside one of the many skylights. Kaida pushed her short black hair back out of her face as she placed a hand on the box's steel cover and closed her eyes to concentrate. A faint glow enveloped her hand, barely noticeable in the swirl of neon colors around them. Nary an onlooker would believe that anything magical was afoot.

Jack crouched next to her and surveyed the festivities before peering deeply into the showroom below. His movements exuded a natural grace and confidence bordering on the supernatural. He shot a quick glance at Kaida probing the metal box and turned back to the skylight. Jack never tired of seeing her in action. Though small and fragile looking, Kaida's magic allowed her to effortlessly mesh her mind with anything electrical, permitting her to control whatever she interfaced with and even manipulate its inner workings. Wherever electricity could travel, she could follow, reading the bit-sized braille formed by the electrical impulses.

Seeing her work always aroused Jack's curiosity. Her gifts made his abilities seem dull in comparison. Sure he could make himself faster, stronger, and nigh invulnerable—yet he still envied her. Jack briefly entertained the idea of switching his own physical gifts with hers, if it was possible, but discarded it. The potential for mischief was there but he couldn't escape the notion that he'd have to start wearing horn-rimmed glasses and a pocket protector as well. He shrugged to himself. Slowly he raised his hands until he could see the shadow it cast on the floor of the exhibit hall and proceeded to…

"Stop it, Jack!" Natalie warned. She quickly grabbed his arm, forcing him to lower his hands. "You're so juvenile sometimes. What if someone saw?"

"Relax, Nat. No one's around." Jack grinned widely at his partner. "Don't you like my animal shapes? I thought the last one was a pretty good goat…"

"Will you be serious? This place could have cameras everywhere."

"Oh, please. I doubt security is that tight. Only grey haired old farts with monocles and severely spoiled pet cats would ever consider stealing anything from this place."

"Old men like Vaughn and Leo?" Natalie countered.

Jack considered carefully for a moment. He knew all too well the powers both men possessed. It was on Vaughn's order that they were at this tumbleweed fair, and if Vaughn wanted something Leo would certainly try to stop him from obtaining it.

"Whatever," Jack said at last, rolling his eyes at his fiery companion.

The wind blew Nat's long, loose, auburn curls playfully around her face. She was grinning now, her eyes locked onto Jack's face ready to pounce at the first sign of weakness. Jack shrugged and leaned back against the skylight casing, eager to change the topic. He hated when she was right, which was much too often. With another quick glance around he focused on his other partner again. Kaida certainly wasn't as flashy as Nat, although, her curves were in exactly the right places. His curiosity piqued ever so slightly as he watched her.

"Say the word, Kaida, so we can start the show and get out of here," Jack whispered, unable to keep a note of concern out of his voice. London was foreign to him, constantly reinforced by the odd sights, smells and sounds around him. The din of London's traffic and crowds of people constantly mobbed his senses. He longed for the open plains of his childhood. He just wasn't comfortable here.

Kaida opened her eyes and stared at Jack a moment before responding. Her bob of black hair stirred in the evening breeze.

She opened her mouth just as Natalie cut in.

"Awww... Past your bedtime already, Jack?" she teased mercilessly, clearly trying to provoke another clash. "If you'd like to go find some milk and cookies, Kaida and I can handle this." Her wide smile intensified her mocking tone.

"The last time I left you two alone, you flooded half the city and you had every police officer in the area chasing you," Jack said.

"Don't worry, I doubt we'll be close to any water here."

"That's too bad. You could use a bath."

"What!?" Natalie shrieked, her good-natured teasing quickly turning to open hostility.

"I'd volunteer to do it myself but..."

"Listen here, goat boy!"

"Who're you calling *goat boy?*"

"I believe I've located the gems." Kaida's quiet statement rocked the combatants. With a final few nasty glances and nose wrinkles, both returned to the business at hand.

"According to the security cameras they appear to be located in a small room on the main floor," continued Kaida. "Once we drop in follow me—and please try to remain quiet. Let's not forget why we're here, okay?" Kaida looked meaningfully at her unruly companions.

"Let's go," Jack added. "The sooner we finish here the sooner we can meet up with Vaughn and Alana." *And get away from this mind-numbingly boring place!*

His companions nodded in agreement. Natalie seemed to be making a great effort to hold back a quip, saving it for later. She merely smiled as they carefully opened the skylight.

Chapter 3

On the Prowl

Soft white light burst through the open skylight into the dark night. A thin black rope dangled into the auditorium. Below the rope Kaida knelt beside Natalie. They were waiting for Jack near the top of the stairs leading down to the main floor. One of Kaida's hands was firmly pressed against the wall near a series of switches as she continued divining the building's hidden secrets. The floor creaked as Jack dropped from the rope, landing beside them. Panicked, Natalie quickly glanced around to confirm that no one else had heard the noise. Kaida had skillfully blocked the building's security system from registering the open skylight but there was little she could do against actual security guards. Live guards always worried Natalie the most. She didn't have Jack's strength to subdue them, or Kaida's ability to confuse them, leaving teleporting them away, far away, as her best option. That didn't stop them from calling for backup, however. Automated guards were so much easier to deal with. Power cords could be easily teleported out of their sockets and sensors could be easily fooled to see what wasn't there.

"Why not ask a security guard for directions already?" Natalie said. "It'd save us some time!"

"Oops," Jack replied sheepishly, giving Nat his best 'I didn't mean to' expression. However, she didn't believe it.

Fresh air trickled through the open skylight and mixed with the finely air-conditioned fragrances around them. The lights in this part of the building were dimmed for the evening, creating shadows along the decorated displays and walls. With another quick glance around, Jack let one hand hover over his jeweled belt buckle, a present from Vaughn, and gave the rope a quick jerk with the other. Faint light sparked from the buckle along Jack's body and up the rope. A moment later the rope dislodged itself from the frame above and joined him on the floor of the balcony. Another quick flash and Jack held the rope, coiled neatly, in his hand.

Kaida knelt quietly against the wall, waiting for her companions to settle themselves. Thanks to her unique ability to 'speak' with computers and other electrical devices, she was now completely enmeshed with the security system, focused on erasing any trace of their presence and keeping them one step ahead of the guards. Through the cameras, the main jewel display cases in a meeting room just off the central corridor could be seen.

"Okay?" Jack paused and looked at Kaida.

With a slight nod, Kaida sent yellow sparks from her hand up the wall, signaling the building to close the skylight.

"The guards are just finishing their rounds. We should be safe if we hurry." Kaida's voice was little more than a whisper.

"You're sure?" Natalie sounded skeptical.

"It's what the cameras tell me."

"Cameras, eh?" Jack grunted.

"Don't be alarmed. We can move freely. I've taken care of them."

Neither Jack nor Nat could help looking up and into the nearest security camera guarding the interior of the building.

"This way," Kaida indicated, and slowly, confidently began to lead her companions towards their goal. Jack and Nat followed close behind, scanning the surroundings for possible danger. "Phat Lewt awaits."

"Did she just..." Natalie looked worried. Kaida's speech de-evolving to Leet Speak, the short-hand dialect favored by hard core computer geeks everywhere, meant only one thing. Her adrenalin was kicking in.

"Yeah..." Jack's usually serene companion had a tendency to lose her natural reserve when high stakes competition called. Images of the trouble caused the last time Kaida uttered those words flashed through his mind. The destruction of the landmark arcade in Japan, the crying gamers nursing their bruised egos, the piles of loose change everywhere in the street...

So not good.

"Hey, Miss Hyde," Jack prodded Kaida, "You know this isn't a game, right?"

Kaida froze. Slowly she turned to Jack. Her face retained its normal tranquil expression with the exception of her eyes, two dark liquid-brown orbs that blasted Jack with icy fury. Instinctively, Jack found himself examining the floor tiles, feeling quite blue in the face and longing to be only three apples tall.

"Call the whaambulance already. Let's go," was all Kaida said before turning and proceeding down the stairs.

"Nice one, goat boy," Nat chided with a wide grin, swatting Jack across the chest as she crept past.

***

"They're on the west stairs," Maude confirmed. She made a quick scan of the room. Every officer from Terra Protectra was present. Together, their black uniforms seemed to absorb the light in the room.

"The room's ready. Everyone to their places! We only have one shot at this," Mark ordered as he completed his final survey of the room.

The meeting room had been emptied of its usual tables and chairs to make room for the display cases arranged in a semi-circle facing the door. The walls were covered in posters detailing the histories of the gems on display, where they came from, what their shapes meant, who originally owned them etc—a perfect haven for jewel enthusiasts everywhere. A single glass door, centered in the middle of a glass wall, connected the room to the rest of the complex. The locks on the display cases were shiny and new, almost as shiny as the gems they were protecting. However, they were not the only safeguards protecting the treasure within.

Maude quickly took her place in one of the false floor compartments scattered around the edges of the room; just one of the surprises Terra Protectra had added as part of their special security precautions. The other being lining the walls, ceiling, and floor with Misorbium. Hope sparked inside her, as she contemplated their coming victory. Thanks to their leader's improved refining process, never before had they been able to employ so much Misorbium. She cupped one hand in the other and let her fingers trace the bulky Misorbium knuckles of her gloves Such remnants were no longer necessary now that they could craft flexible Misorbium as thin as paper while still retaining all its potency. Coating the walls had been time consuming, but concealing it along the glass wall and door had been grueling.

Finally, they had taken great care in modifying the security cameras to filter out the presence of Terra Protectra officers in the room. Each camera had its own lenses modified and tweaked. Anyone wearing a Terra Protectra uniform was automatically scrubbed from the video feed. In effect, they were walking blue screens, invisible to the electric eyes monitoring the rooms.

"Let's go! Let's go!" Mark commanded. His voice was steady, betraying nothing that would signal this was his first solo stake out. "You all know what to do. Be ready to move on my signal."

He could barely contain his excitement.

Over a dozen officers, the bulk of the Terra Protectra organization, took up positions along the walls of the room at even intervals. *I wish we had more men,* Mark thought. Those who had the gift of absorbing mana were rare even in ancient times though. Almost in unison, they sealed their hiding places and promptly disappeared. No trace could be seen of them, by un-magical means anyway. They would get Vaughn this time for sure. After a quick final check, Mark too concealed himself across from the door so he would have an unobstructed view of the action. *They will come and I will catch them,* Mark promised himself. *Escape is impossible.*

Chapter 4

Tricks and Traps

Nigel and Frank leisurely went about their rounds on the upper floor of the auditorium, their coffee cups at the ready. As expected, nothing was amiss with any of the displays. Candies to candles, pewter figurines to pottery, all seemed to be in their proper places.

"Hmm. The blooming air conditioner must be broken again," Nigel observed as he was struck by a gust of cool air.

"…Or someone left a window open," Frank chimed in, chuckling to himself.

Nigel considered it for a second. That would be highly unlikely. Except for a few skylights, there were no windows in the main auditorium. Their offices didn't even have windows. No—it must have been maintenance again—always overdoing it, hot in the winter, freezing in the summer. Still, it wouldn't hurt to leave them a note in the morning.

"This Ethiopian Sidamo is a tad citrusy for my liking. What do you think, Nigel?" Frank asked as they rounded a pedestal displaying a vintage gown. Frank's palate was finely honed. He could detect even the most subtle flavors in a cup of coffee thanks to Nigel's expert tutelage.

"Truthfully, it's not my favorite either, but by the time we finish up here, there should be a new pot brewing," Nigel remarked as Frank deftly dumped the remainder of his cup into a nearby potted plant.

***

Kaida kept her companions moving quickly and decisively to avoid the caffeine-craving guards. Being able to see through the eyes of the building's security cameras had its advantages. She led her companions across the auditorium floor, past expensive watches and designer sunglasses, to the room containing their prize. Before moving into the room, she stopped and inspected the glass door, trying to determine if any traps awaited them.

***

A trickle of sweat ran down Mark's forehead as he watched three shadowy figures stop just outside his door through the tiny camera, cleverly placed by his team to watch the door. It wasn't connected to the main system. Only the tiny screens in their secret recesses could access it, another of their subtle upgrades to the room. *Impossible!* There was no way they could know, yet they stopped. A spasm worked its way through his gut. He clenched his teeth in frustration. *There's no way!* The three intruders stood and moved to enter. *They're still coming!* Mark suppressed a very large sigh.

***

Kaida checked the door again. Nothing! Everything seemed to be in order. Carefully they opened the door and made their way to the cabinets in the middle of the room. As they approached the display cases, she could see dozens of brilliant gems lying on soft black velvet. The room's lights were low, but each case had its own internal bulbs, illuminating the treasures within. Kaida, Jack and Nat pulled out tiny flashlight devices from their pockets and shined them at the gems. Quickly they scanned the collection, looking for the brightest stones.

"Here they are," Kaida said as she motioned towards the display case in the middle. The display signs indicated it was full of diamonds but when viewed with the special light in Kaida's hand the jewels glowed bright reds, greens, blues, purples, and yellows. Looking closely at them revealed tiny engravings, runes of some sort circling the gems that also shimmered in the special light. Jack dispatched the locks on the case with ease.

"Quickly!" said Natalie, "Let's get them and go."

"That's far enough!" The words streaked through the air.

Their heads jerked towards the voice. On cue, the walls began to glow dark purple, casting an eerie glow over everything.

"It's a trap!" shouted Natalie.

Lids sprung open in unison as half the guards rushed to surround the thieves, their bodies emitting purple auras of their own. The remainder hung back, focused on activating the Misorbium panels lining the room, exponentially augmenting their abilities. As the glowing surfaces increased in intensity, they unleashed their powers on their prey. Waves of magical energy began billowing away from the intruders.

Jack could barely hear Natalie's words as he instinctively charged towards the nearest glowing goon. *Ambush, eh?* He lowered his shoulder and focused stored mana from his belt buckle onto his jacket, hardening it to a density many times that of steel. Using this much mana he had smashed through cement walls as if they were paper.

From across the room, an officer lined Jack up with his straightened arm, focused his ability through his Misorbium gloves and stripped a globe of mana away from Jack and shredding his defenses.

The globe whizzed back toward the officer's glove and was consumed by the rare metal as Jack tumbled to the floor, winded and disoriented.

Dazed, Jack rolled behind one of the display cases for cover and looked up just in time to see Nat sending a shimmering bolt of raw magic into the wall. The wall absorbed the bolt without the slightest sign of weakening.

Frustrated, she fired again at one of the officers. The magical bolt splashed across his chest, stunning him momentarily, but doing no real damage as it was quickly absorbed. Her blast was answered by a choir of shots, as officers attempted to drain her mana, sending her crashing to the floor next to Jack.

Nat's patented 'What now?' look raced across her face as she struggled to sit up. Jack forced himself to think.

"It is useless to resist." Mark stepped forward, bathing his captives with his malicious grin. "It may not look it, but you are completely encased in Misorbium, as well as surrounded by our troops. Soon your energies will be completely absorbed. Fighting will only weaken you faster so please continue to waste what precious little magic you have left. Face it, you're defeated. There is no escape."

Jack exchanged worried looks with Nat. Both glanced at each other's gemmed accessories, noting the fading glows emanating from them.

Mark walked forward to inspect his prisoners. His eyes gloated with every step. *Oh yes, finally you're mine.*

***

Jack thought quickly, *if they couldn't fight with magic…*
"Blondie has a point," Jack quipped. "Nice to see your

— 27 —

hair's grown back, Mark, although the shade is a bit off... I suppose that's what happens when you consult a veterinarian instead of a real..."

"Silence!" Mark's face was turning redder by the second.

"Hey, Mark," Natalie followed Jack's lead, trying to salvage some pride of her own. "That big throbbing vein in your forehead must drive all the other baboons wild."

Mark stared at her, his face conveying instantly what words never could.

"I'm almost impressed. I didn't think you could actually plan something like this," Nat taunted.

"Well, maybe not entirely by himself," chipped in Maude as she stepped away from the wall to get a better view. She smiled slightly and offered a mocking wave to their captives.

"Figures. I knew you couldn't have done all this by yourself." Jack's enthusiasm pressed exactly the right buttons. "Heck, I bet she even dresses you in the morning."

"Don't you dare mock me!" Mark's anger flared. "I'm not the one who will be dying tonight. Soon you will be nothing more than a bad memory and the world will be much better off for it."

"Oh good, I hate long waits." Jack rolled his eyes, hiding his inward uncertainty. *We're so screwed.*

"Is that a new rug, Maude? I hear they're all the rage these days," asked Natalie.

"Actually it is. I picked it up just last week at..." Maude replied.

"Maude, shut up," Mark hissed. "Don't concern yourself with them. They won't be here much longer."

"Sweet. I can't wait to get out of this purple play house of yours and wrap my hands around your scrawny neck," Jack said as he met Mark's gaze.

"Poor, Jack, you misunderstand me." Mild amusement played across Mark's face. "When this field gets through with you, you'll be dead. Your bodies have been saturated with magic for so long I doubt they can bear to function without it."

"Yeah, yeah. Could you be more jealous?" Jack boasted, or tried to at least. Already nausea was setting in and his skin was beginning to feel tight around his chest. A spasm gripped his arm. *This is bad.* He looked around the room. All the guards were grinning confidently at each other. *If only...*

"Very well then, shall we go?" Kaida's voice seemed to come out of nowhere. They all turned to give her their full attention. "We have what we came for."

The display case was empty. Kaida cradled the bulging bag of gems close to her chest. She carefully shifted the bag to her left hand, freeing her right which slowly dropped to one of the work lights inside the display case.

"Uh, sure thing, Kaida," Jack replied, still confused as to what she could possibly do in this situation. *What could she...* Understanding hit him as she beckoned her companions closer.

"It's been fun, Mark, Maude. Lets do this again—not," Natalie crowed sarcastically at the would-be heroes, as she moved closer to Kaida.

"You can't be serious. You're completely enclosed in..." Mark muttered in disbelief as he lowered his gaze to Kaida's hand and the lamp it was resting on. His eyes traced the lamp's cord down to a power bar on the floor, across the floor, to a power socket, and through the Misorbium lined walls they had constructed.

Abject terror gripped Mark. *How could a detail like that go unnoticed?* The barrier was not complete. They had failed to isolate the center of the room. *Could this girl possibly do something to take advantage of such an insignificant opening? Could she?*

Mark's mind raced at the possibilities. She was a mage after all.

"The cord! Cut the cord! Don't let them escape! Shoot them!"

The air around them filled with glistening chrome light as Kaida dematerialized their bodies, transforming them into binary electromagnetic particles, and whisked them away through the lamp's power cord. Jack didn't even try to contain his victorious smirk as his body dissolved before Marks eyes.

***

As the captives' transformation continued, Mark raced towards the cord.

A few officers tried to absorb the energy before they completely disappeared, but they were too late. The last Mark saw of the trio was the tip of Natalie's tongue sticking out at him as blinding light dissolved the thieves and sucked them through the power cord to freedom.

"What?!..." Mark screamed. *How could things have gone so wrong!* Sweat rolled down his face. His heart beat furiously as he waited for an answer.

Maude stood stock-still for a moment as she quickly scanned the building for any magical energies, "I can't sense... Yes! They're still in the building—near the main security station."

"This way!" Mark commanded. Booted feet pounded out of the room in a mad frenzy. The game was still afoot. Mark led his troops up the stairs towards their prey.

***

The lights flickered in the employee coffee room. Nigel had just sent Frank around with the rubbish and was currently replacing the filter on the coffee maker. He had come across a bag of Sumatra beans and was dying to whip up a pot. Colin's nightly kip had taken a more serious turn than usual and had him snoring soundly in the next room. Humming to himself, Nigel fixed the filter into position. He reached for the bag of coffee beans and jumped as a loud pop filled the room, followed by a blinding flash of light.

"Bleeding lights on the fritz, too," Nigel mumbled as he lifted his head to check the situation. Standing before him were two young girls and a young man. Two of them looked rather bewildered, as if they didn't know what had just happened either. Behind them, sparks were flying out of the wall's electrical socket.

"I'm sorry. This is as far as I can go," Kaida wobbled slightly as she spoke. "I can't keep all of... coherent... Natalie will have to take us ... Vaughn." The strain of dematerializing three people after fending off that deadly trap was extremely apparent.

"Hang in there, Kaida," Jack said as he reached out to steady her. At his touch her knees buckled and she slumped backwards against him. He caught her easily and gently lowered her to the floor. Her cheeks were extremely pale. The sound of heavy footfalls on the cement floors echoed through the door.

"Um, guys..." Natalie had finished surveying the room.

"What, Nat?" Jack sighed impatiently, turning to follow Natalie's gaze. "The wonder twins will be here soon." He finally saw the elderly security guard, tightly gripping a bag of coffee beans, standing next to a table heaped with doughnuts. The older man simply stared at them, completely dumbfounded.

"Get a fix on Vaughn already, Nat," Jack scolded, ignoring the guard.

Jack swallowed hard as he watched Natalie fumble the

Waystone Vaughn had given them before the mission out of a jacket pocket and juggle it briefly. Once under control, it began to glow silently in her hands as her magic activated it. He sighed, inwardly relieved to be leaving. A faint smile crossed his lips as Natalie cursed silently at needing the tool to augment her own powers. Jack new how hard it could be to admit a weakness. Those attuned to magic could instinctively sense others of their kind. The range varied greatly from one to another, however. Vaughn had been careful not to criticise her abilities, but just giving her the stone said enough. The locator runes twinkled before Nat's face for a few seconds before settling on one pattern of flashing lights.

"Who… are… What… are…" stuttered the guard, trying desperately to form a coherent sentence.

Jack turned towards the shaky voice and smiled. "Hey, are those custard donuts?" Using magic always made him hungry. More accurately, he was always hungry.

"Y-y-y-y" the guard stammered, looking from the boy to the pastries in confusion.

"Oh please, we don't have..." hissed Natalie.

"Mind if I steal one?"

"Jack!" Natalie's rage boiled over as Jack reached over and nabbed a rather plump donut from the table. He paused for a second, then grabbed another one and offered it to Kaida.

"Eat up, a little sugar will help," he said softly as Kaida took a small bite.

"P-please, by all means, help yourselves," the guard droned with sudden hospitality. The shock of three people suddenly appearing in front of him showed no signs of wearing off soon. Sounds of heavy footsteps echoed through the door from down the hallway.

"Cheers," Jack toasted the guard. "You ready yet, Nat?"

"Yes!" Natalie replied, giving Jack a look that could have pulverized solid stone.

"Well, what are you waiting for?" Jack asked, taking another bite of donut.

Natalie was about ready to give Jack a long deserved piece of her mind, but the sounds of footsteps were rapidly becoming louder. Squelching her retort, she took a last look at the gizmo she held in her hand, noted the destination it was marking and closed her eyes to concentrate. The tracker suddenly changed its pattern and gave off a confirming burst of light. Natalie, Jack, and Kaida winked out of the room.

***

Mark was breathing hard as he entered the coffee room. In the middle of the floor stood an aged security guard holding a bag of coffee beans. Alone. The room was otherwise empty and quiet. A dozen men quickly entered behind Mark.

"Where did they go?" Mark shouted at the guard.

The guard fought through his bewilderment and tried to form a comprehensive response. "I... I... don't know. Unless, disappearing into a ball of light counts as somewhere..."

"Damn it," Mark swore. He was consumed with an inner rage. *Of all the stupid things to overlook... What am I going to tell Leo? Where is he anyway...?* There was no point staying here any longer. The operation had been a failure. Remaining would only lead to a lot of questions being asked that he didn't want to answer.

Maude's hand on his shoulder tried to comfort him. "It's not your fault, M...".

He recoiled at her touch. Mark turned abruptly, leading his men out of the break room.

Chapter 5

Unexpected Confrontation

The reddish glow was already fading from Vaughn's hands as Ethan's withered body crumpled to the ground. The soul transfer was a success. Again. Vaughn flexed his hands. No longer were they wrinkled and boney. His hair, once white and wispy, was now full and jet black. Outwardly, he was a man of thirty again, no twenty. He straightened himself, testing what his revitalized body had to offer. At his feet lay a gnarled corpse, barely recognizable as a thirteen year old boy. Vaughn snapped his fingers and his walking cane rose to meet his hand.

"How do you feel?" Alana inquired from a few feet away. She had been keeping watch as Vaughn completed his grim task. Alana studied him now, concern evident on her ageless face.

"I feel—young," Vaughn stated as he continued to hold his cane in both hands, clenching his fingers around it. "It seems like a long time since I've felt this way."

He let his gaze linger on his victim before turning to face Alana. "Well then, shall we…"

Suddenly, in great pain, Vaughn doubled over. His breathing was rapid and shallow. His eyes lost focus as he spoke. "My dog... I need to find my dog." His legs buckled, sending him tumbling to the ground. "Aaaarrrrgh!"

Alana watched in horror as Vaughn fought to regain control. She had never seen such bad side effects from the transference before. Draining a person's soul was probably the vilest act one could ever perform. It could extend your life, but the merging of another's soul with your own goes against nature and is not without consequences. Her mind raced, trying to think of what to do, how to help. Thankfully, the fit passed as quickly as it had begun. Vaughn fell silent. He was on all fours, not moving a muscle. Slowly he straightened-up with Alana's help, his breathing once again slow and regular. Taking a deep breath, he looked at Alana, his face once again calm and serene.

"I'm fine," he said at last. Color slowly returned to his face as he spoke.

"You're sure?" Alana had her doubts. Stealing someone's soul to revitalize your own was not something done lightly. Of course she had done it many times as well. Yet each time she did so, she found herself having to justify it again. It was a necessary evil if their work was to continue.

"I know that look, Alana," Vaughn tried to comfort her. "I'm fine."

"Mmm hmmm." Alana wasn't convinced. "Come on, we should be going. The others will…"

"I knew you would be up to something." A chilling voice shattered the stillness of the night. Vaughn and Alana turned in the direction from which the sound had come, facing the darkness unflinchingly. "Only one act I know of would light you up as bright as a Christmas tree like that. You look well. I may be late but at least I'll have the pleasure of depriving you of your ill-gotten bounty."

"Hello, Leo," Vaughn said. It was impossible to detect any hint of emotion in his voice.

"I was sure you'd have gone to the fair, but now I understand why you didn't. I suppose it's poor timing on my part." Leo's eyebrows knit together on his smooth face. His tall frame radiated defiance, with enough meat on his bones to make him look dangerous, despite his age. Only a few errant strands of grey were apparent in his short chestnut brown hair.

His grey eyes, like the sea after a terrible storm, were fixated on his prey. "You knew we'd be there and you used it as a diversion, didn't you? Did you really think I wouldn't be able to detect your shenanigans? With the magnitude of power being transferred? Not even the activities at the fair could cover that up. Sending your kin to their deaths to save your own skin—you're as ruthless as ever. Tonight I'll ensure you've killed your last victim."

A dark purple aura engulfed Leo as the Misorbium in his uniform telegraphed his intentions. In one smooth motion he extended his arm and flicked his wrist. A shining mana globe emerged from Vaughn and streaked towards Leo. Abruptly the globe stopped before Leo could absorb it. A gentle chuckle escaped from Vaughn.

"Your technique has improved, Leo. Thankfully, Alana has been practicing as well." Even as he said this, Alana was directing the stolen ball of energy back towards Vaughn. As it made contact with his body, it pulsed rapidly and burst, covering Vaughn in a shower of magical particles. "Yet, you seem surprised. Perhaps I underestimated you?"

"Have you forgotten how I earned my command?" snorted Leo.

"I remember the oaths you swore upon accepting it."

"Those words are nothing but sands scattered by the winds of time. Your actions have seen to that."

"I, at least, have remembered my oaths."

"Yours? Your blasphemy and betrayal has produced your own doom. If you had any honor left, Vaughn, you would cease your vain self-preservation and accept your fate."

"Humph... At least he's not some delusional hypocrite,"

Alana protested.

"How dare…"

"Yes, well, I'd love to stay and chat," Vaughn cut in, "but as you already know, this has been a very busy night. Perhaps, some other time?" Vaughn looked bored, yet gave his adversary a courteous smile.

"I don't think so," Leo said as he prepared for another attack. "You've been living on borrowed time for too long!"

***

Leo's body went unexpectedly rigid. Shock covered his face as his aura flared, fighting to absorb the magical bindings holding him. *How?* Leo thought. *Alana!* He was speechless. Every muscle in his body refused to obey him.

Alana shook her head. "Tsk, tsk. Old age must be affecting you, Leo. Wasn't it you who taught me to always keep track of my opponent's actions? Magic may not affect you, but it certainly can affect the air around you." She tried to suppress a smile but failed miserably. "It was good to see you again. Do try and stay out of trouble," she added with a wink as she moved back towards Vaughn.

"And now we must depart," Vaughn declared. "I'm sure you understand. Schedules to keep, people to see, that sort of thing."

He turned to Alana, "Got them?" She pulled a Waystone from her coat and consulted it, frowning as she deciphered the display.

"I have… but they are significantly further away than they should be." She spoke quietly so only Vaughn could hear. "Has something happened?"

"We shall see." Vaughn reached for the device. Its display

showing their three companions brought a concerned look to his face. "No matter. We will resolve this when we arrive."

Nodding a brief farewell, Vaughn added, "Leo, you'll have to forgive me if I don't accept my fate just yet." They turned to go, leaving Leo in his paralyzed state.

"There is no hope for you, Vaughn. My men have recovered the Oracle of Y'alan—what's left of it anyway."

Leo's words had their desired effect. Neither Vaughn nor Alana could conceal their surprised horror.

"Is that so..." Vaughn replied, after regaining control of his senses. "That is good news. I strongly suggest you turn it over to us before you hurt yourself."

Mocking laughter erupted from Leo. "Why would I give you the power to destroy everything all over again? Once we study it, and destroy it, all that will be left is ensuring you die a gruesome death."

"Tell me," Vaughn replied smoothly, "my dear friend; do you have any idea what the Oracle of Y'alan actually is? Do you really expect it to still work after all this time? It took the greatest mages of our age to use it and you honestly expect it to…"

"I'm not a mage. Terra Protectra doesn't NEED mages. The world is better off without mages!" Leo shouted. "And when we do learn the Oracle's secrets, its destruction will ensure the world is safe from your kind."

"The Oracle survived the destruction of Baurum'tatus, it will survive you!" retorted Vaughn.

"Enough! We will discover its secrets." Leo was yelling now. His face was as red as a blast furnace. "You know as well as I do what it was used for. I swear it will never be used by any mage ever again. Take my advice, Vaughn, leave. Just go. Your time is over. The future belongs to us."

Silence filled the space between them. They glared at one

another, refusing to give way or show any sign of weakness.

"We shall see, won't we," Vaughn said simply.

Without another word, white light enveloped Vaughn and Alana. A flash and a slight pop later and they were gone.

***

Leo fumed. *That good-for-nothing swindler! Too long he has run free. I will see Vaughn and the rest of them dealt with if it's the last thing I do. Only then will I be able to rest.* It took another moment for the shackles Alana had wrought to expire. Gingerly, he rubbed his arms to help their circulation return.

"We shall see, won't we," Leo echoed Vaughn's words. He turned and headed towards the fairgrounds.

Chapter 6

Snow Day

It was a cool day in Westbrook. Fresh snow blanketed the small town. Snowy rooftops sparkled as the midmorning sun peaked through the clouds. Radios and televisions everywhere were tuned to the local weather reports by residents hoping for a hint of relief from the early winter onslaught. It had come as a surprise to most people in the town, but snow was not unheard of this early in October.

It had snowed particularly hard the previous night. Road crews were still struggling to clear the major streets in Westbrook. In parks and side alleys sled races had begun, and cheery snowmen populated neighbourhood lawns. On Pinetree Lane, street hockey was the sport of choice. Snow was piled high along the freshly cleared sidewalks and walkways. Vehicles parked on the street were encapsulated in natural igloos. Residents, unable to drive due to the abundance of snow clogging the streets, had no objections to the congestion created by hockey nets and shouting teenage boys.

"He shoots, he SCORES!"

The wind picked up as Andy fished a frozen tennis ball out of the net. The score wasn't even close but he didn't care. The teams had been fair at one time, but that was before Greg Millen was shepherded away by his parents and Randy Que was called in for supper. Of course, they had tried to even out the teams by exchanging token players, but the score wasn't changing as fast as the players were. The atmosphere was a mix of stoic resignation and carnival frivolity.

"C'mon, Andy, we'll get it back." Brett Maddox tried to sound confident, but both boys knew the odds were against them. He held his stick between his knees as he retied the hood of his ice blue jacket.

"I should have had that one, guys," Ryan said miserably. "Sorry."

"You suck, Ryan," Lance taunted. "You're mom is better in net than you are, loser."

Andy and Brett did their best to ignore Lance. "Don't sweat it, Rye-man. We'll get them yet." Andy tried to sound reassuring but didn't quite succeed.

"Where's Nick?" Brett asked.

"I think he buggered off," Josh said. "Probably sick of losing." He couldn't hold back a grin.

"Hey, man, I'm probably gonna half'ta take off soon, too," Lance said. "It's my turn to make dinner tonight."

"You can't leave. We're just starting our comeback," Brett cried as he slapped his stick on the snowy street.

"Ya, sure you are. Ha, ha. What's the score again?" Josh added sarcastically. He scrunched up his face, miming a look of deep thought, then held up his right hand, slowly counting on his fingers.

"Tell ya what, next goal wins," Jeremy said. "Okay?"

"Phhhht. We don't need your charity." Andy was resolute.

"Don't sweat it. It's not like you're gonna, score anyways," Lance said with a grin.

"You'd need a fireball to get past Jeremy," Josh said as he plugged his brother in the arm. Jeremy grinned modestly.

"He's been lucky so far," Ryan said, trying to sound brave.

His face said otherwise, however.

"Fine, bring it on!" Brett said in exasperation. "Next goal wins."

Josh and Lance smiled at each other as they set up for the face-off. Brett lined up with Josh to start the show while Andy positioned himself behind the center mark on Brett's right wing, across from Lance. *I'll show them a fireball*, Andy thought to himself.

Due to the traditional referee-free street hockey rules, those taking the face-off banged their sticks together three times before making a swipe for the ball to start the play.

Once, twice, on the third crack it was Brett who got his stick on the ball first and passed it back to Andy. Josh and Andy were both surprised that Brett had won the face-off. Lance, seeing Andy's hesitation, immediately charged towards him. Andy recovered just in time to flip the ball over Lance's groping stick and race towards Jeremy's waiting net. Lance recovered quickly and ran after Andy. Panting, Andy passed the ball to Brett hoping he'd have better luck. Josh was sticking to Brett like glue, giving him no room to maneuver. Beyond them, Jeremy tracked the ball, keeping himself square to it at all times.

They were at an impasse. Brett could keep Josh at bay all day but that wouldn't help them get the ball any closer to the net. Something drastic had to be done. Andy realized the only way to get a clear shot on goal was to get away from Lance. He weaved back and forth, but Lance read every move and followed his every step. Not knowing what else to do, Andy turned and ran straight towards Brett, Lance trailed just steps behind. At the last moment, Andy veered off and began running circles around Brett and Josh. Lance muttered a curse under his breath and chased after Andy. After his second loop, he gave Brett a slight nod. Suddenly realizing what Andy was going to do, Brett returned the gesture. Half way through his next pass Andy slowed just enough to let Lance get right up his tail. Suddenly, he pivoted and ran in-between Brett and Josh. Lance instinctively tried to follow but only succeeded in slamming straight into Josh and knocking both of them off balance.

"Clear!" Andy yelled after he had widened his lead by a few meters.

Brett shot the ball through Josh's legs towards Andy. His pass was tape-to-tape perfection and Andy cradled the ball with his hockey stick. Jeremy finally noticed Brett no longer had the ball and started to move across the net to block Andy.

"Shoot!" yelled Brett.

Andy raised his stick. *Fireball... fireball... fireball... I need a...* He swung. The ball rocketed through the air straight towards the net. There was a soft 'poof' as the ball met the net and continued on without the slightest sign of slowing down. Finally, about a block and a half away, it disappeared into an alley between an old coin-op laundry and a small dental office.

"Ha ha ... you missed a wide open net." Josh couldn't stop laughing. "You should really stick to sports you can handle, like checkers or tic-tac-toe."

"This is hockey, not golf, man, " Lance added dryly, leaning heavily on his hockey stick.

"That ball is out'a here," Brett said, awe creeping into his voice.

"Screw you, Josh," Andy protested. "I hit the bloody net. Check it."

"Check what? That ball is gone, man!" Josh exclaimed as he waved his arm.

"Whoa, check this out!" Jeremy was holding a piece of mesh from the back of the net. Several of the strands were severed and blackened, as if something had burned its way through them.

A hole large enough for a tennis ball was readily apparent.

"What are ya talking about?" Josh asked. "How'd that happen?"

"I don't know but it wasn't there before," Jeremy said. He always took great care of his gear.

"It went through the net? No way." Brett crouched to examine the net as well.

"That was awesome!" Ryan cheered as he ran to meet the throng.

"I guess this means we win?" Brett's grin was infectious, if not cruel. The other team froze for a moment before turning to Brett, Ryan and Andy. They weren't happy.

"Whatever." Lance was already brooding over the loss. "I gotta go anyways. Later, guys."

"Yeah, me too. Besides, we know who really won that game anyway," Josh said. He picked up one side of the net as his brother grabbed the other. Equipment in hand, they headed for home.

"Yeah, US!" exclaimed Andy to the retreating players.

"Who's getting the ball?" Ryan asked, obviously not wanting to volunteer.

"Whoever burns it, returns it," Jeremy chipped in. "Later, Andy."

"Ya, ya, I'm going," Andy said, sighing. "Guess I'll see you guys tomorrow."

They said their goodbyes and started for home. Andy continued down the street after the ball, kicking piles of snow and chopping at imaginary pucks with his stick. It started to snow again. He pulled his toque down over his ears. His body cooled off quickly now that he wasn't exerting himself. A few minutes later he found himself standing in front of the laundromat. A large neon sign read *Mom's Laundry* in big green letters. Further on, a backlit blue and white sign declaring *Dr. Perrywhite's Dental Practice* glowed peacefully. The hum of washers could be heard through the laundromat's walls as Andy walked by and turned into the alley. The ball should be easy to find, or so he thought.

The alley was a blizzardy mess. Snow drifts a solid three feet high lined either side, hiding the concrete walls of the shops. *There should be a hole somewhere in the snow.* He began inspecting the snowbanks for any sign of disturbance. His own footprints were the only marks he could see. No one had been here for days it seemed. Perplexed, he stopped to readjust his toque as a spot on the wall caught his eye. There it was. The tennis ball, about a foot above the highest drift, charred and half melted to the wall. *How the heck did that happen?* Andy moved forward a few steps to get a better look.

A brilliant flash of light illuminated the alley, knocking him off his feet in surprise. Blowing snow stung his face and a chill that had nothing to do with the weather ran down his spine. He sat motionless as three people materialized before him, two girls and a guy. They appeared to be about his age but he couldn't be sure. One of the girls seemed to be injured.

What the... Andy stared in amazement, thankful he was concealed by the snowdrift.

***

"I said find Vaughn, not Santa Clause," Jack griped as he shivered in the cold. Their sudden arrival kicked up tons of snow, creating billowing white clouds around them that threatened to cover everything.

"Where are we?" Natalie sputtered, ignoring Jack.

"See, this is why you're never allowed to drive," Jack said. "Do you even know how to use that thing?" He brushed off

Kaida as well. She shuddered at the cold but made no move to remedy the situation. Her eyes were closed, her face serene. Their previous ordeal had seemingly sapped every ounce of vitality from her body.

"Shut up, I know what I'm doing," Natalie retorted. "He has to be around here somewhere." She gave her Waystone a swift thump with her free hand, but nothing happened.

For a moment Jack stood there, examining the little alley in which they stood. The snow fell quickly, smothering everything in a thick layer of fluffy, frozen winter cheer. Oddly, one greenish, blackened clump refused to be covered, melting any snow falling near it.

"There's something you don't see everyday." Nat bent over to have a closer look, discovering the smoldering remains of a tennis ball. Puzzled, she leaned closer to examine it further. *My teleports have never done that before.*

"Who's there?" Kaida's return to consciousness sparked new life into her companions. They turned to see what she was looking at. All eyes fixed on a rather large man-shaped lump of snow, spread-eagle in the chilly afternoon. Slivers of bright red were peeking through where the head appeared to be, giving the snowy creature a striking resemblance to a Bonhomme. It blinked under their intense scrutiny.

"Did he see us?" Jack asked.

"Of course he did," Nat replied icily. "Geez, you're thick sometimes."

Jack considered the situation for a moment. Slowly he half-turned away from the snowman and carefully moved a hand towards his belt buckle. A second later the snow covering the mysterious visitor exploded, leaving not a trace on him. Kaida found herself sitting across from a thickly dressed young man with big green eyes and tufts of strawberry blond hair sticking out from under his red toque. His eyes bulged with surprise at the disappearance of the snow covering him.

"Hello, there," Natalie tried to sound as friendly as possible. "You haven't seen an elderly man around here, have you?"

"Uh, no... , " he stammered.

"Is this your work?" Jack pointed to the remains of the tennis ball. "Barbecued tennis ball never worked for me. Too rubbery for my liking."

A quick jab in the ribs by Natalie shut him up.

"I don't think so, at least I didn't mean to." Confusion raced across his face. "Err, who are you guys?"

"We're looking for someone," replied Nat.

"What's your name?" Jack asked flatly.

"Andrew, err Andy"

"Andy, do you have any ideas how this tennis ball wound up like this?"

"I shot it," Andy said, trying to sound confident, "with my hockey stick. I think."

Jack's confusion was mirrored on his companion's faces, prompting Andy to relate how the hockey game had ended and his discovery of the ball in its present position.

"Hmmm..." Jack shared an uneasy glance with Nat.

"It's all right. He's one of us." Confidence flowed from Kaida as she stared at Andy. "Nice beanie by the way."

"Are you sure?" asked Natalie.

"Of course. Can't you sense it?" said Kaida.

Natalie, for the life of her, couldn't see anything special about the boy. She tried fiddling with her Waystone to buy some time.

"Should we test him?" Natalie shot a skeptical eye towards Jack, then Kaida, and finally Andy. The question hung in the air.

No one wanted to answer.

***

Taking the initiative, Kaida beckoned Andy over to her. Puzzled, he rose up to his hands and knees, crawled over to Kaida, and sat in the snow next to her. She pulled out the bag of gems they had recently acquired and sifted through them.

Andy's jaw dropped as he saw the bag. *Who were these people?* Never before had he seen such wealth.

After fishing in the bag for a minute, Kaida found what she was looking for and pulled out a large gem with especially brilliant red light swirling inside it. When she held it in the palm of her hand the fiery light emanating from it entranced Andy. Silently, he swore that it was calling to him.

"Hold your hand above mine, palm down," Kaida instructed. With a slight hesitation, Andy settled himself on his knees and did as he was asked. "Close your eyes and focus on the gem with your mind. Imagine the light within the jewel. Try and feel it as it swirls around inside the gem. Once you have that picture firmly in your mind, try and sense that light flowing from the gem into your hand."

Andy closed his eyes and focused. Nothing happened. *This is silly. I'm not a freak like these guys,* he thought. Yet he continued to focus. Suddenly, the presence of the others became very prominent in his mind. Even though his eyes were closed, he could make out their shapes and postures wrapped in pale auras he couldn't explain. Natalie and Jack watched him curiously, waiting to see what would happen. Kaida was staring at Andy's face, trying to read his thoughts.

"Don't block yourself. You have to want it to happen," Kaida instructed. "You have to crave it more than anything."

He squinched his eyes shut tighter. Slowly, the image of

the swirling light formed in his mind. *Come here you stupid light.* As if on cue, a short tendril of orange light formed above the gem. Andy's hand began to feel warm and he opened his eyes at this unexpected sensation. His eyes lit up when he saw the dancing light above the gem. This small accomplishment made him nervous. *Whoa! Am I really doing this?* Unconsciously, he leaned back to put some distance between himself and the bright light before him.

"Great, Andy, now try and pull it towards your hand."

"No problem." He closed his eyes again, silently hoping he wouldn't succeed. *This is crazy.* The fiery energy was perfectly clear is his mind. Andy could distinguish every twist of every strand. He concentrated harder. In his mind the ball of fire grew larger and larger. He gasped as the tendril stretched upwards and began to mimic the image in his mind. Its intensity increased from a mere slice of orange to a roaring white geyser.

Come to me.

With this thought, the fire consumed his mind. The ball of energy erupted in a flash and surged into Andy's hand. The shock knocked him backwards onto the ground. A blazing aura enveloped him as his body struggled to ingest the energy. A moment later the aura faded, leaving wisps of steam rising from his prone body—the only proof that the transference had occurred.

"Wow," was all Jack could say.

"I've never seen anyone absorb so much energy on a first attempt," added Natalie. Surprised, she reached to examine the gem.

Kaida couldn't tear her eyes away from Andy's smoldering body. When she managed to look at the gem again her eyes widened in shock. The dancing energy once contained within the stone was completely gone. A lifeless piece of glass was all that remained. Where brilliant light used to dwell there was now merely a murky cloud, as if the energy had completely burnt out.

Groggily, Andy sat up. His head felt like it had been used as a dance floor at an elephants only night club. The aches echoing from the rest of his body weren't far behind. He tried wiggling his fingers and toes to confirm they were all still present. Each joint struggled to respond, but they all checked out fine. Every part of him felt like lead, yet strangely, he felt more alive than ever. His arms and legs groaned as he tried to move them but slowly they obeyed his commands. At the same time, he felt solid, almost indestructible. The world seemed more vibrant than ever before. Something had changed within him but his mind couldn't grasp just what it was. He looked at his hands, slowly clenching and unclenching them, trying to detect any differences.

"I have no problem sensing him now," Jack said wistfully.

"Same here," Nat agreed.

"I feel so—warm," Andy said.

"Well, I sure don't," Nat complained, looking at her snow-covered clothing.

"We should get going. We may have been followed." Kaida's words brought them back to reality. They were no longer anywhere near the fairgrounds but with all the mana being hurled about it was impossible to predict if anyone had discovered them.

"Where are we anyway?" Jack asked. He looked at Natalie expectantly.

"Westbrook," Andy volunteered.

"Where's that?"

"Uh… Canada…"

Their eyes glazed over in unison as Andy named their

location. Finally, Jack looked at Natalie and said, "You're SO busted."

"At least it explains the snow."

"Can you sense Vaughn?"

Natalie consulted her Waystone again. She pushed a button, spun a knob and sighed. "All I get is the half-pint here."

"Vaughn will come to us," Kaida stated positively, "once he realizes where we are. We should just play it safe and wait for him."

"No way I'm waiting here," moaned Natalie. "I'll freeze before he comes.".

"Hey, Squirt, you know a place where we can hang out for a bit?" asked Jack.

"Yeah, there's a little donair place some of us hang out at around the corner."

"Great, lead on."

Chapter 7

Repercussions

Mark's foot slammed into the wall paneling of the private jet, sending vibrations through the thin skin of the aircraft and projecting into the hanger beyond. Ground attendants paused their flight preparations at the sound, trying to determine the source of the ruckus. The night's activities had taken their toll on Mark. His hair was a mess and his uniform was undone, revealing his white undershirt. Anger management had never been his strong suit. *Another failure.* His fist continued his foot's attack against the wall, leaving another shallow indentation. Wearily he leaned forward and rested his forehead against the smooth surface.

"Damn them!" he cried, his fist punctuating his anger, enlarging the wall dent.

Maude sat silently across from him on a beryl and beige leather couch. Her eyes wandered every so often from the fashion magazine in her lap to Mark and back, like an experienced parent keeping an eye on an errant child. This wasn't the first fit she had witnessed. She could easily recall a dozen repair bills from similar circumstances. However, these outbursts seemed to be coming more frequently. A worried expression creased her face. *He's never been this bad before,* she thought. *We've had other setbacks but... Something else is wrong this time.* The twins were alone as their subordinates scurried around preparing for their departure. Silently she wished the others would hurry so they could leave this whole disaster behind.

"It's not your fault, Mark," she reassured him.

"It's somebody's fault."

She closed her magazine and sat up, curling her feet under her. She let herself stare at Mark as he leaned against the wall. His weariness was obvious. Neither of them had been sleeping regularly since they had arrived at the fairgrounds. It seemed that he was carrying all their failures on his shoulders, never forgetting them, never letting them go.

"It was an accident," she said dismissively. "We'll get them next time. I'm sure they won't stay hidden for long." Which was true enough. As long as Vaughn and his cronies were alive, they would keep popping up, spreading trouble and mayhem in their wake.

He turned to face her. With great effort, Mark straightened his shoulders and composed himself. His facial features relaxed and softened. Outwardly he was a picture of serenity. Only Mark's eyes now showed the inner turmoil and the chaos tearing at his soul.

"There have been enough accidents." Venom dripped from his voice as he spoke. "We examined every inch of that room, planned for every contingency. And *still* they got away."

She shrugged, knowing it was pointless to argue with him in this state. "Stuff happens."

"Is that all you have to say for yourself?"

"What do you mean?" She gave him a quizzical look.

Mark came at her point blank, holding back nothing. "You were the one in charge of preparing the wards in the vault. You failed in securing the room. It's your fault."

Maude cringed at the accusation. Her shock instantly changed to outrage. *How dare he!*

"Just what do you... they beat us, Mark. Deal with it.

Maybe if Leo had been…"

"So this is MY fault! You little…"

The door banged as Leo entered. Mark instantly cut off what he was about to say and stood at attention, saluting as Leo walked in and sat opposite them. Maude remained seated, attentively studying Leo for any hints as to how his night had fared.

"Report."·

Mark launched into a scathing review of the nights events. Their quarry's sudden appearance at the auditorium. The failure to contain them. The ineptitude of the security guards who could only think to offer them pastries before they escaped. Leo listened in stony silence. His face remained rigid as he absorbed it all with barely a blink of acknowledgement. Maude stretched out on the couch, not the least bit interested in analyzing everything again, and started flipping through another magazine. Mark's summary soon turned into a rant after the facts were presented. He was blaming Maude for the mishap when Leo cut him off.

"That will do, Mark," he said finally. "Do you have anything to add, Maude?"

"No." She glowered into her magazine, raising it to hide her face.

"I see. Don't distress yourselves too much. You're not the only ones to taste defeat tonight." He related his encounter with Vaughn and Alana to them. Mark couldn't suppress his rage as he heard Leo's story. Maude listened impassively as he spoke. Only the furrowing of her eyebrows betrayed any emotional connection to what was being said.

"We have much to do. We may have been unable to stop Vaughn from performing his vile acts once again, but we still have a few cards up our sleeves. First, we must take heart that most of the mana gems they use as batteries were depleted either by the Misorbium or by their escape. If what you say is accurate, they spent a lot of energy escaping. This means it will be essential for them to recharge theses gems and themselves as soon as possible. All known cracks in the great barrier need to be monitored. I want every man we can spare at the larger ones to monitor them personally. Secondly, we need to ascertain how to utilize the Oracle of Y'alan at once. I want our best researchers on it around the clock. Once we understand it, we can ensure that this state of magical abstinence is permanent."

"We should destroy it," suggested Mark.

"No. We can't be sure what effect that would have on the barrier," Leo explained. "Until we know more, it's wiser to study it. For all we know, destroying the Oracle will destroy the barrier preventing mana from reaching the Earth as well." He looked from Maude to Mark, "Anything else?"

"No, sir," the twins answered together.

"Then get going. You have your assignments."

"Aye, sir!" They snapped their salutes in unison and headed to pass on Leo's orders.

"Maude, a word please." She stopped and calmly pivoted to face Leo. Mark looked back at her and sneered as he walked through the hatch.

Leo waited for Mark to leave before continuing, "Now, tell me what really happened tonight."

"It occurred just as Mark described," Maude confessed.

"The Misorbium panels, they functioned adequately?"

"Yes, better than expected actually. If only…" She stopped awkwardly, pretending to examine a spot of dirt on her shoe.

Grunting, Leo sat back on the couch and fished in his pockets for his pipe. They both fell silent as he lit the tobacco, permeating the cabin with the aroma of Cavendish, cocoa with a touch of vanilla.

"I see," he said at last. "Maude, I don't blame you for what happened. I want you to know that. The very nature of magic is to court infinite possibilities making it virtually impossible to plan for every contingency. Our only edge is wit—being able to out think our opponents. Now that we've seen this particular trick, we must remember it and plan for it next time. We must be patient. Sooner or later they will get sloppy or run out of tricks. Then victory will be ours. Magic itself may be infinite in possibility but they are not infinite in ability..."

Maude stood stoically as Leo spoke. She knew he was trying to reassure her but it wasn't necessary; she didn't blame herself. *I may have set the wards, but Mark is the one who checked them.*

"You look tired, Maude."

"Oh, I've just been on the look out for magical manifestations for a week. I don't see how that could POSSIBLY be tiring," she snapped at him.

"Fine, I'll be quick. If there's nothing else you wish to add, I'll let you go."

"No, Sir, except... have you ever considered alerting the general population to these murderers? Surely with government support we could find Vaughn, and his cronies, easily and end this stalemate."

Leo paused as he considered her words. Drawing long and hard on his pipe he sent a torrent of thick smoke swirling around his head as he exhaled. He looked straight at her with a twinkle in his eye before responding.

"Alerting the authorities would cause more problems than it would solve, primarily by having to explain how we know all this, ensuring we'd be under the same scrutiny as our quarry."

"But..."

"Wouldn't they be able to help?" Leo finished for her.

"What would they do if they did find a mage? Only we can sense their presence. Only we can negate their magical abilities. Sending a mundane soldier against them would be like sending an ant against a lion. I can't imagine the terror or panic we might cause by announcing there is magic in the world. Human memories are short. Better to let them think magic is good for card tricks or pulling rabbits out of hats and nothing more. Have no fear, child. We are the protectors of this world and we will prevail."

He spoke his last words with increased enthusiasm. "Now get out of here and let an old man smoke his pipe in peace." Both of them were smiling now. "And get some sleep."

"Yes, sir," Maude confirmed as she turned and exited through the hatch.

Chapter 8

New Alliances

For the second time, bright light bathed the alley behind Mom's Laundry. Two figures, dressed in long woolen jackets, searched for something. The woman shuffled her feet and rocked her shoulders in the cold to warm herself while the man busied himself studying the remains of a scorched tennis ball. With a quick nod they walked briskly and confidently into the open street as if following something only they could see.

***

"… so then she starts running back with a bottle of shaving cream and says..."

"Shut up, Jack," interrupted Natalie.

"No, she says… "

"Shut up, Jack!" Kaida and Natalie yelled in unison. Their simultaneous solicitation was finally enough to muzzle Jack, but not enough to wipe the smug smile from his face.

Andy was sitting with a bemused grin on his face across from Jack. He wasn't really sure what to think of his new companions. Sure, they claimed they could use magic, *as if magic really existed*, which would make the stories Jack was telling almost believable. His own experiences in the alley, the burnt tennis ball, the sudden warmth and euphoria from the little 'test' they performed weren't enough to convince him of his own abilities, although he couldn't think of any other explanations for what had happened. At least here at Uggabuga's Donair Shop magic was something that wasn't a pressing concern. The food was greasy and the arcade games were old, but its comfortable booths and jovial atmosphere made up for its shortcomings. It was this combination of addicting entertainment and unhealthy snacks, away from the surveillance of prying parents and nosey teachers, which made the spot so popular with Andy and his classmates.

"I'm still hungry," Kaida said, picking up the menu again. Two malt cups sat empty before her already.

Natalie looked enviously at Kaida, her wheatgrass smoothie sat half empty in front of her. In spite of its image, Uggabuga was experimenting with a few trendy, healthier choices, adding wheatgrass, and herbal supplements like Echinacea, Ginseng and Bee Pollen in an attempt to appeal to non-school-age customers.

"Aren't you afraid of getting fat?" Natalie asked Kaida.

"Give it a rest, Nat," Jack sassed. "Just because you think wheatgrass is tasty, doesn't mean we all do. You shouldn't worry so much. Besides, even if you did put on a few pounds you could always just teleport them off, right?"

"It doesn't work that way, Jack," Natalie answered politely. Slyly adding, "But, maybe you'd like to help me experiment? You could stand to lose a few pounds yourself." Her eyes sparkled at the prospect of humiliating him again.

The waitress, a short girl with dark hair in two long ponytails, and a long white apron sauntered over and enthusiastically began clearing their empty dishes. She didn't even blink when Kaida ordered another malt. Instead, she added, "They are good, aren't they?" Andy smiled as she returned to the kitchen.

"Don't look at me," Jack pleaded, holding up his hand. "It's Kaida who's going to be needing your help. Anyways, I'm sure she'd love to work with you on that. Think of it as a girl bonding experience."

Kaida was not amused. A chilly glance was the only warning Jack earned before a loud pop echoed through the cafe. Powdered glass fragments rained on Jack from a broken light high above him. Not one piece of debris missed him thanks to a few quick magical manipulations from Natalie. Jack sat perfectly still as the white crystals accumulated on his head and shoulders. His eyes flicked between the two girls as he tried to decide who was guiltier. In the background he could hear Andy laughing at him.

"Laugh it up, half-pint."

"Face it, you've been burned," Andy managed between chuckles.

"I'll get you yet, your highness, and your little lackey too," threatened Jack, half-heartedly.

"What?" Kaida batted her eyes, innocent as a newborn lamb.

"Now this is a bonding experience!" Nat was all smiles as she elbowed Kaida.

***

In spite of it all, Jack was grinning too. Watching them taunt and tease one another, Andy got the impression this sort of thing happened a lot. Like people who grew up together, there was a bond between them that seemed to go beyond mere friendship.

"Wait, why did you call her 'your highness'?" Andy asked.

"Well, 'cause she's a queen," Jack answered. "Well, a former queen anyway."

Andy could hardly believe his ears. First he'd learned he could use magic and now he was hobnobbing with royalty. Could things get any weirder?

"Where are you from Kaida?"

"I was born in Osaka, but I grew up in Kyoto."

"You're Japanese? I never would have—I mean, I didn't think they had a queen?"

"My father moved around a lot because of work," explained Kaida, an amused grin on her lips. "He married a native but he was originally from the states."

"Of course Japan doesn't have a queen," Jack butted in. "She's the queen of Sylgara, land of dragons!"

"Huh?" Andy was totally confused.

Kaida looked distinctly annoyed.

"You know, Sylgara, from Dragon Masters, the computer game," continued Jack.

"Are you kidding? Everyone knows that game!" Andy had many friends who were addicted to Dragon Masters. It had taken the online world by storm when it came out two years ago and it was considered one of the pillars of the role-playing game community. Its graphics were superior to any other game and its player vs. player combat was legendary. In fact, only recently had someone managed to kill the final boss monster, Queen Xulalita, the dragon ruler.

"Wow, you used to work on that game, Kaida? That's awesome! Everyone used to say that monster was under human control. It was way harder than anything else in the game. A lot of people gave up trying to beat her but finally my friend Lance did a few weeks ago."

"What?!" Kaida gave Andy her full attention.

"Yeah, Lance said they must have reprogrammed her or something because her fighting style became really predictable and he could exploit it."

Anger boiled up within Kaida as Andy spoke. Her face went rigid and her hands clenched one of the empty cups in front of her. The warning signs were clear to Jack and Natalie, who exchanged worried looks, but Andy kept going.

"I'm sure everyone will be beating her soon. Lance said it's pretty easy once you know how. He posted a big guide in the game's 'how to' forums." Andy's companions were silent. Jack and Nat watched Kaida expectantly.

"I'll kill him," she stated finally with the same nonchalance as a doctor diagnosing a stubbed toe.

Andy bust out laughing. The serious expression on Kaida's face didn't change, however. Startled, his voice caught, "What! Why?"

"Kaida didn't program the character, she WAS Queen Xulalita," Natalie informed him. "Her magical specialty is controlling electrons and technology and stuff. When Vaughn found her, she was actually living inside the game. In the original version, there was no Xulalita at all. Kaida created her to defend the dragon lands. Those who fought Queen Xulalita were actually fighting Kaida. Naturally, there was no way for them to win."

Andy's jaw hit the floor as he listened to Natalie. *Magic, queens, living computer characters, next they're going to tell me that the Tooth Fairy is real.* His mind reeled with the possibilities, as a part of him desperately tried to reject the scene before him.

"Ya, right... what were you doing inside a computer game?" Andy asked cautiously.

"Hiding," Kaida replied.

"Hiding?" Andy looked confused. That was the last answer he had expected.

"Vaughn overheard someone talking in some cyber-café about how impossible this character was, and that even those who tried to hack the server to beat her were utterly destroyed," Jack cut in. "Vaughn's own curiosity got the better of him, so he tried the game himself and discovered Kaida controlling the queen. He contacted her soon after that. Once Vaughn was able to convince her that he could use magic inside the computer game too, she came around pretty fast."

"Oh, how'd he do that?"

"He killed her character," Jack stated triumphantly. "Vaughn was the first to beat the great Xulalita but he was using magic so you could call it cheating, I guess. Then again, she was using magic too so…" Jack shrugged as he trailed off, trying not to provoke Kaida.

"Anyways, right afterwards, Vaughn disappeared for a week and when he returned Kaida was with him," Nat added.

"Where did he go?"

They all looked at Kaida expectantly. She ignored them and took to studying one of the menus on the table. When it was clear she wasn't volunteering anything, Nat continued, "We don't know. She's been rather tight-lipped about that."

Andy sat still, trying to digest what he had just heard.

"How long have you all been together?"

"About five years for me," Natalie offered. "Kaida joined up about a year after I did and Jack…" she smiled mischievously as she spoke his name, "Jack's the baby. He's only been with us about a year."

"And it's a wonder how you guys survived without me," he said.

"Get over yourself. We've been covering your bungling ever since you got here."

"Two words Nat-illa: Water-park Rumble."

"What-ever…"

"Are you with these guys, Andy-Pandy?"

Nat's scathing rebuke drew more attention than she anticipated. A trio of boys, wearing letter jackets marked Westbrook High, were approaching their booth. In the middle was the master of mayhem himself, Lance.

"Hey, Lance, your mom let you out early after dinner again?" Andy said. "I'm surprised you managed to make it across the street without her. At least you have Randy and Conner to hold your hands."

"Aww, you're so cute when you're trying to be cool," replied Lance. "How much are you paying these people to be your friends?"

"Absolutely nothing. I was just telling them how I scored the winning goal in today's hockey game." It felt good to grind Lance's gears for once.

"Oh, ya?" Lance couldn't believe his ears. "That was luck, not skill."

"Let me guess," replied Andy, "You were tired, and there was snow in your boots?"

"Bah, we had your team cold." Lance gave a dismissive wave. He half turned to survey the restaurant, losing interest in the conversation.

"Was this before or after he shot one right through the net?" asked Jack.

Lance lost some of his bravado as he turned; his full attention was on Jack, still covered in glass slivers and shavings, sitting calmly smiling up at him.

"What are you supposed to be? Some kind of Christmas ornament?" asked Lance, confused.

Jack's expression soured instantly but Nat cut him off. "I think he's a hero," she added and snuggled up to Andy. "You guys did say last goal wins, right?"

Stunned, Lance just stood there, unable to comprehend that his barbs had actually backfired for once. He looked to his companions for support but even they were busy looking elsewhere, anywhere but at the people sitting in the booth in front of them. Gritting his teeth, Lance sneered at Andy, trying to salvage some of his pride.

"Whatever. Let's go, guys. I want to beat my high score on Bojo's Revenge tonight. We'll settle this next game. Then you'll see who the real champs are around here."

"Anytime, man, anytime," Andy replied, grinning.

As the trio left, and made their way to the arcade games in the far corner of the restaurant. Jack fidgeted in his seat. Nat gracefully un-entwined herself from Andy, causing him to blush. She smiled at this modest complement and shot him her signature don't-get-any-ideas look.

"What is Bojo's Revenge?" Kaida asked, still watching the boys as they started to play.

"It's the latest fighting game. No one has really mastered it yet. Lance is pretty good though. Best around here anyways."

"I'll pwn him," Kaida replied as she started to get up. "Consider him fragged."

"You think that's a good idea?" Jack asked, sensing another arcade assassination in the making.

"Ab-so-lute-ly," she replied and set off across the floor.

When she was about half-way there Jack leaned across the table and asked Natalie, "Think he has a chance?"

"None whatsoever," Nat replied matter-of-factly.

They moved on to other things. They talked about traveling and hobbies. Andy confessed to never having been away from Westbrook, except for the rare occasions he had gone to visit relatives in Vancouver with his mom. They all agreed that a two hour car ride didn't actually constitute having been somewhere. Andy was amazed at some of the things Jack and Nat had done. They told him about when they had been to Monaco and had caused a rude hotel clerk's face to appear in the hotel's most prized painting. On another occasion they'd brought a statue to life in Naples to scare away a street hustler. Throughout their discussion they could hear muffled cries of anguish from the game players across the room. Being so enthralled by their conversation, they barely acknowledged the waitress when she returned with Kaida's malt.

"Your malt, madam."

"Actually she's…" Nat started but stopped when she recognized the waitress.

Her black hair was done up in a bun, accenting her rosy complexion and large, deep blue eyes. Behind her stood a young man with equally dark hair and eyes. He looked familiar but Natalie couldn't quite place him. Alana took Kaida's spot in the booth, her eyes twinkling in delight.

"In that case," Alana bubbled before she took a quick taste. "Mmmm, this is good."

"How did your gig with Vaughn go?" Jack asked. "Where is he anyways?"

"Why I'm right here, of course." Vaughn stepped closer to the table.

"Wow, they're really doing miracles with Botox these days," Jack quipped.

"My HMO hates me," Vaughn grinned. "Membership has its privileges though." He made a slight waving motion with his right hand. On cue, Jack scooched over, allowing Vaughn to sit across from Alana.

"Tell me, my young apprentices, what difficulties did you encounter at the fairgrounds that forced you to jump all the way out here?"

"Well," Nat began, "We were looking for you actually... But instead we found him." She wiggled her thumb at Andy.

"Indeed." Vaughn raised an eyebrow as he set his gaze upon Andy for the first time.

"One moment." Alana drew their attention as she snapped her fingers. The air around the booth shimmered for a second before reverting to normal. There was a noticeable muting of ambient sounds around them. "Just in case someone is trying to overhear us."

Natalie quickly turned from Alana to Vaughn, who merely nodded in agreement. Then she began telling the whole story of their recent encounters. How they had escaped into the night only to find a snow covered teenager instead of their ailing leader. How he passed their magical test with flying colors, and how they had learned that Queen Xulalita had finally been defeated.

Vaughn took in every detail, shifting only to acknowledge Andy when his name was mentioned. When Natalie finished he looked down for a moment, digesting what he had heard. Finally he said.

"How's she taking it?"

Ah, priorities. Jack thought. *Here we sit with a boy who may be the most powerful wizard we've ever discovered and Vaughn wants to talk about video games.* He looked across the restaurant and saw Kaida engrossed in the game she was playing. A small crowd had gathered around her. He couldn't see Lance's face, but from the way he was standing he didn't look too happy.

"As well as can be expected..." Nat offered.

"Has she killed anyone yet?" Vaughn asked, an amused look on his face.

"She's in progress as we speak." Jack chuckled.

"Is that what she's up to?" inquired Alana, staring at the

mass of bodies huddled around the Bojo's Revenge machine. "Public executions always draw a crowd."

The five of them couldn't hold back their smiles and exchanged knowing glances. These weren't the first newbs ganked by Kaida's wrath.

***

"So tell me, Andy," Vaughn began again, "how long have you been able to use magic?"

The smiles were casually replaced with an assortment of inquisitive looks. Suddenly the center of attention, Andy found himself unable to speak. He moved his mouth but no sounds came out. Jack promptly gave him a stiff shot in the arm, enabling Andy to squeak out, "I haven't, I mean, today was the first time."

"I see. Perhaps you should start by telling us a little about yourself," Alana prompted.

"Well, there's really not much to tell there but..." Andy began to tell how he came to live in Westbrook. How his parents divorced soon after coming here and he had stayed to live with his mother. He told them about school and summer and winter and the vacations he'd taken. If fact, strangely, he couldn't stop talking. He told them everything, even about his favorite cereal and his lucky socks. He talked until his head was completely empty of anything to say. Dizzy, he finally stopped, and took a deep, slow, breath.

"Well Andy, it's apparent you've accomplished quite a bit in, how old did you say you were again?"

"I'm fourteen," Andy said brightly.

"Yes, of course you are," Vaughn asserted. "In any case, it seems you're more than ready to join us and learn how to control your magical abilities as my student."

Andy was stunned by what he had just heard and he wasn't the only one. Everyone was looking at Vaughn in surprise.

"May I have a word with you?" Alana asked Vaughn.

"Of course."

The two of them rose and commandeered a neighboring booth. The air seemed to lighten as they left. Jack and Natalie waited till they were seated at the next table before congratulating Andy.

"That was quick," Jack said with a smirk. "Usually they interrogate people for days, although, they don't all babble as readily as you do. I wonder who will be baby-sitting first, Nat?"

"Welcome to the team, Andy," congratulated Natalie. "And, the only person in need of baby-sitting is you, Jack."

"You wouldn't know what to do with a baby if one crawled over and...."

"Thanks." Andy cut Jack off, hoping to avoid another light bulb shower. "But what does that mean exactly? What do you guys do?"

"Well, my young friend, it means you're going to be trained to control your magical abilities for starters," Vaughn said as he returned to the booth. "It is our duty to preserve what magic we can, and to pass it on to those who can use it. For, well longer than you can imagine, Alana and I have been eluding those who would see magic snuffed out forever."

"What do you mean?" Andy was thoroughly fascinated by Vaughn's words.

"In the old days, when humans were still new to the word, magic was everywhere. Those who could wield it were easily found. Youngsters would regularly test themselves against their friends and family for status and honor. They called themselves the Vir, or 'heroes' in today's English. But another kind of mage also existed, much rarer and more specialized than the Vir. Instead of wielding and channeling magical energies, they could devour them, thus preventing people from using magic. These people were known as Econtravir or 'anti-magi'. The Ruling Council of the age formed the world's first police force from these anti-magi. The most capable were hand-picked to join the nation's elite royal guard. But that was then..." Vaughn's voice trailed off.

Andy looked confused. "So, these anti-magi, like this Leo you mentioned earlier, don't they use magic too?"

"Yes... and no," replied Vaughn. "They are opposites. Much like hot is the opposite of cold. In essence they describe the same thing, temperature, but in practice, fire behaves very different than ice. It's similar to what we do. The way we shape and manipulate the energy of the world is called magic, whereas, the way that energy is destroyed is described as anti-magic. Certainly they are related, but they are not the same."

Andy was silent. *That makes sense, I guess.*

"Today, the energy needed for people to activate their abilities and use magic is very scarce," Alana picked up the story, "Even though people are still capable of using magic, it is much more difficult to spot them. There isn't enough magical energy in most places to allow magic to happen. Only those with specialized natural traits and abilities, such as Kaida's ability to control computers or Natalie's teleportation ability, have a chance of developing those abilities because the magical energy needed to use them is far less than normal. In the ancient academies, it would take someone years of study and practice to do the same feats, yet Kaida and Natalie do them instinctively. Detecting people who can use magic requires them to use it. Since the energy to do so is so scarce, many people who could use magic never develop their abilities."

"So, my ability is controlling fire!" Andy blurted out

excitedly. His mind instantly recalled the flames he saw during the test and the melted tennis ball stuck to the wall in the alley.

"That is quite possible," Vaughn confirmed. "It will require a bit of study to determine your exact potential, but it seems like a perfect place to start."

Chapter 9

Dreams and Plans

"Have you seen my dog? He's a white Maltese named Scooter."

Vaughn woke with a start. Perspiration stuck his nightclothes to his body as he instinctively checked his surroundings. The single bed creaked as he threw back the teddy bear covered duvet and stood up. A clock in the shape of a shaggy blue monster holding a cookie flashed 4:00 a.m. in bright red numbers. He could only make out vague shapes of furniture, model cars, and other belongings occupying the room. Carefully he walked to the door, making sure not to disturb Jack, who was curled up in a red and blue sleeping bag on the floor. Vaughn's blue and brown striped pajamas clung to him as he moved. Slowly he turned the door handle, trying to be as silent as possible. After the previous day's harrowing events he wanted everyone to get as much rest as possible.

Andy's mother had been very gracious to let everyone "sleep over" for the night. On Vaughn's coaching, he, Alana, Kaida, Natalie, and Jack pretended to be visiting exchange students. It didn't take much effort to make Alana and himself appear younger than they were to Ms. Cache. Over the years they had many opportunities to practice this particular skill. The main problem lay in finding room for them all. A spare cot was added to the guest room to accommodate Alana, Kaida, and Natalie. Andy had graciously offered up his room for the guys, thus relegating himself to a prime spot on the living room couch.

Vaughn slipped through the doorway and gently shut it behind him. He moved silently down the short hallway towards the washroom. Pictures lined the walls on either side of him. He couldn't see what they were exactly, but he deduced they were mostly family pictures of Andy and his mom. Andy had not mentioned why his parents divorced but it wasn't a subject Vaughn felt comfortable pursuing. He flicked on the bathroom lights after a few fumbling tries. The dream kept flashing through his head. At least he hoped it was only a dream. The process of absorbing another person's soul was not without its difficulties. Entwining body, soul, and magic so tightly was never recommended, even at the best of times. He rubbed his temples and took a hard look at himself in the mirror, forcing himself to remember that he was Vaughinlus Stormbaur the VIII, High Chancellor of...

"Jack snoring tonight?"

Vaughn whipped around to find Alana in the doorway leaning against the frame. She was wearing a yellow T-shirt and matching boxer shorts. Her hair was braided in one long plait hanging over her shoulder and her arms were crossed over her chest.

"You don't approve of my late night escapades?" Recovering from his initial shock, his body relaxed once again. "You seem to be having trouble sleeping as well."

"I'm worried about you."

"How so?"

"It's not like you to be so trusting so soon. Don't you think we're moving a little fast here?"

"I have no doubt that he is one of us." Vaughn turned way from her, preoccupied by his reflection in the mirror.

"We don't even know what his innate abilities are yet."

"I have an idea as to what those powers entail," Vaughn

assured her.

"Oh, really." Alana was clearly annoyed that she had missed something. "A boy heats up one little tennis ball and you think you've got him all figured out?"

"From the stories the others told it's obvious he has some ability to control fire. His recollection of his test confirms at least that much."

"You suspect more though?"

"It's too early to say. However, I doubt it was totally accidental that Natalie's Waystone locked onto him instead of me," Vaughn continued. "It would be reasonable to assume that his powers rival my own. What I do know is that we must train him as quickly as possible. If Leo really has found the Oracle of Y'alan we must retrieve it at all costs. If Andy really has the ability to control fire we may at long last have a formidable weapon we can use against those Terra Protectra buffoons."

"Is that all you see him as? A weapon?" Alana asked crossly.

"What Leo has in his possession could doom us all."

"Why is it so important?"

Vaughn stopped his facial examination and turned to her. He smiled.

"It's been so long. I forget you were only a child back then, when it happened." He paused. "Even I do not know the legend's true origin but they say that during the Time of Woe, our first Emperor, Eldoran Kalridge Y'alan the Great, summoned all of his strength and cast a monumental spell to save our lands from a devastating storm. When the spell had run its course, all that was left was a crystal statue about the length of a man's arm in the shape of our beloved Emperor as he stood posed to fight the storm. Our scholars studied it intensely and believed a fragment of the old emperor's spirit remained, locked within the crystal. In times of great need, legend states that the statue would speak to those around it, offering warnings of the hard times ahead. This is how it became known as the Oracle of Y'alan. But it has been ages since the Oracle last spoke. The only other fact that I know is that it is also an unparalleled power focus. Many powerful magical rites would not have been possible without it. There are rumors that the Oracle can also… Well, they're just rumors. I don't put much stock in them. If it holds any other powers, no one has been able to confirm them."

"I can see why Leo would be interested in it," Alana agreed, "but surely it was destroyed along with everything else during the destruction of Baurum'tatus."

"I assumed so too, but who knows for certain?"

Vaughn's voice grew distant and he paused to collect his thoughts before continuing. "There's one other thing you should know. It is believed that the Oracle was used in the disaster that destroyed Baurum'tatus." Alana straightened at this. "Trust me on this, Alana, but that is not our only worry. If Leo did manage to activate the Oracle, and that is a big if, he could also use it to find the sleeping chambers we have kept hidden for so very long."

"What? Impossible. How can you know that?" Alana looked suspicious.

Vaughn ignored her question. "We must recover it before Leo learns its secrets or worse, destroys it. Personally, I have no doubt it was used in the catastrophe that destroyed our city and erected the barrier preventing magical energy from reaching this planet. I don't know of any other objects that would have the power to do so. Possessing the Oracle's power is probably our only chance of restoring magic to this world."

They stared at each other at length. "Very well," Alana finally conceded. "Do you have any idea how to get it? We don't know where their headquarters is much less where the Oracle would be kept."

"If we can't go to them then we must bring them to us," Vaughn said.

Alana raised a wary eyebrow, clearly not liking where this was going. "How?" The word dripped out of her mouth, conveying her reservations about what Vaughn was about to suggest before he even said it.

"It's easy to catch anything, really," he said mildly, "if you use the proper bait."

"And which one of us do you propose to use as this 'bait'?"

"My dear, there is only one of us whom they won't shoot on sight. The rest of us are too well known."

"Do you really think he'll go along with it?" Alana asked.

"He doesn't need to know."

"And you're certain he'll come with us?"

"He's young. If it's one thing I know about young people, it's that they love new things. With us, he'll be able to experience much more than this little town could ever offer. Besides, he needs us. No one else can train him to use his magical gifts. I dare say that's an offer not easily passed up. And, of course, if we are unable to rescue him afterwards, he won't be of much help to them."

She considered what he had said. His plan was as simple as it was barbaric. There were so few mages left that to casually sacrifice one on a whim— yet, if this Oracle was as important as Vaughn said is was...

"There has to be another way," she said at last. "Your plan seems rather brash, does it not?"

"Certainly, but time is of the essence. We cannot allow

Leo to damage the Oracle in any way. The fate of the world may depend on our 'brash' actions."

"I understand," Alana said as she turned to leave. "Vaughn, I really hate you sometimes."

Vaughn smiled as he watched her go. *That, my dear, is the least of my worries.*

Chapter 10

Magic in the Air

The morning sun shone brightly through the kitchen window. Outside, the sky was clear blue as far as the eye could see. Inside, the kitchen table was covered with dirty bowls and leftover ingredients. The dining room table had been commandeered for breakfast. Its oak tabletop had ample room to accommodate everyone thanks to an extra leaf pulled out of a nearby closet. Jack and Kaida were busy making Belgian waffles, to Ms. Cache's delight, allowing her to sit and enjoy a meal for a change. Although, it was obvious that Ms. Cache worried that some of her guests were a little young to be drinking coffee. Hungrily they wolfed down their waffles, heavily coated with maple syrup, fresh fruits, and icing sugar.

"Another waffle, Ms. Cache?" asked Jack.

"I'm good, thanks. And please, just call me Susan. Every time I hear 'Ms. Cache' I feel twenty years older than I already am."

Alana struck up a brilliant conversation with Susan about tea blends and their health benefits before Ms. Cache was forced to rush off to work. With her gone, the others got down to business.

"Well, we should be off, as well," Vaughn said as he rose to his feet.

"Already?" Andy looked disheartened. He greatly enjoyed their company. In the short time they had been together Andy already considered them friends. For once he was around people who weren't talking about how he dressed or what would make a good after-school snack. They were talking about life and death adventures and important missions. *Leaving already? I thought they were going to teach me some magic?* thought Andy. Somehow, his world seemed emptier now that they were leaving.

"Time waits for no man, Andy," Vaughn quoted dryly. "Our adversaries will track us eventually. It's best to keep moving."

The trio finished tidying up and gathered around Andy to say their farewells. Although they had barely been together a few days, a bond had formed between them. Alana stood off to the side, seemingly resigned to their departure.

"Will I see you guys again?" Andy asked.

"Well," began Jack, "with the way Nat teleports..."

"Definitely," Vaughn eye's twinkled as he assured him. He seemed certain of this. Andy wished he had his confidence though. "Come with us, Andy."

The words sent goose bumps down Andy's spine. That wasn't what he had expected Vaughn to say at all. Not in a million years. Thoughts of wild adventures and amazing magical feats danced in his head.

"C'mon, Andy," Jack prodded. "I could use a wingman. You know, someone to watch my back around these two." He jerked his thumb in the direction of Natalie and Kaida.

"At lest you're right about the 'needing help' part," Natalie said as she eyed Jack critically. "Come with us, Andy. We could definitely use someone who's IQ is bigger than their shoe size."

Jack shot Natalie a menacing look.

"I'd like you to come too," said Kaida, her calm voice diffusing the fiery stares between Jack and Natalie.

"We need you, Andy," Vaughn continued. His tone was

serious. "There aren't many of us left. We need everyone we can get."

Andy felt his heart longing to go with them. He kept remembering the melted tennis ball stuck to the wall and wondered what else he was capable of doing. The possibilities seemed limitless. His life until now seemed drab in comparison. *Getting up, going to school everyday, doing homework, brushing my teeth before bed. It was all so... ordinary. Yet...*

"I can't." His answer stunned him almost as much it did them. "I mean... my mom... and school, there's no way they'd just let me leave... even if I wanted too."

His answer echoed in the room, drowning out all other noises, and dampening the cheery atmosphere that had existed a moment ago.

"Andy," Vaughn said slowly, "Do you want to come with us?"

"Well, I guess, but..."

"Do you want to learn how to control your abilities?"

"Of course!"

"Then join us, Andy," said Vaughn. "Become what you were meant to be."

"But what about..." he began to protest.

"We can take care of everything, Andy," Alana spoke up. "If you want us to, that is."

Andy didn't speak for a few minutes as he wrestled with the decision. The thrill of learning magic, real magic, weighed heavily against school, hockey... "Okay, I'll come, as long as you can square it with my mom. I don't want her worrying about me."

"Naturally," Vaughn reassured him, "I'm sure she'll be delighted as well."

Andy was skeptical about that but he was eager to get

started. *I'm going to learn real magic!*

"Welcome aboard!" Natalie slapped Andy hard across his back. "Let's rock this town."

"Good choice, squirt," said Jack, enthusiastically.

"Welcome to the team, Andy," Kaida added.

"Let's get to work, shall we?" Vaughn began laying out the plan.

***

Susan Cache's day had never been busier. The fourth floor of the Westbrook town offices was already humming with activity as she entered that morning. A stack of fresh audit reports awaited her as she entered her cubical. The unexpected weather was playing havoc with the transportation budget and, as usual, only she could make sense of what was going on.

She barely registered the announcement that someone was there to see her.

"Susan Cache?"

"Yes?" she replied, from behind a mound of paperwork. She felt momentarily lightheaded before acknowledging her visitor. The speaker was an elderly gentleman in a plain but well kept grey suit. He wasted no time congratulating her on her son's acceptance to the very private school he represented. He apologized profusely for arriving so late in the term as the application paperwork was held up for some reason or another, but everything was straightened out now and Andy could attend with a full scholarship. He praised her profusely on raising such a 'fine young man' and said they expected great things from him at the academy.

Ms. Cache couldn't help feeling incredibly proud of her son and grateful for this new opportunity, although, she couldn't remember applying to any private schools. She was thankful such a distinguished school was interested in Andy and worried about holding him back if she refused to let him go. She would miss him dearly but putting her son's interests before her own was every parent's responsibility. With a tear, Ms. Cache signed the papers, making way for Andy's new school term to commence.

She walked the headmaster to the empty elevator when they were finished. As he stepped into the lift he bowed and apologized once again for disturbing her before the doors closed. On the ground floor a single woman with long dark hair exited the elevator and briskly left the building.

***

Duncan Singleleaf had been the principal of the Westbrook Jr. / Sr. High School for almost fifteen years. During that time he'd thought he had seen everything. That was until a well-dressed older woman walked into his office, informing him of Andy Cache's acceptance into a very prestigious academy, to which he would be transferring immediately. When Duncan mentioned that she must be mistaken, and that he couldn't remember Andy being on the honor roll even once, she merely looked at him questioningly and assured him that he must be thinking of someone else. She assured him that they had already contacted Andy's parents and just a few clerical matters remained.

Principal Singleleaf looked at the armful of paperwork she pulled out for him to sign, and sighed. All of it looked very proper and official. When it was finished, she gushed, saying how lucky they were to be accepting such an outstanding student and that they were expecting great things from him. Duncan remained skeptical, but if this grand academy wanted Andy they were welcome to him. There were plenty of other students to look after. He escorted the woman out of the school, thanking her for taking the time to come in person to tell him the good news. *If some school I've never heard of wants to poach one of my students then good riddance,* he thought. As Principal Singleleaf walked back to his office, he glanced at the pictures and plaques identifying past honor roll students and citizenship award recipients along the wall of the administration room. He stopped and stared, not believing what he saw. Andy's name and picture were on every one.

Chapter 11

Home is where the Magic is

Andy materialized on a sandy beach, surrounded by his new companions. He ran his hands over his body, reassuring himself that everything was still attached in its proper place. Convinced that everything was where it should be, he examined his new surroundings. Clear, sparkling water reflected the sun high in the sky. Small waves washed ashore, bringing pieces of driftwood with them. Beyond the narrow stretch of beach, all he could see were tall palms scattered amongst the sand and underbrush. The air was fresh and mild, a pleasant change after all the cold and snow back home. His companions were already walking down the beach, chatting freely amongst themselves. Andy ran to catch up.

"Where are we?" asked Andy.

"We be home, mon!" Jack exclaimed in an imitation Jamaican accent. "Well, as close to a home as we have."

"We keep moving around," explained Vaughn, "to stay ahead of Terra Protectra, but we come here every so often for extended stays."

They soon left the beach, following a narrow trail into the brush. With Jack in the lead, they made good time traipsing through the dense jungle-like vegetation. Andy was surprised to see a house at the end of the trail. It was a small, one room dwelling, made entirely of hand crafted wood planks with a thick thatched roof. Andy couldn't help thinking that his mother's garden shed was larger, and a fair bit sturdier than what was before him now.

Above the door the phrase, 'Welcome to Arcadia' was burned into a raw plank. Peeking through the open entrance, Andy spied a collection of reed mats covering the floor and a single wooden stool occupied a far corner. Not knowing what else to do, Andy nodded and smiled as he wondered how the six of them could possibly share this cramped little room.

"It looks cozy," he said with a worried grin. "I've never been camping before."

"Really?" asked Vaughn, amused. "If your training goes well we may be able to find time to take you."

Puzzled, Andy smiled weakly and mumbled, "Great," under his breath.

"Follow me," said Vaughn. He walked into the cabin and knelt in the middle of the room. The others followed in single file and took up positions around him. Andy jumped in surprise as a circle of sparkling light formed on the floor, centered on Vaughn. Strange symbols formed in the air around Vaughn. They revolved around him for a moment and then vanished as quickly as they had appeared. A second later, two of the floor mats in front of Vaughn disappeared revealing a deep hole. Vaughn stood and strode briskly into the darkness below. Andy followed him and the others into the earth, eager to see what was about to unfold.

An earthy smell engulfed him as he descended. It took a moment for his eyes to adjust to the dim light. The tunnel stretched out before him, sloping deeper into the ground, much further than he expected. The walls were just over an arms length apart on either side of him. Speechlessly, he watched small round stones on the ground along the tunnel path glow as Vaughn passed them, creating two solid strips of soft bluish light to guide them. The light created eerie reflections as it bounced off the tawny-orange humite walls. They followed the tunnel for some time until at last they reached a grand furnished chamber with a number of smaller tunnels branching off from it.

"It's not much, but it's home," Alana said warmly. "Welcome!"

A large fireplace occupied the center of the room, encircled by a pair of half-moon tan suede couches. Wooden shelves filled with old books with strange writing on the covers lined one wall of the room. A pair of writing desks were set against another wall. Pictures of odd places, at least places Andy had never seen before, depicting large stone buildings and glowing people suspended in mid-air covered the walls. Burned into the rock were large runes at random intervals. Looking back down the tunnel, Andy noticed that runes covered every wall in some form or another, even those in the tunnel they just walked through.

"The runes help disguise our little hide-away," Alana stated, guessing the source of his curiosity. "They prevent magical energy from leaking outside where others may detect it.

"If you like," Alana continued, "I'm sure Kaida would be happy to give you a quick tour while Vaughn prepares your room."

"Oh yes, I'd like that," Andy replied.

"Certainly," Kaida said. "This way."

"I'll come too," Natalie said. "Just so he knows to STAY OUT of MY room."

Laughing, Andy let Kaida steer him through the tunnels. She showed him the work rooms and meditation rooms where they worked their magic and practiced their skills. Andy marveled at the ingenious system of small skylights and mirrors used to light the rooms. Where light couldn't reach, glow globes, magical balls of light, were used instead. As the tour continued, Kaida led him through the library, kitchen, lounge, exercise room, game room, which Andy supposed was Kaida's favorite, and even an underground pool. *Nothing like roughing it,* thought Andy, understanding why Vaughn had reacted to his camping comment the way he did.

"This place is huge! It's like having a hotel in your backyard."

Kaida smiled as she led him up another hallway towards where Vaughn and Jack stood. "And finally," she said, "your room."

Andy had almost forgotten. With everything Kaida had shown him, needing a bed was the last thing on his mind.

"Come, let's get you a room." Vaughn beckoned Andy down one of the side passageways. "I'm just about ready."

"That was quick," said Jack as he leaned against the wall. Next to him, a door marked with big bold letters read, 'JACK'S PLACE, Enter On Pain of DEATH!' The sign drew scoffs and smirks from Natalie and Kaida. Andy looked at Jack who only shrugged.

"Hey, you've gott'a protect your turf with those two around." Jack jerked his thumb towards the girls. Andy suppressed his laughter but failed to restrain his smile from peaking through. "Honestly, you'll be begging for a sign of your own soon."

The girls continued on down the hallway, whispering to themselves.

"Yes... well... in any case," Vaughn started, "about here should do, don't you think Andy?"

Puzzled, Andy looked from Jack's door to the blank wall where Vaughn was standing.

"Um, sure, I guess so."

"Stand back then." Vaughn said as he raised his arms. His hands were already glowing with soft yellow magic before Andy and Jack could relocate themselves out of the way. Vaughn squared himself with the wall and extended his arms straight out toward it.

Andy could feel the energy pouring out of Vaughn as an energy induced euphoria swept through him. *This must be very strong magic,* he thought. *Someday I'll be able to do this I bet.* A door sized chunk of the rock wall was glowing bright yellow now yet Vaughn continued to channel more energy into it. Hairs on the back of Andy's neck stood up, resonating with the energy around him. The area turned to a molten liquid, folding inwards upon itself, boring deeper into the rock wall.

A minute later it was done. The light faded away revealing a large opening where solid rock used to be. The tingling sensation he felt began to disappear as the remaining magical residue dissipated. Andy moved towards the door and peeked inside. A large empty oval room had been carved out of the rock, complete with runes of protection on the far walls.

"Alana should be by soon to help with the furnishings. I don't have an eye for that sort of thing," Vaughn said with a wink before leaving.

Jack examined the new room with a critical eye and marched out after Vaughn. "Hey, how come his room is bigger than mine?" he shouted down the hall.

Andy couldn't help laughing gleefully. Vaughn made it look so easy, and he was going to learn how! This was the best day of his life. With all the excitement he barely had a chance to let everything sink in. He wondered how his mother was handling this. Would she miss him? Andy walked into his new room and examined it more closely. The walls were the same color as the hallway and extraordinarily smooth to the touch. It felt empty and unfamiliar, but intoxicating at the same time.

"Now then, you can't sleep on the floor," Alana said as she appeared in the doorway. "Let's do something about that, shall we?"

A bed, desk, dresser, wardrobe, and a few other knick-knacks later, the room was ready. "Enjoy your new room, Andy." She turned to leave. "Oh, I almost forgot!" With a wave of her hand a door appeared. "There you go. Dinner should be ready soon." Andy took one last look around and followed her out of his room. As he closed his door he noticed it read, ANDY'S PLACE.

Chapter 12

Training Begins

The evening flew by as everyone lounged on the sofas around the fire, telling stories and discussing magic. Jack regaled them with stories of pirates and lost treasures, as they hung on his every word. Vaughn told them all a delightful tale about how much trouble Alana used to get into when she was young, to her obvious displeasure. Jack and Natalie laughed along with Andy, even though they'd apparently heard the story many times before.

"Vaughn never tires of that one," Natalie managed between giggles. As the fire burned low, Vaughn ended his story telling with a long yawn, signaling to everyone that it was time for bed. Andy lay in bed wide awake for a long time thinking, *I'm going to be learning magic tomorrow,* before finally drifting off to sleep.

The next morning, Andy was so excited he hardly touched his breakfast. He chugged a glass of orange juice and grabbed a handful of frosted Wheaties before running down to the work room. It had been decided yesterday that Vaughn and Alana would tutor him themselves so he could quickly learn the basics of magic and understand what Jack, Nat, and Kaida were studying. Vaughn would teach him how to control and manipulate his abilities and Alana would instruct him on how to sense mana in others and focus his own powers.

The workroom was bare except for an ancient stone table

against one wall and a half dozen wooden chairs. The massive table was a good eight feet long and four feet wide, with carved runes around the edge and down its legs. The chairs were simple and slender with high backs and stout arms, reinforcing the no nonsense atmosphere Andy felt as he entered the room. The other half of the room was empty, perfect for practicing. Vaughn motioned for Andy to take the chair next to him as he entered.

"First," Vaughn began, "I think it's important to stress what magic is not. Magic, real magic, does not rely on fancy words or gestures. It's not about waving your hands in the air or mumbling exotic phrases. Some people do use slight gestures to aid their focus but if I hear so much as an *abracadabra* out of you, I'll throttle you silly." He paused for effect, winking slyly at Andy who sat gazing at the table anxious to begin. Vaughn followed his gaze towards the runes covering the edge of the table and smiled. "You've noticed the runes have you? I'll get to those later. For now though, remember, the only thing required for magic is your mind. With our thoughts we can tap into the magical energy, or mana, around us and manipulate it to do what we want."

"What can we do?" asked Andy. "Anything?"

"With practice, time, and enough energy, the extent of what we can do is very great. However, there are a few things we cannot do, and probably were not meant to do. These include raising the dead and controlling another person's mind. Both are dangerous and the results are never what you expect. We can certainly reanimate a corpse, but infusing it with a soul, giving it life, is beyond our power. As for the mind, another person's thoughts are very complex things. What they mean to you may differ completely from someone else's perception of them. That is why we consider it off limits. Instilling strong emotions, thoughts or desires into another is too unpredictable."

"So, you're saying we can read other people's minds?"

"Read? Yes. Understand? Hardly."

"But, how would I stop someone from.."

"I wouldn't worry too much about it, Andy," Vaughn said with a chuckle. "Average minds are not easily read, and the minds of wizards are much more complex. If another mage was powerful enough to read you're mind, he would also be powerful enough to seal your fate at least a dozen other ways, none of which you could avoid. And certainly these other options would be more efficient than attempting to control your mind."

"Okay, if you say so," Andy managed with a slight smile, trying to hide his confusion.

"Don't worry, Andy, there are a lot more fun things to do with magic other than using it to sit around and catch all the latest gossip swirling around in someone else's mind."

Andy's smile broadened. "Now you're talking."

"Apparently you have an affinity for fire. Shall we start there?" suggested Vaughn. Reaching into his robe he withdrew a half dozen blazing stones. "These are mana gems. They allow us to carry mana with us wherever we go. Quite practical really, and somewhat of a necessity these days." He handed them to Andy. "Now then…"

"Vaughn, where does this mana come from? What is mana? I mean—I must have used it to set that ball on fire. But how?"

Vaughn nodded his head slowly. "Andy, you have to understand that the world was not always as it is now. Long ago, magical energy was everywhere. In the air, the sea, it was a part of life. But, as they say, all good things must come to an end. To be honest, we really don't know what happened except that something went very, very wrong. Something, or someone, caused a barrier to be erected around the Earth, isolating us from the mana in the universe. Before, as energy was used, more would automatically flow in to compensate. Not so anymore. Most of the world is devoid of mana these days. Thankfully, the barrier has developed a few cracks in it over the years, allowing a trickle of energy through. We call these places mana pools and use the energy around them to recharge our mana batteries. Some cultures have recognized these places over the years. The early Hawaiians thought these spots were sacred. Others build monuments on them. One of these places just happens to be above that fabulous donair restaurant you used to 'hang out' at."

"Whoa— seriously?" He'd been sitting under a mana leak for years and hadn't known it. How was that possible? Yet, as he thought about it, it all made perfect sense. He remembered the first day he had walked into Uggabuga, the warm, tingling sensation he felt when he sat down in the booth. *Could that really be why I could do that?* "But why did I..."

"Crank a tennis ball up a few thousand degrees?" finished Vaughn. "Only the most gifted wizards can manifest something in the barren magical world we live in now. Those who can wield magic have very specific traits that allow them exceptional influence in certain areas. It is reasonable to assume that your area of expertise is fire, since that is how you first discovered your powers. This discovery wouldn't have occurred unless you really wanted something, Andy. How badly did you want a fireball?"

"More than anything!"

"Exactly," replied Vaughn. "You had the energy to do it from your accumulated time in the restaurant and you had the desire to use it. The result is, as you say, history."

Andy pondered this revelation before answering. "Something always felt good about that place. Homey, you know? But, I really didn't know what I was doing. It was just luck that it happened. I wouldn't know how do to it again."

"Luckily," Vaughn smiled, "You have also met someone

who can teach you these things, and I think I know just where to start. Hold out your hand."

***

By lunchtime Andy could summon and dismiss a tiny ball of fire from his hand at will. It had been hard work though. Even with Vaughn's guidance he really hadn't been sure what to expect. Andy's success buoyed his confidence and removed his doubts that he had made a mistake deciding to learn magic. Relieved and excited, he ran to find Jack in the kitchen and tell him the news.

***

Alana was already in the meditation room when Andy arrived after lunch. She smiled and motioned for him to join her on the Tami mats in the middle of the room.

"I hear you made excellent progress this morning," Alana said as Andy sat before her. "I expect equally impressive results from you. What you learn here is even more important than your lessons with Vaughn. In fact, what you learn here will quite possibly save your life."

Andy's back straightened at these last words. *Save my life?* Until now, he had never considered magic to be dangerous. Andy watched her intently, determined to master whatever she was going teach him.

Alana reached behind her and brought forth a deck of cards, placing them on the mat between the two of them.

"Together we are going to practice control and concentration. It is essential to be able to control your abilities at all times, under any circumstances. We will use these cards to begin. As you become more experienced, the tasks will become

— 94 —

more challenging. For now, all you have to do is keep a card standing straight up for as long as you can, like so." The top card instantly jerked straight up into the air and stood balanced perfectly on top of the deck.

"Now, I want you to concentrate and try to feel the energy I am using to hold the card in place. If you can sense the energy flowing from me, you should be able to duplicate it and hold the card yourself."

He concentrated on the card. Nothing.

"I don't see anything," Andy said, frustrated.

"Try again," encouraged Alana. "Relax, you have lots of time."

Andy closed his eyes and took a deep breath, forcing himself to remain calm. Once again he focused on the card, picturing it in his mind. *It looks like an ordinary card, yet...* Something was different. Faint yellow light encircled the base of the card. Now he knew what to look for. As he studied the card, the energy became brighter and more pronounced and a small tendril leading away from the card became visible. Finally he could see the intricate pattern of woven energy around the card. *That's what I need.*

"I see it now."

"Good, now you hold the card," she said as the card flopped back onto the top of the deck.

Andy nodded in acknowledgement and, in his mind, recreated the pattern he had just seen. Next, he formed an image of the card and projected mana towards it. The magical pattern wrapped around the card at once, lifting it from the pile. Slowly, Andy opened his eyes to confirm his success. On the floor, between himself and Alana, stood the card. Success!

"I did it!"

"Excellent, Andy, now keep concentrating. Don't let it

fall."

"Sure, it's easy now that… Ouch!" Andy exclaimed as the card fell to the ground. His forehead stung. It felt like someone had flicked him hard, with her fingers.

"What was that?"

Alana cracked a wide smile but otherwise held her composure.

"Let's try again," she suggested.

"That was you?" asked Andy, incredulous.

"Of course. Being able to concentrate in the midst of distractions and discomfort is a very important skill. What were you expecting?"

"I — I'm not sure. I wasn't expecting anything, I guess."

"Well, now you know. Ready?"

"Okay," Andy confirmed. *It's going to be a long afternoon.*

At dinner, Andy had trouble chewing his meal of roast beef and baked potatoes. His cheeks were sore and stiff from Alana's 'distractions'. He had managed to progress past the forehead flicks and cheek tweaks and had graduated to pinches and scratches to his arms and back.

"You look rough, Andy," Jack said as he sat down to join him. "Vaughn's really putting you through the ringer, hey?"

"No," replied Andy, "but Alana sure is."

"Figures," Jack reminisced for a moment. "I remember her lessons. They went better after I started defending myself."

"Defend myself?" Andy asked. "I thought I was just supposed to focus on keeping my concentration."

"You know what they say, Andy, 'All's fair in love and war', and that one definitely loves starting wars," Jack added with a wicked grin. "Try and notice the mana flows she gives off when she's about to ding you, copy them and send them back at her."

"That sounds like a lot of work," conceded Andy. "It'll be

awhile before I can do that."

"It's easier than is sounds," Jack encouraged. "I can give you some pointers if you want."

"Yeah, for sure."

"Bring your food. We'll practice in my room."

The next afternoon Andy was very tired from his morning session with Vaughn and his late night practice session with Jack. The extra practice had paid off though. Andy could sense when mana was being directed at him, although he still lacked the ability to recognize what that energy was intending to do.

"Hello, Andy," Alana greeted him warmly. "You look no worse for wear. I won't be going easy on you today so I hope you're ready." She winked at him and motioned for him to sit. The deck of cards was already before her.

Andy sat and cleared his mind, allowing his senses full access to his faculties. He reached out and held the top card and waited. Instantly, something slapped his cheek. His focus on the card didn't slip but he doubled his efforts to sense what she would do next. Again his cheek was slapped. For a second he thought a magical pattern was visible, almost. *C'mon*, he thought to himself. At least he knew where to look now. Crack! He almost yelled aloud as his other cheek stung from a deft blow. The energy pattern was still murky but he seized it and projected one of his own, copying Alana's as best he could. Blindly he lashed out with the magical pattern, praying it would reach its target. Whack!

"Oh!" Alana squeaked.

Andy's eyes burst open at the sound of her voice, hoping he hadn't gone too far. Alana sat calmly in front of him rubbing her cheek. Her eyes were studying him intently.

"Well, Andy, let the games begin."

Chapter 13

Reminiscing

"Did she give you any trouble?" asked Leo.

"None, Sir," replied the officer. "In fact, she seemed very eager to help us."

"Your report states that she's rather young. Do you believe she's reliable?"

"She claims to be working first hand with a gnome and a dragon. The details she has passed on seem accurate and do support her story."

"Very well. Set up surveillance and have her report in regularly."

"Yes, Sir."

"Dismissed."

Leo waited for the door to close before allowing himself to relax. He sifted through another stack of papers piled on his desk. His best efforts to restore order to the cluttered desktop had failed. It was the one place in his otherwise immaculate personal library he was unable to keep clean. The paneled shelves lining the walls stretched to the ceiling, filled with books and journals. A notebook clattered onto the hardwood floor before Leo could prevent it from sliding off his desk. Reports from Terra Protectra and his various legitimate companies kept coming in much more quickly than he could process this evening. The number of agents in the field stretched their resources to the limit. Despite his best efforts to concentrate on the problems before him, Leo's mind kept drifting back to the Oracle. At least having too much to do was better than too little.

His centuries of experience traversing the globe gave him unrivaled insight into where rare antiques and valuables may be hidden away and provided a major source of income for Terra Protectra. Over the years his philanthropy, through various aliases, had produced some of the most startling discoveries. Thanks to his sponsorship, museums around the world were displaying mummies, pots, jewels, and rare ancient wares of all kinds. His generous patronage generated a constant stream of petitions for his help, enabling Leo to pick the ablest minds and the most prized resources to further his search for Vaughn.

He sucked deeply on his pipe and dropped the papers on the desktop, exhaling a slow steady stream of smoke. The reports from his officers echoed the previous ones, and the ones before them; no signs had been found of their quarry. His eyes stared blankly through the skylights at the clear evening sky. Leo let his gaze linger a moment on the distant stars before he lowered it to the crystal statue, his most cherished prize, across the room. No progress had been made on that front either. His best men could not solve the puzzle of how to activate the Oracle. *Maybe Vaughn was telling the truth.* He considered this a moment, then quickly discarded the thought. Too much had happened; too much had changed between them for him to take anything Vaughn said at face value.

Slowly he reached down, opened the bottom drawer of his desk and withdrew a lacquered cherry wood chest. It was unadorned with a silky smooth finish. He set it down on the desk and rested his palm on the lid. With a slight pop the box opened to his touch. From the papers inside he withdrew an old photo. His face drooped as he studied it. *Vaughn, I will miss you when you're dead.*

A double knock broke his quiet reflection.

"Enter," Leo commanded as he placed the picture back in its chest.

Leo turned towards the door. Mark stood straight and proper on the threshold of the study, waiting to be acknowledged.

"What's on your mind, Mark?" asked Leo, waving him in.

Mark swiftly closed the doors behind him and strode towards the desk. Without further invitation, he took a seat across from Leo, his expression revealing nothing to indicate the business at hand. Leo waited for Mark to begin.

"Do you know what time it is?" asked Mark.

Irked, Leo studied him a moment. "If you have something to say, out with it. I don't have time for childish games."

"Is it childish to prepare for the future?"

"I'm listening." Leo leaned back in his chair, studying his pupil. Judging by Mark's self-control, he had obviously given what he was going to say some thought.

Emboldened, Mark leaned forward. "I just wanted to reassure you, Leo, that I'm ready for anything Terra Protectra asks of me. My sister and I owe you everything. I can't imagine how we would've turned out if you hadn't adopted us from that orphanage."

"That was a long time ago, Mark. Your sentiment is appreciated, but if there's nothing else…"

"You're not getting any younger, Uncle. Perhaps it's time you named your successor? If something should happen…"

"I assure you I am quite healthy, thank you very much," Leo cut in, letting his annoyance show.

Mark snapped back into his chair. "I'm sorry, sir. I meant no disrespect, but, I just… I feel I'm capable of more than is being asked of me. I wish only to serve to the best of my ability."

"For now, I will decide what is the best way you can serve Terra Protectra. I admit you show promise. Both you and Maude do. I... have favored you two for some time now. But, you have yet to justify my giving you the responsibility you have asked for. Mark, you are a capable team leader, but running Terra Protectra requires much more than that."

"I know I can, Sir, if I only had a chance to..."

"You had a chance at the fair. How did that turn out again?" asked Leo. He watched as Mark retreated into his chair, his hands clenched around the armrests, fuming at Leo's words.

"That wasn't my fault. I..."

"You were the Team Leader. Everything that happens under your command is your responsibility." Mark was silent. "You want another chance. Is that it?"

"Yes, Sir!"

Leo thought for a moment, trying to remember his own tribulations when he was Mark's age. Would his mentors have been so forgiving? "If you really want to prove yourself beyond all doubt, to me and to the other officers you serve with, do something none of the others have and I'll consider naming you my successor. But fail again..."

"I won't, Sir, I swear," Mark replied eagerly.

"Then go, and see that you don't fail."

"Yes, Sir!" Mark rose and saluted before heading straight for the doors. Leo stared at the closed door, wondering how much of himself he really saw in Mark. Before turning back to his work, he causally picked up the photo again and studied it. *Some things do change.*

Chapter 14

The Strain of Learning

Vaughn kept him longer than usual that day. Only after the sun had long set was Andy allowed to pack it in. Weeks had past since he had begun his training. Every lesson learned led to another challenge. At times it seemed never ending.

The lights in the kitchen were low and the chairs and tables were empty. Glowing embers were all that was left of the familiar fire in the lounge. Wearily Andy made his way towards his room. *It must really be late,* he thought. *Everyone else is already in bed.* A door slammed down the hall. *Or not.*

His door muffled the voices but they were obviously Jack and Alana yelling at each other, about what though, he couldn't tell. *I'm sure I'll hear about it in the morning,* Andy thought as he climbed into bed.

Near morning, Andy lay awake in bed, not ready to get up and face the day. To help relieve some of his claustrophobia living underground, Alana had enchanted the boarder along his walls to show the position of the sun as it traveled across the sky. It hadn't quite worked, but it did brighten up the room. A one foot strip below the ceiling now flaunted the moon's image setting in a distant corner and the sun still hiding behind the horizon.

A firm hand clamped over Andy's mouth. Startled, Andy jerked left and right, trying to shake off his assailant.

"Shhhhh, it's me."

Andy recognized Natalie's voice at once. His alarm turned to irritation. The hand over his mouth loosened

"What are you…"

"Shh!"

Andy waited for an explanation but didn't get one. Instead, Natalie teleported him. Fresh air greeted them as they reappeared on a tropical beach.

"Where?"

"Buck up, scrub! We're just on the other side of the island."

"You got me out of bed for what? Dawn sand inspection?"

"Over here," said Jack, waving his arms towards them.

"You said by the forked palm!" said Nat.

"It was," explained Jack. "It's in the water now."

"What's going on?"

"We're taking a vacation!"

"Current working conditions have necessitated taking affirmative action," said Jack. "C'mon."

"Huh?" replied Andy.

Together, Jack and Natalie lifted Andy to his feet and led him down the beach. The sun was peaking over the horizon now. Andy scanned the beach for—something—anything that would give him a clue as to why he was here. As he watched the morning sun reflecting off the water, he spotted it. A hundred meters from shore Kaida was sitting on a large raft. She waved to them cheerfully.

"I ain't swimming out there," Andy sighed. It was much too early to be up, let alone cold and wet.

"A little hocus pocus will do the trick." Jack hitched his thumb behind his gleaming belt buckle. Blue and green sparks spurted from the belt buckle and surrounded their feet.

"C'mon, it's better to sail with the tide." Jack and Nat made straight towards the waiting raft. Andy watched them go. *I sooo don't want to go.*

"Andy! Let's go!" Jack called back to him, half way to the raft already. Andy watched him turn and continue on before his brain registered what was going on. Jack was walking on water.

"Am I going to get in trouble for this?" he yelled after them.

"Probably!" replied Nat.

"Figures." Andy briefly looked back before proceeding. *Of course, if I don't go, they'll probably...* Before he could finish his thought, water was licking his bare feet. He was out over the water, being pulled by someone's magic.

"Lovely."

"Oh, you're on strike too?" asked Kaida as Andy stepped onto the raft. She continued to lounge beside a giant cooler and other equipment.

"Huh?" Andy threw a questioning look at Jack. "What's going on?"

"Relax, Andy," Jack assured him. "We're just gonna have a little fun today. Those slave drivers can cram it for a change."

"What did...?" Andy began. Vaguely, he remembered the odd banging last night.

"They've been working you pretty hard too, right?" interrupted Natalie.

"Yeah, but..."

"Andy, sometimes you have to stand up for yourself," said Jack. "Since we're all being overworked, it's important we all stick together on this. You understand, right?"

"Sure." Andy didn't have a clue, but the idea of a day off seemed well-deserved.

"Just think of it as go'n fishin'." Jack gave him his best

smile and thumbed his belt buckle again, propelling the raft rapidly over the clear ocean waters.

Jack watched the waves gently rock the raft as the afternoon sun reflected off the clear blue water. A finer day for a little fishing there never was. Andy, Nat, and Kaida lazily soaked up the sun's rays while Jack tended to his fishing lines. He was determined to catch something, even if it meant using himself as bait.

"Why are you trying to catch something anyway?" asked Nat. "Sit back and enjoy yourself."

"I am enjoying myself. The fish are down there. I can sense them," Jack retorted. "If you want to waste your day away go right ahead."

"I'm not wasting anything! Check out this tan."

"Oooh, fascinating!"

"I sense sarcasm, you witless dunderhead."

***

Andy stretched out again and turned his head away from his bickering companions. Despite their heated debates, he was enjoying himself. It felt really good to just sit back for a change, listening to the rolling waves and watching the seagulls high overhead. *If only they'd shush.* Andy began to formulate a truce when a loud snore silenced both combatants. They all turned towards the source of the outburst.

"Kaida! Stop that! You'll scare away all the fish."

Another loud snore was her only response. Andy moved closer to wake her.

"Kaida!" yelled Natalie.

Instantly Kaida sprang to her feet, oblivious to those around her, knocking Andy off the raft in the process. A loud splash alerted everyone as he floundered in the water.

"He knows how to swim right?" asked Jack.

Nat shrugged.

"Oh geez," Jack sighed.

Chills enveloped Andy as his head sank below the surface. Everything seemed to be happening is slow motion as the bright lights of the surface faded, drowned out by the murky blackness below. Faint shapes beneath him faded in and out of his vision. The realization that he was sinking finally hit him. Desperately, Andy thrashed in the water, trying to claw his way back to the surface.

One of the shapes, a deep cobalt blue spine, brushed his toes. Andy instantly curled his feet and legs to his chest. He watched it circle him, all thoughts of escape forgotten. *It was just a fish. It had to be a fish.*

As though sensing Andy's panic, the beast rushed at him. At the last minute Andy rolled as the fish passed him, barely managing to avoid its sharp jaw, but not quick enough to avoid being draped against its giant, dorsal fin. The giant fish convulsed recklessly, trying to shake him off. Desperate, it raced towards the surface, determined to throw Andy off.

Blue skies greeted him as they broke the surface, soaring high into the air before plunging back into the ocean, sending water spraying everywhere. The raft rocked in the strong wake of the fish. Through the turbulent waters, Andy could see the shock on his friends' faces as he frantically rode the fish, bounding and bucking for freedom. On one leap, he barely heard Jack mumble 'best blue marlin' as he stared in envy, transfixed at the sight.

The rapid ascents and descents were taking their toll on Andy. The short breaths of air barely filled his lungs, making him lightheaded. The world seemed to pass him by as if in a trance. He had managed to reorient himself into a sitting position, allowing him to hang on while the marlin tried to buck him off. *Let go! Just let go! End it!* Andy thought. His muscles had other ideas, however.

"Andy!"

Through the haze of motion around him, somewhere deep inside Andy grasped Kaida's voice, jarring him momentarily from his reverie. His grip on the fish slackened for a split second. The marlin bucked savagely, sending him flying into the ocean.

Firm hands, and a little magic, hauled Andy onto the raft where he lay gasping for breath.

"Andy!" Kaida shouted again.

"Andy, are you all right?" asked Jack.

Slowly, Andy's eyes opened, signaling his return to consciousness. He looked at his rescuers and smiled.

"Am I alive?" asked Andy, to a round of collective sighs.

"Dude, that was awesome!" Jack said in amazement. "Do it again!"

***

The day passed without further incident. Jack even caught a fish, not a marlin, but still something he could be proud of. The ocean rumbled as they made their way to shore. The sun had almost set and the cool evening air guided them along the trail as they returned to their cabin. Alana and Vaughn were sitting near the fire when they returned home. Alana merely looked at them as they walked past. Vaughn seemed not to notice them at all.

"I trust tomorrow will be business as usual?" asked Alana as they were about to enter the hall.

"We'll sleep on it," was Nat's only reply.

***

Alana slept on it as well, getting up earlier than usual to prepare a spot on the beach for her eager pupil. She was just finishing her warm-ups when Andy joined her on the sand.

"I hope you had a good night's sleep. Today is going to be a long day," she began. Andy groaned in reply. She really wasn't angry at him, not anymore anyway. No need to let him think otherwise though.

"Since you like the water so much, I thought it would be fun to try a few aquatic exercises," said Alana. Andy sighed again. "Follow me." She waved him forward and into the waiting surf, explaining what they were going to do along the way.

During high tide that afternoon, Andy keeled over on the beach, exhausted.

"That's it for today. I'm heading back to take a bath. You've come a long way, Andy," Alana said as she wiped her brow. Her clothes were covered in sand that had been kicked up during their battle. A ring of leaves, shells, driftwood, and other debris littered the beach around her, a testament to how far her student had come in the last six months. "I'm not sure how much more I can teach you. I'll have to think of something really diabolical for tomorrow."

"Great." Andy let out a long sigh in reply as Alana set off towards the cabin. His body burned from the sun and from Alana's daily training sessions. Gone were his toneless arms and torso, replaced with new sinewy muscles. He brushed the sand off his bare chest and back as he rose and headed to the cabin.

***

They had moved constantly over the last few months, never spending more than a few weeks at a time in one place. Partly to stay ahead of Terra Protectra, partly because they needed to keep recharging their mana gems, but mostly because it was fun. Andy learned of a dozen hideaways, scattered around the globe. Most were near the equator or the ocean, but a few were in more temperate climes. The changes in scenery made up for the monotony of his lessons.

Both of his teachers marveled at his progress. Under Vaughn's tutelage he now found balls of fire simple to create. He could make all kinds of shapes out of burning ether, from cubes and pyramids to complex objects like plants and animals. Andy delighted his comrades by acting out their favorite scenes from books and movies with characters composed entirely of fire and light. His abilities to control multiple magical manifestations were more Alana's accomplishment than Vaughn's, however. Their friendly sessions soon turned into all out wars as she kept thinking of new tasks for Andy to perform and new ways to distract him. Andy's repertoire of card tricks was first rate thanks to her guidance.

And thanks to his unofficial mentor, Jack, Andy had become an expert at detecting magical signs. Alana's torments were easily recognizable as soon as he saw them, making it virtually impossible for her to catch him unaware. As his control grew, he graduated from moving cards to books to stones to parked cars.

To his relief, neither Vaughn nor Alana had ever questioned him about his role in the impromptu vacation he had taken with the others. They seemed to have written it off as a 'teenager-thing'. Jack, Natalie, and Kaida certainly felt closer to him than ever before, and Jack's redoubled help made his sessions with Alana almost enjoyable.

How to survive his sessions wasn't the only thing Andy was learning from Jack. After enjoying a few weeks of watching Andy do all his chores by hand, Jack and Natalie caved-in and began teaching him how to do them using magic. Not only was it easy to enchant a dishcloth to wash dishes, it was faster too, allowing Andy to do two or even three things at once. Now he could lounge in his favorite chair as invisible hands made his bed, cleaned his room, and washed his clothes. If this magic thing fell through, at least he'd be able to get a job as a first class butler.

Andy found that he could apply Jack's lessons to other people as well. He discovered the patterns Natalie used to teleport around the globe after seeing her perform only a few times and Jack's ability to increase his strength was easy to understand too. The only person he had problems with was Kaida. Her abilities to work computers scrambled his head when he tried to watch them in motion. Andy had numerous opportunities to observer her.

After learning of her beloved dragon queen's downfall, Kaida was determined to never let it happen again and had reprogrammed Queen Xulalita to be more ferocious than ever. She even added special subroutines to detect when Lance was playing and hunt him down. After making a few attempts to unravel her methods, Andy decided that playing computer games was a lot more fun than cheating his way through them.

***

While Andy was studying, Jack, Kaida, and Natalie were equally busy—off on errands for Vaughn or Alana. Life wasn't all work and no play, however. When they were together, the four of them played beach volleyball to pass the time. Andy had tried to teach them hockey, but Natalie and Kaida didn't understand why someone would bother running around when they could just enchant their hockey sticks to play for them.

Mages! Andy rolled his eyes.

Conceding defeat, Andy resigned himself to volleyball. While it wasn't as exciting as hockey, the contention between the teams rivaled that of any in hockey. Andy enjoyed playing with them, although their competitive side wagers made winning almost as dangerous as losing.

From Vaughn, Andy also learned other essential skills such as how to mask his own magical aura, although crudely, and how to detect mana sink holes, what anti-magic users normally created by their presence. In his short time with the others, he had mastered the basic skills his companions depended on everyday.

That evening Andy heard an unexpected knock at his door. Opening it, he found Alana carrying an armful of books.

"I've got a treat for you," Alana said as she entered. "You've applied yourself well. Because of this, Vaughn and I have decided that it's time to teach you some more advanced topics."

She sat down on the bed and spread the books and papers out around her.

"What's all this?" asked Andy. "You're not going to make me write an essay are you? That's so lame."

"Hardly," replied Alana. With a sly grin she added, "Although, that might not be a bad idea."

"Lovely." Andy was horrified at the thought of giving her more ideas with which to torment him.

"Vaughn says your abilities to control fire are very advanced," she began. "What you are going to learn now is how to make things store your magical thoughts so that others may understand what you've recorded. There is a system of glyphs that…"

"Wait," interrupted Andy. "Aren't magical thoughts unique to the caster? Vaughn always said that we sculpt magical energy in our own way, that no two mages do it exactly the same."

"You are correct, Andy. How we focus the energy is different but the end result is the same. You've demonstrated for months, quite well I might add, how you can copy my magic patterns. Did you think you were doing the exact same thing as I was? The results were the same, yes, but not the means."

The sudden insight stunned him. *Why didn't I realize that before?*

"Now then, these glyphs I'm going to show you literally record the thoughts of the writer. Any magician can activate them to learn what they contain, but having the glyphs magically transferred to your mind destroys the original transcript. You must be able to recognize what the symbols mean without using magic."

"You're teaching me a whole new language?" asked Andy. "I don't know about this. I was never even that great at French."

Alana smiled. "This is much easier. There really isn't that much to it. By now you already know a great deal about how to use your talents. We can start by writing things you already know, that way they will be easy to recognize. Then, you will be able to see these basic forms in more complicated drawings. Let's get started."

As Alana drew the first symbol, Andy felt a strange déjà vu come over him. Spelling was one of the few classes he had never enjoyed in school—probably because all the fun words were never on the spelling lists. *I guess magic isn't all fun and games.*

***

It was late when Alana left. Andy's head ached with all the symbols she had shown him. He wasn't sure how he was ever going to remember them all and doubted it would be any easier the next day. He cleared his bed and slipped into his pajamas. As he tucked himself in and drifted off to sleep, his mind danced with strange glyphs.

"I am proud of you, Andy," Vaughn said the following morning. "You are ready to take the next step in your education."

"Thanks. What are we doing today? Pulling rabbits out of hats? Sawing old ladies in two? Don't start holding out on me now."

"Don't worry, I won't leave anything out," Vaughn reassured him with a broad smile. "But for now, to mark your progress, it is time you started on your own robe."

"A robe? You're teaching me how to sew?" Of all the magical topics Andy pictured learning from Vaughn, needlepoint was not one of them.

"Not exactly, although sewing does come in handy," he continued in a matter-of-fact tone. "It is tradition for apprentices to make their own robes as a mark of their accomplishments. Styles of robes vary considerably these days. Long flowing gowns are traditional but not necessarily the most fashionable. The structure and appearance is up to you, however, what really makes a wizard's robe is the mana he imbues it with."

"What do you mean?" Andy asked.

"The greatest asset a wizard can have is his robe. By storing a portion of his power in the garment he can protect himself or do other things even when he is cut off from any mana. Almost everything you can do with magic can be patterned into your robe. However, you must remember that the energy your robe needs to perform the tasks you want it to must still come from somewhere. It takes the same amount of energy for your robe to do something as it does you. By now I'm sure Alana has shown you that every wizard has a distinct magical signature that can be used to trace him. Because each signature is unique it's also possible to make glyphs that only respond to your personal commands."

"I see. So only I can use my own robe?"

"Exactly, Andy. Usually, if your robe performs magic it uses up the power associated with that action," he paused before adding, "but there are ways around that too. Let's just keep it simple for now, shall we?" Vaughn drew out an old white wool sweater and handed it to Andy. "You can start practicing with this until your design skills become ready for the real thing. I'll show you. Hold the sweater like this," Vaughn spread it between his outstretched hands, "and focus on creating a ball of fire. But instead of projecting the image outward, send the image in your head into the sweater."

Vaughn concentrated for a moment and a tiny orange orb circled by four lighting bolts appeared in the wool. It was about a centimeter across in size. After examining it, he tapped it and a globe of fire as big as a softball launched out of the sweater and hovered before them for a few seconds before dissipating into nothing.

"Now you try."

Andy grasped the sweater like Vaughn had done and concentrated. He closed his eyes and formed the image of the sweater and of a fireball in his mind. Slowly he merged the two together. The fireball melded delicately with the cloth and seemed to sit there waiting to be released. Opening his eyes, he found that his globe wasn't the delicate little ball Vaughn's was but almost the size of his entire hand.

"In time, as you learn greater control, your images will shrink in size," Vaughn assured him. Andy tapped his ball and it sprang to life, surging upwards in a blazing ball of fire.

"Very good, Andy, now we need to discuss triggers," Vaughn instructed. "Just now we manually released the stored energy but we can also set it to activate on a predetermined signal or event."

"Like what?"

"Anything you can think of. From the time of day to a bird flying by; if you can dream it, you can make it. It's for this reason that magical robes are considered your greatest protection. You can plan something to happen when an enemy attacks even if you are asleep or unconscious. Many battles have been won not by the strongest, but by the most prepared. Try another and I'll show you how to link glyphs together."

"So I can activate more than one glyph at once?"

"Close, linking glyphs together allows you to use them more than once by connecting them to a mana battery. You can use one battery for many glyphs or have many different batteries. Whatever works for you. For large reserves though, I recommend embedding gems into your robe like so." He opened his coat to reveal a half dozen glittering jewels fastened to the lining. Andy could barely see the delicate spider's web of glyphs that criss-crossed the jacket connecting them all together.

"The difficulty lies in drawing the energy to make the batteries. Very few substances can store mana for any length of time, hence the gems."

"Show me how to do that!" Andy pleaded excitedly.

The rest of the day flew by as Andy worked to master this new skill. By the time the sun set he could focus enough to create one of each type of glyph. He had a lot more work to do, but he was off to a good start. The moon was rising by the time he crawled into his bed. Sleep came the instant his head touched the pillow.

Chapter 15

Stress

Maude stifled a sneeze. The room smelled of disinfectant and mothballs. How that could be healthy she wasn't sure, but it wasn't a good sign.

After the failure at the fair, everyone from Terra Protectra was caught up in a bad mood. Tempers ran short all around. Leo had recommended a little time off for everyone. Maude was reluctant to go—she didn't need a break. Focusing on her work seemed the best way to move on but this "little spa in the mountains," as Leo described it, sounded too tempting to pass up. She made sure her reservations included a complete relaxation spa package. Plus, the Rolling Ridge Health Resort offered excellent horseback riding, something she was longing to do again.

She crossed the small suite that was to be her home for her week-long stay and opened the windows wide, confident the fresh air would do wonders for the room, before heading down for dinner.

The evening meal was being served in the outdoor dining hall. Small tables were scattered amongst large broad-leaved shrubberies, fulfilling the spa patrons' lust for everything natural and adding a touch of privacy for their more discerning clients. The main course had just been served. Maude was savoring a delightful broiled salmon with steamed greens when her head exploded with swirling colors. These blazing imprints could mean only one thing. There was no mistaking it. There were mages present.

Quickly she glanced around, but the foliage prevented her from spotting anything amiss. Maude felt very exposed and unsure of what to do. *What would Leo do?* she wondered.

Quietly Maude picked up her ice tea and left her half-eaten dinner to move to the resort lobby. She managed to find a seat in a large, Victorian arm-chair and tried her best to conceal herself behind a travel magazine. From her seat she could keep an eye on the main doors, the restaurant, and the elevator. She didn't have to wait long before her instincts paid off.

The double doors to the lobby swung open, revealing Jack, followed by Natalie and Kaida. They walked straight to the front desk and began chatting with the attendant. Three on one were not the odds Maude was hoping for. *Why would they be here? And why isn't Vaughn with them?* Puzzled, she watched them check in and get on the elevator. Maude counted to one hundred, as slowly as she could, before leaving the lobby herself. She needed to think—to plan. Her watch chimed musically, starling her. She had forgotten all about her hot rock massage, just the thing to help her relax.

Unfortunately, Maude's massage did little to improve her mood. She had managed to tune out most of their presences, allowing her head to mute the myriad of colors each one induced, but the question of what to do still haunted her.

Calling Leo would be the smart move. He would mount up and ride in with the cavalry. Together, they would certainly be able to capture them. Another idea lingered though. *What would Mark do?* Not that he was that special or anything, and his career was looking rather bleak of late, maybe even enough for Leo to recognize her with a little more respect. Kicking Mark when he's down was not really her style, but the idea of presenting Leo with three bounties was not something to be easily passed up. Mark would certainly charge straight in, guns blazing, daring fate to deal him any unfavorable consequences. The glory of the success was lost on Maude, but not the respect it could earn her. Sure she was gifted in the arts, maybe even more so than Mark, yet everyone always assumed he was the leader. Perhaps this was her chance to prove them all wrong.

Maude concentrated on the colors in her head. Satisfied that they hadn't moved since she saw them checking in, she decided to turn in early. Rest was something she would need, and she felt safe enough knowing that the lack of mana around her was more than enough to mask her presence. Besides, she would know if they went anywhere.

***

Morning greeted Maude with the dull buzz of her room's alarm clock. She stretched under her sheets and rolled over, enjoying the peace and quiet around her. Startled, she bolted upright. The clock read ten AM, not the seven AM she had set it for, meaning she had missed her morning pedicure—but more disturbing was the realization that her head was clear.

They were gone.

Cursing herself, she jumped out of bed and dressed in jeans and the oversized wool sweater Leo had given her on her last birthday, and stormed out of the room. Startled people stopped and stared at her as she burst out of the elevator and ran through the lobby. Outside, Maude stopped by a map of the resort and strained to detect any sign of them. A faint echo pulsed from one of the horse trails. Determined not to let them get away, Maude ran to the stables and commandeered the first saddled horse she saw, a beautiful roan mare with white markings on its face and hooves. All thoughts of calling for backup were forgotten as she galloped through the trees and down the trail.

What could they... there must be a mana pool around here, thought Maude. They'd come to fill their mana crystals. She couldn't let that happen. *If I could at least destroy the crystals...*

The path snaked through pine trees on the mountainside, climbing only to disappear into another valley. Just shy of an upcoming ridge on her right, she stopped. She sensed her quarries lingering on the other side of it. The heightened mana in the background gave her goose bumps. Maude slid from the saddle and tied her horse to a tree before heading into the woods and climbing the ridge. It wasn't long before she was at the top. In the vale below she could see Kaida collecting gems and adding them to a velvet pouch she was carrying. Jack was lying in the grass at the base on the ridge. *If I jump, I could easily land on him,* thought Maude. *But where is...*

An unseen force sent Maude sprawling to the ground, gasping loudly. Shocked, she started to push herself up only to be sucked into the ground and buried up to her head in dirt and gravel. She sputtered desperately, trying to catch her breath.

"See, I told ya, someone was coming!"

Maude recognized Natalie's voice at once. Dirt sprayed into her face as Nat landed beside her.

I'll never doubt your sense-fu again," replied Jack, heading toward them.

"Or your tree climbing ability," added Kaida. "See any squirrels up there?"

"You can both show your gratitude by doing my chores for a week. Whada'ya say?" replied Nat, ignoring Jack's last comment.

Kaida just looked at Jack before replying.

"I don't think so."

"You'll come around," goaded Nat.

Maude struggled to turn her head to see the three of them standing over her buried form. "How?"

"Isn't it obvious?" asked Natalie. "Just because you absorb magic, doesn't mean the ground under your feet does. If all that dirt suddenly gets, say teleported away, you still fall down, go splat. Or, did you really think you could—Leo must not have trained you very well. There's enough energy pooled here to make you stand out like a sore thumb."

Maude exhaled slowly and rested her chin on the ground. Her body was sore everywhere.

"Anyway, it was nice seeing you again, Maude," said Jack. "Be sure to say hi to Mark-o for us, okay?"

"Wait! Don't leave me," Maude struggled to say, but it was too late. White light was already washing over her and then silence. She was alone. Slowly, Maude let her face fall to the ground again, tears flowing freely down her cheeks.

Maude awoke as she was being pulled free of her earthen prison. She hadn't heard the transport arrive or the troops from Terra Protectra running towards her, or even Leo ordering them to dig her out.

Leo stood before her now, his expression a mixture of concern and anger. Looking around, Maude could see others planting a monitoring station but Leo immediately grabbed her full attention.

"Are you all right?" he asked.

"I—I think so." Maude sighed as she dust herself off. An awkward silence stretched between them. Leo seemed to be waiting for something.

"So did you manage to learn anything useful?" inquired Leo.

Maude squirmed under his intense glare. "Natalie likes trees," she offered, trying to be helpful.

Leo's grimace only deepened. "I'm very disappointed in you, Maude," he continued. "Frankly, this is the kind of reckless behavior I would expect from Mark. I would have thought you'd be more sensible and at least, check in before running off like this. You're lucky the resort called us when you didn't show up for your appointment. After that it wasn't too hard figuring out where your went. Not many guests here ride off on a horse at full gallop."

Maude was speechless. The weight of her failure pressed down on her.

"Let's go," said Leo and turned toward the transport. Maude followed him without comment. The ride home was going to be very long indeed.

Chapter 16

Bump in the Night

The sun had long since set as Alana stormed into Vaughn's room and flung her travel bag on his desk.

"It didn't go well?" said Vaughn as diplomatically as possible. He watched from his corner chair and closed the book in his lap as she threw herself in the chair opposite him.

"Nothing!" Alana rubbed her temples. She tried to contain her frustration. The last few days had stretched her patience to its breaking point. "He says there isn't any more he can do. There isn't enough energy left in the Oracle to detect it."

"That's not really surprising. However, it would have been nice if he would have admitted as much months ago."

"After all this time, he still has his pride."

"Which isn't helping us at the moment. We've wasted enough time. It seems that the boy is our only chance now."

"I still don't like it."

"It's a necessity."

"Is it?"

"If you have any other ideas…" Vaughn let his voice die out. She could tell he was watching her carefully. "We've discussed this before. Now is not the time to get cold feet. Much depends on our success."

"I know." She threw her head back and stared at the ceiling. "It's just that…"

"You like him, don't you?"

"I know you do as well. Don't try and deny it," she added defensively.

"Whatever I may feel towards him, it doesn't change what we have to do. We may already be too late. Do you want to live like this forever?"

"No… we swore to the sleepers that none would be sacrificed."

"True, and none of THEM will be."

"Hmmm," was her only reply. Intensely, Alana studied the ceiling, hoping to find an alternative in its simple patterns. Vaughn continued to watch her before adding.

"Alana, before the great accident, I swore upon taking the office of Chancellor to serve in the best interests of every citizen, to protect every inhabitant of Baurum'tatus, and to do no harm against any of them. That is a pledge I am still bound by today. I can not let Leo make me break my oaths. Too much is at risk. So, are we agreed?"

Alana stood up and slowly walked towards Vaughn's desk. Her face was a turbulent storm of emotion. What Vaughn was proposing was tantamount to treason. The idea repulsed her yet she couldn't see any other way. She grabbed her bag and headed towards the door. Pausing on the threshold she said, "Agreed."

Chapter 17

Extracurricular Activities

BAM! BAM! BAM!

Andy sprang from his sheets at the sound, anxiously looking to see what was going on.

Bam! Bam! Bam!

His door shook with the force of the blows. A quick glance at his clock told him he had slept in, and today was his turn to cook breakfast.

"Okay, okay, I'm up!"

Andy dressed in a flash and rushed out of the room, arriving in the kitchen just as Natalie was joining Jack and Kaida at the table.

"Get a move on, you bum! We've got a big day ahead of us," she scolded. "I want a bowl of Honey O's with skim milk, shaken not stirred, a large glass of fresh orange juice and step on it, chop chop!"

"Just coffee and a donut for me, Andy," Jack said. "And have you seen a newspaper around here?"

"I can get you one," Nat said.

"No thanks, I pay enough Nat Tax as it is," Jack said.

"Why you…"

"I'll have steak and eggs, and cup of green tea, Andy," Kaida said as Jack and Nat looked at her. "What? I'm hungry and he makes great steak you know."

"Coming right up."

Alana walked in dressed in her light grey traveling robe. Her hair was pinned back in a severe knot that matched the serious expression on her face.

"Nat, Jack, Kaida, you three are with me today. Andy, you're with Vaughn," she stated crisply. "We have a lot to do so let's go. No time to dilly dally today."

"Andy was late this morning, so can't we leave after breakfast?" Nat whined.

"Very well then, eat up. And some lemon water for me please, Andy."

"Right away," Andy acknowledged as he set a bowl of Honey O's and some donuts on the table. With a little magical assistance everything was soon served. The smells of warm food drifted through the kitchen. His customers fed, Andy slumped in a chair next to them. "So, where you all off to today?"

"Top Secret, kiddo," Jack avowed. "We're off to save the world, and pick up a few groceries, too." Winking, he stood and ran his hand through his hair. His tangled locks sprang back almost instantly.

"Don't worry, Andy," Kaida said as she too stood from the table. "Vaughn will have a fun day planned for you I'm sure."

"You're going to have to learn more than just cooking before you can play with the real McCoy," Nat said as she finished her breakfast.

Vaughn walked in.

"Everything ready, Alana?" he asked in a businesslike tone.

"Affirmative," she said with a mock salute. "Let's go everyone." As they filed out, Andy cleared the dishes and started washing them.

"Hurry, Andy, we have a busy day ourselves," Vaughn said as he grabbed a glass of water for himself. He was wearing his long wool traveling coat, something he never wore unless he was leaving the island.

"Sure, more glyphs today?" Andy asked skeptically, hoping they were going somewhere too.

"No. We have an errand of our own today, a rather important one, I might add. We'll be away from the island for a while so I'd like you to wear this." He held up one of his own robes. It was an older one, quite traditional, styled more like a hooded bath robe than a traveling cloak. Its dark brown cloth was covered in the same web-like maze of symbols as the inside of his coat. In the light it seemed almost alive as the glyphs pulsed and throbbed across its surface.

"I can't wear that. It's yours. There's no way I could control it and you know it," Andy protested.

"That's true, but it will hopefully mask you from anyone who might be watching for us."

"You think Terra Protectra will be watching for me?"

"It's unlikely, but it's better to believe they will."

Andy recalled the stories the others had told them about Terra Protectra, and how they were committed to exterminating anyone who used magic. Some of the stories were comical, scripted right out of a movie. Other meetings were more dire, including the circumstances leading to Jack, Nat and Kaida finding him in the first place. Perhaps that's where the others had gone, to strike a blow for the magically enabled. Andy imagined them all charging in like the cavalry of old, swinging swords and throwing thunderbolts.

"What are we doing that's so important?" Andy asked.

"We are coming to the end of your training, Andy. Your abilities are improving steadily. There's not much more we can teach you. What you need now is experience, and fast. Today you will learn the most important thing we can teach you: how to refill the battery gems we use to contain our power. Without the gems we wouldn't last five minutes against anyone from Terra Protectra, and even with them it's still a gamble. We'll be going to one of the largest mana pools, where the barrier around the planet is cracking, and filling as many as we can today. Your lessons have drained quite a few. More than I assumed they would. I never imagined you'd come so far so quickly. It's time to renew our supplies. The others have been doing it off and on for some time now to prevent us running dry completely, but everyone must be able to do it. It could mean life or death for us."

Realizing how essential the skill Vaughn was teaching him today would be, Andy took the robe from him and put it on with no further protest. Where they were going sounded dangerous, but knowing Vaughn would be with him eased his fears. The robe was much too long for him, but he managed as he rolled up the sleeves and tied the belt. The aura of Vaughn's magic imbued within the robe weighed on him, stiffening and slowing his movements. It took a little getting used to.

"I'm ready," he said at last.

"Take my hand." Andy clasped Vaughn's hand and together they disappeared in a flash of light.

The sun shone brightly in the clear sky as Vaughn and Andy materialized. They were on a different island with tall palm trees and crystal blue water lapping gently against white sandy beaches. A lone seagull flew high overhead, a distant blur in the morning sun.

"This way," Vaughn gestured. Andy followed him off the beach and through the trees towards the center of the island. Soon they came to a small dirt path, heavily overgrown with wild grass and small yellow flowers. Andy couldn't see any signs that it had been used recently. As they walked, Vaughn pointed out sporadic sugar cane stands and wild coffee plants nestled in the brush. Andy could feel the path slowing sloping upward for a long distance before steeply descending. They had been walking for about an hour when the trail opened into a central plateau covered in short grass. In the distance Andy could see the edge of a small lake. "Almost there," Vaughn reassured him.

They stopped at the lake's edge. The beach was strewn with odd sized rocks and dead plants.

"This is the spot," Vaughn said at last. "Can you feel it Andy? There is a crack in the anti-magic shield high above us. Mana is slowly seeping through it down to this spot. It's one of the most active mana pools so you should have no trouble sensing it."

Andy reached out with his newly trained senses. His body began to feel warm and tingly. *There is mana here,* he thought. *Lots of it.*

"What now?" Andy asked.

"One moment, let me adjust your robe," Vaughn volunteered. "I'll activate it." He reached out and touched Andy on the chest with the palm of this hand. Instantly, dozens of patterns erupted in silvery gold flares while others disappeared completely. Andy could feel the changes. The robe was lighter now and less solid, almost breezy against his body.

"Now, take these." Vaughn reached into a royal blue velvet bag and handed Andy a handful of gems. They shone dully in the sunlight. "These should do for now."

Andy weighed the gems in his hand. They looked so insignificant in his palm yet his mind raced with the potential power they represented. He tightened his fist around them.

"You know how to tap them," Vaughn was saying "to draw power out of them. Now you will learn the reverse, how to deposit energy into them. It's rather simple in theory, first you need to open yourself to the mana around you. Then, as your body begins to absorb it, you channel it into the gem. Like so."

Vaughn held a stone in the palm of his hand. Soon, energy condensed around the gem and slowly swirled into it. "Easy, right?" Vaughn grinned.

"No problem," Andy replied, admiring the energy torrent churning in Vaughn's hand.

"The catch is that you can only fill the gem to the same power level as you can hold in your own body. Of course, as you become more experienced you will be able to embrace more power within yourself and fill the gems more completely, but that is neither here nor there. Just do your best. That's all I ask."

"All right, I'll get right on it," Andy assured him.

A large rock jutted out of the ground near them. Andy walked over and sat on it, trying his best to get comfortable on the hard surface. He set all but one of the gems on the rock beside him and held the remaining one out in front of him. Ready, he opened himself to the energy around him. The familiar warm tingling sensation greeted him as his body prepared itself. Finally, he reached for the gem with his mind. The gem was unexpectedly slippery to concentrate on at first. The energy he directed at it seemed to have a life of its own, wanting to fan out around him instead of converging in a controlled stream. He focused harder on the jewel and reluctantly the energy began to deposit within the battery. *This is hard. No wonder they left this lesson 'til last,* he thought. Content in his achievement, he sat there at one with the mana around him. So engrossed in his task he became that he almost didn't hear Vaughn say, "You're doing great. I'll be over here if you need me, going to stretch my legs a bit...."

As the day passed, he lost track of time, only pausing briefly to change gems once he could not fill one any further.

***

The remote monitoring station sprang to life. The strength of the magical signature was unmistakable. It noted the location of the signal and automatically sent the information to Terra Protectra headquarters along with a brief note. Vaughn had been found.

Officer Nigel Coleman sat at his duty station. A steaming cup of fresh coffee sat before him as he reminisced. After the dust had settled from the fair fiasco, he and a number of other security personnel had found themselves without jobs. Apparently, those in charge didn't care for his story of how the intruders simply vanished right in front of him, or that he was busy in the coffee room when it happened. The only one who seemed vaguely interested was an officer from Terra Protectra.

This officer, unlike Mark, was older and seemed to respect the experience of others, something Nigel could relate to. He had introduced himself to Nigel only as Leo at the time. To his surprise, not only did Leo believe his story, but he offered him a job on the spot. "We need people like you," Leo had said. Apparently, they were short on people who had actually encountered real magicians in the field. At first he had been skeptical. At his age, Nigel wasn't keen on relocating either. Only after Leo mentioned that Terra Protectra maintained a private coffee plantation near their headquarters and that Nigel would be welcome to pick a few coffee beans for his own personal use did he agree.

The job itself was easy enough. The machines did most of the work for him, letting him sit back and enjoy his own personal brew. Presently, the display he was responsible for monitoring began blinking. Quickly, Nigel paged the duty officer in charge.

"Sir, you should look at this," reported Nigel. "One of our remote monitoring stations from sector 9-G just reported in. The signature seems to match..."

"Give me that!" Mark hissed. He snatched the report from Nigel's hands and scanned it hungrily.

"Sound the alarm!" Mark shouted. "I want every available officer on the transport in two minutes. Wake-up Maude, but don't disturb Leo. We can handle this ourselves."

"B-b-b-but, sir," stammered Nigel, "Standard procedure clearly states that Leo…"

"DID YOU UNDERSTAND WHAT I SAID?" shrieked Mark, punctuating every word. All activity in the operations room ceased immediately. Nigel sat helplessly at his desk, riveted to his seat by Mark's unbridled fury.

"Yes, sir," he replied, his voice a faint echo of his usually self-assured nature.

"Good! Just—Do—It—Then." Mark let his fury seep into every word. Almost as an afterthought he added, "Vaughn's gotten cocky. It was only a matter of time before he made a mistake. We will get him this time for sure."

"Yes, sir!" Nigel managed to sound a little more enthusiastic. Mark, satisfied that his will would be carried out, dashed off to the hanger, leaving a room of very pale faced operators behind him.

"Yes, sir," Nigel echoed as Mark disappeared down the corridor.

***

Two minutes later, the co-pilot was about to shut the transport door when a very ragged Maude hauled herself inside sporting a world class case of bed head. Her uniform was freshly pressed, but her jacket was undone and her undershirt was not tucked in.

"What's going on?" she asked.

— 131 —

"Move it!" Mark screamed. "I won't lose Vaughn because of you again."

Maude eyed him critically as though about to say something, but decided not to. Taking a seat near the back, she began reading the field reports.

"It can't be him," Maude said in disbelief. "Vaughn would have to be flying a whale or something to be radiating this much energy. He knows we're watching for him. Has he lost his mind? There must be a mistake."

"Why should I care," was Mark's only reply but Maude could see the thoughts of revenge clearly on his face.

Frustrated, she flipped the com button and asked, "What's our ETA, pilot?"

"Two hours, forty-one minutes," he replied.

Two hours, forty-one minutes to figure out what the heck was going on, she thought. A minute later they were soaring towards their unwitting prey.

***

Andy set the full gem on the rock and picked up another. Three gems now sparkled with fiery intensity at his side. Beads of sweat dotted his face. The heat of the afternoon sun was getting to him. He ignored it as best he could, hoping the wind would change again and bathe him in a cool breeze from the water. Holding the next gem in his hand he took a deep breath to clear his head before focusing once again on his task.

***

Ten thousand feet above their target the transport circled while everyone on board went through final preparations.

"We are using pattern Orange," commanded Mark, "pattern Orange everyone. Spread the containment vortex at one thousand feet and we should take him by surprise. We can't afford to fail again. I want everything by the numbers. Follow my lead. Maude has the rear guard position. Let's go everyone!"

Maude adjusted the harness on her energy-chute, one of Leo's many inventions. Once they jumped there would be no room for error. The containment would be tricky. Their flight suits had Misorbium bands sewn into them, running up one sleeve, across the back, and down the other, allowing team members in formation to pool their abilities. Together they could perform at a far greater capacity and precision than they could individually. The deadliest and most difficult maneuver was the containment vortex.

She had managed to tone down her appearance from natural disaster to severely windblown over the course of the flight, but nothing could ease the queasiness in her stomach. *Vaughn's no fool. Is he setting a trap for us?* As the warning klaxon blared, signaling the beginning of the operation, she took her position in the formation and waited for the drop door to open.

"Here we go!" yelled Mark. In a synchronized rush of movement they jumped out the open door into the blue sky. They formed a giant ring in the heavens directly over their target as the wind whipped past them. Purplish sparks from the energy-chutes crackled behind them as each member struggled to maintain proper placement in the formation. Wind whipped through Maude's hair, lashing it against the sides of her face as she plummeted, and the steady buzz of the chutes droned behind her.

At fifteen hundred feet their energy-chutes throttled back, spreading purple glows around them and slowing their descents from recklessly insane to utterly neck breaking. At one thousand feet they began to channel, the Misorbium glowed brightly, drawing strength from each member in turn. The ambient energy drifting through the crack in the great barrier high above them began reacting with the Misorbium ring, filling the empty space between them with a great swirling purplish vortex of energy. As they continued to fall, it slowly billowed upwards like an enormous balloon, slowing their descent further. At one hundred feet the Terra Protectra soldiers aimed their vortex at their target. The ground shuddered as mana was sucked into the vortex with an ear shattering, thunder-like clap. Earth and flesh alike instantly released their energy, which was greedily consumed by the vortex.

On landing, Maude examined their handiwork. In the center lay a man in a dark robe; he was slightly shorter than she expected. What once had been rocks and vegetation around him had been pulverized by the force of their attack. A shallow indentation in the ground marked where the vortex had touched down. Mark, flanked by two guards, was already running to confirm their handiwork.

"Darn it!" Mark cried as they rolled the prone body over. "It's not him. Be on your guard. Find Vaughn!" His anger seethed, casting a stormy cloud over the once sunny day.

"I can't sense anyone else," Maude stated.

"He's still alive," a guard confirmed, bending over the body.

"He should be dead!" Maude exclaimed, running over to examine the body herself. Her eyes fixated on the rosy cheeks and fair hair of the youth at her feet. "What have we done?" *But how did he survive? Is he that powerful?*

"He's still one of them, Maude," Mark countered. "We're just doing the world a favor. Let's finish him off and get out of here."

"No!" Maude barely interjected herself between Mark and the unconscious youth before he could carry out his threat.

"What?" Mark turned on her, grabbing her by the arm and shoving her away. She desperately hung on and managed to spin him away from the prone boy. "Pull it together, Maude. This is what we do."

"Wait!" Maude was frantic. Surely Vaughn was evil, Leo had told them enough stories about him that there could be no question about that. But who was this boy? "We should question him. Maybe he can give us some information that will lead us to Vaughn."

"Of course he knows Vaughn!" Mark bellowed, losing his patience. "They're all working together. Do you really think he could make that robe himself?"

Maude crouched and examined the robe for herself. Grasping it in one hand, she could clearly make out the distinct signature of its creator.

"We won't catch Vaughn by accident," she replied. "We need to know what he's up to. This boy can help us."

"Do you really think we can let a wizard of such power live? It took nearly all of us to knock him out. If he wakes up it could be disastrous for us!"

Maude looked down and studied the boy's face again. *Who are you?* The wind picked up around her, swirling the sparkling remains of the gems on the ground. Overhead, the sun came out from behind a cloud, bathing the boy in warm sunlight. Next to the unconscious boy, her eye was drawn to sparkling flecks in the sand. Curious, she moved closer to examine them. Playing a hunch, she opened the robe of the unconscious young man. On the inside there were similar specs scatted about. Encouraged, she inspected the boy's hands.

"He's not that strong," Maude said at last. "He was refilling his batteries when we attacked. The jewels must have born the brunt of the vortex, saving his life. Even the ones attached to his robe were destroyed. It's just luck that he survived."

Mark looked at her, furious that he hadn't noticed the powder deposits himself.

"Very well. Prepare the body for transportation," he commanded stiffly, unwilling to humiliate himself further. "Johnson, call the transport. We're leaving."

A purple bubble enclosed Andy's limp body and lifted him off the ground, as a precaution. It would prevent any mana from reaching him. The troops scattered loose sand and debris around the edge of the small crater left by the vortex to obscure it. When the transport arrived they marched in, floating Andy behind them. As they took off, not a trace was left to indicate their presence.

***

About a kilometer away, high above the sandy beach, watchful eyes peered out from the protective cover of palm leaves as the transport departed. *So it begins,* Vaughn thought to himself. For hours his hiding place had given him a first-class view of Andy as he toiled at his task. Vaughn could feel the magical energy being condensed and stored, which surprised him at first. That much energy would mean Andy was filling the stones to their breaking point. *He's more than I imagined. He could be the one...*

Vaughn observed the boy closely. It was extremely rare for someone so young to be able to channel so much power. He had believed that Andy's own capacity would be much less than that of the gems, yet somehow he appeared to be filling them easily—one after another. Perhaps he had made the wrong choice. Before Vaughn had time to change his mind the troops, from Terra Protectra had arrived.

The troops were not as gentle as he had hoped. He was relieved that Andy had survived and that Maude, at least, had the sense to question him. Everything was going according to plan. He surveyed the little island, making sure that the enemy had left, then, with a wave of his hand, he vanished.

Chapter 18

Trapped

Andy awoke with a splitting headache. He pressed his hands against his forehead trying to drive out the nausea and vertigo. It took a moment for him to realize he wasn't standing or sitting on anything. He straightened his arms, seeking the comfort of a solid anchor but there was none. His eyes adjusted to the dim light and confirmed that he was floating in the middle of a small stone room. The mortar between the rocks on the walls was cracked and crumbling, giving him the impression that this building had been around for a long time. A single light shone softly from the ceiling, but the floor was covered with strange equipment, machines he had never seen before. Some looked strikingly medieval—others looked modern and computer-like. Turning his head he saw rows of bars blocking the only exit. *What the heck?*

He closed his eyes as another wave of nausea washed over him. Andy forced himself to remember. *I was on a beach... I was filling a battery... Then nothing.*

However he had come to this strange prison, it remained a mystery to him.

Well, at least I'm not naked, he thought, searching for a positive note in his current predicament. *I should be able to get myself down as soon as...* Andy's mind finally registered what was peculiar about this chamber: there was no mana. No, there was mana around him but his mind vaguely registered it being there, as if a great distance had sprung up between himself and his most cherished possession. *Was this another test?* Andy tried to focus on conjuring a simple ball of fire. A small flame materialized beside him and puffed out of existence as quickly as it appeared.

"Not bad. Most people like you can't manifest anything inside the field."

Andy looked around. He hadn't noticed anyone entering. Below him, by the door, a fragile looking figure in a black uniform looked up at him. Andy couldn't decide if the person was male or female. The voice and blonde hair seemed girlish, but the uniform was definitely tailored for a man.

"Hey, are you looking up my robe?" he yelled back.

Dark scarlet patches appeared on the checks of his custodian. *Definitely a girl,* he thought. Before they could continue their conversation, two more people entered wearing the same black uniforms. One was blond, like the girl, the other was much older with streaks of grey in his otherwise brown hair.

"He's awake? Good," the older man said.

"What is your name?" the younger man demanded.

"Where am I?" Andy asked.

"We're asking the questions here, scum," said Blondie.

"Did Jack put you up to this?" Andy continued in confusion. "I'm so going to get him back for this."

"Silence!" yelled Blondie. His hand glowed as a purple bubble ripped away from Andy's chest. The pain was unbelievable.

"Hey! That hurt!" Andy sputtered. Another bubble boiled away from his body.

"Mark," the older man seemed to be chastising his companion before turning to their captive. "Listen here, mage, you're being kept alive for one reason and one reason only; to help us find Vaughn and the rest of your kind so we can eliminate them."

"I don't know what you're talking about," Andy lied.

"Where are the sleepers?" barked Mark impatiently. The other two suddenly looked annoyed, but not with Andy.

"No idea." Andy looked confused.

"Come, come, enough heroics. We know you can use magic. You're one of them, aren't you? There is no way you can justify your criminal actions. We of Terra Protectra have been battling your kind for ages. We know all too well the terror and devastation your powers are capable of unleashing, and we will not stand by and let you destroy everything we hold dear."

"Funny, I thought you were the bad guys," Andy sneered.

"Oh, really?" the girl said in amusement, "I'm sure Vaughn told you all about us."

"He said you guys used to be police, until some Leo guy went postal and..."

"Enough!" snarled Mark, raising his hand. It glowed as Andy cried out in pain again. "I will not let you insult Leo!"

"Patience, Mark," Leo soothed. "His confusion is understandable. Vaughn is a master manipulator. Twisting words to suit his needs is his specialty. He is correct, I once served as a 'policeman' as he says but that does not do my job justice. Tell me, my captive companion, did Vaughn ever tell you how the great barrier was erected around this world?"

"No."

"I thought not." Leo shook his head sadly. "He never was good at admitting his mistakes. You see, I was there, like Vaughn, when it happened. When our city, our society, was destroyed and the magical barrier came into being. I was there when Vaughn failed us. It is his fault thousands of people died that day, and hundreds more since then as he vainly clings to life. That day must never be repeated. I will not let it happen again. Now tell us, where is Vaughn?"

Andy was silent, his face contorted in pain and disbelief. He hung before them unmoving, digesting what he had just heard. Finally he said, "I don't know."

"What were you doing at the lake?" asked Mark.

"Delivering pizza," replied Andy.

"Are you always such a smart ass?" Maude questioned.

"Are you talking to me, or the ass?" asked Andy.

"That's strike one, fool," Mark said.

"Sweet, what do I win?"

"This!" Mark ripped another bubble of energy away from him. Andy's body recoiled in pain and his face contorted but his eyes never left his captors.

"Can I take what's behind door number two?" Andy shot back defiantly.

"This is pointless." Maude turned to leave.

"I applaud your courage, boy, but your loyalty is misplaced. I can see why Vaughn is interested in you. Tomorrow the real interrogation will begin," Leo explained. "Think carefully on how you want it to proceed."

"Why?" Andy was indignant. "Didn't you say you were going to kill all of my kind? I assume that includes me."

"It does. However, your cooperation will determine the manner of your death, quick and merciful, or long and extremely painful."

"Lovely. Ya know, if you ever decide to become a motivational speaker, make sure your customers pay in advance."

"Good advice," said Leo, grinning. "Come, Mark. Maude. Let's give our guest time to sleep on our offer."

"It will be better for you if you just give them what they

want," Maude said softly.

"And what do you want?" Andy inquired.

"I…" Maude hesitated, unable to explain why she had spoken. She felt exposed under Andy's gaze. Quickly, she looked away.

"Come, Maude," Leo was already in the hall.

Maude closed the barred door behind her.

***

"Mark, I want you to handle the interrogation personally," Leo was saying when Maude caught up. "That boy knows much more than he's letting on, even if he doesn't know it consciously. We must learn everything he knows. You have permission to solicit his cooperation anyway you see fit but don't kill him, not until we have Vaughn anyway."

"Yes, Leo," Mark replied with a salute. "I won't fail you."

"See that you don't. And Maude, I want you to help in the interrogation as well. Your perspective on the prisoner's responses may prove insightful."

"Certainly."

"I don't need her help!" Mark bellowed.

"Of course you don't," Leo agreed dismissively. "But I need my two best officers to be on the same page and we don't have time to be passing notes like lovesick school children. Together you are far stronger than individually, as are we all. Is that clear?"

"Absolutely," Mark said, seething and still unable to control his temper.

"Yes, Leo," Maude echoed.

"Very well then. Keep me posted on your progress." Sensing Leo was dismissing them, the twins turned to go.

"Just a minute, Mark. Walk with me. We have things to discuss."

"Yes, Sir." Mark fell into step beside Leo. Once Maude was out of sight, Leo began.

"Mark, I'm proud of you. Your judgment in bringing him back alive was excellent."

Mark beamed at this compliment. "I knew you would find him useful. He'll talk. I'll see to that."

"I'm sure you will. Get to it. I'll begin making the preparations for the ceremony myself.

"Sir?" Mark looked confused. "With all due respect, I'd rather just get in there and get to work."

"I'm sure," Leo chuckled. "I'm sure you would. Indulge an old man then, would you? I certainly can't name my successor without a little fanfare, can I? To be honest, I had my doubts about you. What you've accomplished today has convinced me that you do have what it takes to lead this organization."

Mark was stunned. A big dopey grin spread across his face as he realized what Leo was talking about. He bowed his head to Leo saying, "It's an honor to serve you."

"Good. Get to work then."

***

Alone, Leo turned his thoughts to the boy in the cell for a moment. *So young... It can't be helped I guess. The war must be fought whatever the cost.* Turning on his heel, he too left the hall.

***

Andy stared off into space. Moving didn't get him anywhere. Spinning just made the blood rush to his head. In silence he reflected what a fine day he was having. *Get some sleep, ha! I don't even know if it's day or night*, he thought. As if on cue, the light in the cell turned off.

Chapter 19

Desperate Plans

Early morning pyres were already lit next to the Ganges River. People swarmed the river's landings and ancient steps, coming and going in a seamless stream of humanity. Worshipers congregated around the nearest lingam in prayer. Swimmers were already plunging themselves into the river, attempting to cleanse themselves and their spirits. Vaughn's sudden appearance on the wide brick steps next to the river went unnoticed and unquestioned in the morning throng.

Vaughn surveyed the mob of people around him and marveled at how some things never changed. The sun, still low over the eastern horizon, caused the ancient brick buildings to glow with warm orange light. He remembered how the city of Varanasi, now Banaras, was founded nearly 5000 years ago. *Banaras, some things do change,* he thought, chuckling to himself. He set off towards his destination, down the dusty streets crowded with peddlers and customers alike. The smell of exotic spices mingling with sweat and dirt assaulted his nose. His destination wasn't far, but navigating the winding streets and avoiding the local pick-pockets and hustlers was always an adventure. In his peripheral vision, Vaughn noticed several would-be thugs marking him as a tourist. He didn't hesitate to take control of the situation and magically glued their sandles to the stone street. A scathing string of curses followed Vaughn as he continued into the crowds.

He arrived at a shop with a small wooden sign above the

door which simply read: 'Rugs'. Iron bars covered the dirty front window, making the small display hard to see. A hanging sign on the decaying wood door said: 'Closed'. Vaughn pounded on the door anyway. A young girl with dark hair and olive skin opened the door a crack, her shy eyes questioning who would be there at this time of day.

"Hello, there," Vaughn greeted her. "I'm a friend of Sabrina's. I need to talk to her."

"Of course," she answered obediently, "this way. My name is Juana."

"Thank you, Juana," he replied.

The interior of the store was narrow but deep. Just inside the door stood a small counter with an ancient cash register perched on top. Behind the counter, and throughout the rest of the store, rugs hung from floor to ceiling. Racks of rugs of all colors and sizes protruded from the walls making it impossible to see the back of the store from the door. The small girl beckoned him to follow. She expertly wove her way through the cluttered piles towards the back. Another small door separated the storefront from the rear. The girl motioned for Vaughn to proceed alone. The door led to a small office.

"What are you doing here?" Jack asked, surprised to see him.

"I have grave news," Vaughn began. "I must speak with Alana immediately. Where is she?" The answer was obvious, but he asked anyway.

"She's conferring with Sabrina," replied Nat, pointing to a hanging tapestry across from them, separating the room in two.

"How long have they been talking?"

"A few hours now. We finished early and came straight here. I'm so bored," Jack answered, worry creeping onto his face.

He rested his feet on the coffee table before them. "Where's Andy?"

"I must speak with them right away," Vaughn said, ignoring the question. "Wait here. You won't be bored for long."

"What's going on?" Alana's voice drifted through from the other side of the tapestry. A moment later her hand emerged, brushing the tapestry aside. Her gaze swept the room. "What has happened?"

"Andy has been captured," Vaughn explained. He told them how he and Andy had been filling gems at the lake, how Terra Protectra had shown up and captured Andy before he could react. "I was too far away to help him. By the time I got back to the beach they had already taken off."

"Huh?" Jack was clearly showing his reservations to Vaughn's explanation. "Why did you leave him alone in the first place?"

"I thought I detected a new pool of energy on the far side of the lake." Vaughn shrugged. "Andy seemed to be progressing nicely so I decided not to disturb him."

"But," Kaida started. "You told us never to use that lake to refill gems. You said it was too well known to Leo."

"Yes, I know." Vaughn was exasperated. "I thought I could handle it. Given Andy's inexperience I thought the abundance of energy in that spot would make it easier for him to learn how to do the task. I even gave Andy one of my old robes to help mask him, but... I take full responsibility for his predicament. We must find him at once."

"What do we do now?" Nat asked. "We've been trying for months to find their base."

"Things are different now, as I'm sure Sabrina will agree," Vaughn continued. "I must speak to her."

"Agreed," Alana said. "This way." She held the tapestry

while Vaughn walked through. "The rest of you stay here."

"Aye, aye, captain." Jack threw Alana a mock salute before she followed Vaughn into the room. "Things just keep getting better and better," he muttered.

"Shut up, Jack," Nat snapped. She didn't buy Vaughn's explanation either but she wasn't sure what else to do. Kaida quietly sat with a worried expression on her face.

***

The room was barely large enough to hold two chairs and a wooden desk. Throw rugs were scattered across the floor. On top of the desk, upon another pile of rugs, was a tiny desk and chair with a tiny person sitting at it. The muted earth tones of her dress clashed with the bright green hat she was wearing.

"Hello, Sabrina," said Vaughn,

"Welcome." Sabrina's shrill voice fluttered gaily through the room. "I was just telling Alana that we are doing everything possible to find your missing Oracle."

"I'm afraid there's something else we've lost," explained Vaughn. "One of our apprentices has been captured by Terra Protectra. We desperately need your help to find him."

"I doubt there's much I can do," Sabrina said, sympathetically. "We gnomes aren't good with humans. If you had lost a dog or cat I'd be happy to help."

"We're well aware of your strengths, Sabrina," replied Vaughn. "The boy was wearing one of my old council robes. We were hoping you could convince Pheliador to..."

"Oh, I see where this is going," she cut in. "And you know what he's going to say?"

"Sabrina, please," Alana pleaded. "A young boy's life is in danger."

"Not to mention your own," Sabrina cheerfully pointed out.

"Quite," agreed Vaughn. "You see our predicament clearly as always, and we are prepared to be generous…"

"Hmmm…when's the last time you bought a rug from me, eh?" she asked roguishly, provoking sour looks from Vaughn and Alana. "I know, I know, I'll ask, but I won't promise anything."

"Thank you, Sabrina,"

"You may wait here." Without another word, she slipped behind a hanging tapestry. Vaughn and Alana sat down and awaited her return. Alana drew a deck of cards from her robe.

"Care for a game?" she asked.

Vaughn shrugged. "Why not?"

An hour later Sabrina returned carrying a large (compared to a gnome at least) charcoal flower pot. Inside was a single beautiful green flower with a purple stem. The rim of the pot was covered in runes. She set it down on a pile of rugs and beckoned Vaughn and Alana closer.

"Pheliador wants to discuss this matter personally," Sabrina began, "so I brought this Gossip Flower from the nursery. He has another in his lair." As she spoke she watered the flower and waved her hand over the runes. The runes around the edge came to life, glowing pale blue.

"Hail, Pheliador, Keeper of the Auri. I apologize for the intrusion," began Vaughn, "but we desperately need your help."

"You have pestered me often as of late to search for your precious Oracle," Pheliador replied, clearly annoyed. The deep tones of his voice rustled the flower's petals. "Sabrina says a student of yours was captured. Was this accidentally or intentionally?"

"You know me well, Keeper," replied Vaughn, "better than anyone alive."

"I do, hence the question."

"What matters is that we rescue him," Alana said.

"Are you sure he is still alive?" Pheliador asked.

"He was when they took him," Vaughn said. "However, the longer we wait to rescue him, the less likely he will remain that way."

"I will not leave this sanctuary to aid you. My powers are weak. I would not survive long on the surface."

"We ask that you help only in finding where they have taken him," said Vaughn.

"Indeed." Pheliador laughed. His bass chuckle rumbled through the room. "And what is my reward for performing this service?"

"We will gladly increase our supply of batteries to you," Vaughn promised.

Pheliador was not amused. The room shook with his displeasure. "You give me scraps and call it a feast. I should eat you this minute! If you want my help, you know what I require: The Foundation Stone. Consider this the rainy day you have been saving it for."

"That rock is not required," Vaughn replied, not liking where this was going. He knew exactly what Pheliador was referring to and was loathe to give it to him. "I will have my students increase your supplies…"

Pheliador snorted. "Forget it. I can't help you. Find someone else to work your miracles. Or do it yourself if you don't think the stone is necessary. Must I remind you that when you do find the Oracle, and ask me to activate it, and yes, I know you will, I will need the stone to do so. Sooner or later you will give me what I desire. You're a predictable old fool."

Vaughn held his temper, with great difficulty. Pheliador was right of course. He would need access to the Foundation

Stone to activate the Oracle, but Vaughn had never intended to let him keep it. "If you use the stone to find Andy, our lost student, will you still be able to activate the Oracle?"

Silence answered his question. Vaughn's eyebrows knit together in frustration. A deep frown was on Alana's face. Finally Pheliador replied, "Yes. Bring me the Foundation Stone and I will find your lost apprentice."

Relieved, Vaughn let out an audible sigh. "Very well. You will get the Foundation Stone and in return, you will find Andy at once."

"To work such strong magic is dangerous. With the stone I will have the power to find him but I will require your help. The shielding in this place is weak. It will have to be reinforced to keep my powers from being detected."

"Fine." *Safer for you, and safer for us,* Vaughn thought. "Anything else?"

"I'm in the mood for some exotic treats, Sabrina. A couple of zebras should do the trick."

"Of course," replied Sabrina, getting to her feet.

"Very well, I'll make the preparations you require and send for the stone."

"Excellent,"

Hold on, Andy. We'll find you, and a lot more I hope, Vaughn thought. Swiftly he left the room to inform the others of what was to be done.

"Oh," Sabrina said, grinning, "do you like your zebras black with white stripes, or white with black stripes?"

The plant was silent. A moment later Pheliador's amused voice answered, "Surprise me."

Chapter 20

Hard Lessons

"I don't know," Andy whispered.

The pain was excruciating. Purple bubbles smaller than before, but far more numerous, streamed away from his body. Andy's limbs were numb and his senses dulled to everything except the pain running through him. Pain without end it seemed at times.

For the past week his tormentors had taken their task to heart. Andy assumed it was a week, though all he had to go by was the light in his room, on for the day, off for the night. Off, on, pain. That was his routine now. The blond man, Mark, seemed to have a great deal of enthusiasm for his work. *I wonder how many animals he tortured as a child?* Andy asked himself as he received his latest punishment.

Maude had a different approach. Her attempts to reason with him mostly failed, of course, but at least she understood that 'big sticks don't always get results'. She was tricky. Their talks often started out innocently enough, but sooner or later she would get around to Vaughn. He almost preferred the simplicity of Mark's attacks, because he knew to expect the pain that accompanied every question. Maude was less predictable.

At first, he had tried to fight. Andy had picked up a few tricks from Jack that helped him to suppress pain, but the field constantly hindered his concentration making it extremely difficult to focus on them for long. Under the unnatural light his head pounded constantly and his skin felt crispy, almost ready to flake away from his body at any moment. He had tried timing his powers to block the bubbles as they appeared but it was no use. Between the field sapping his concentration and having his energy ripped away from him, Andy felt more helpless than he ever had before. Yet he still clung to hope. The constant pressure to perform had forced Andy to adapt. Somehow, despite it all, over the past days his abilities had begun to adapt to his extreme circumstance. His concentration had improved to where he could occasionally hold a fireball for a few seconds. The constant energy drain had taught him to refine his thoughts. He had progressed from seizing broad columns of energy to thin razors of power to achieve the same results. More complicated acts were still tenuous. Healing himself during the day was pointless. The pain lingered long after the bubbles vanished. There was no way to block it all. The questions kept coming. He stalled when he could but sometimes that just made things worse.

The questions never changed. Where is Vaughn? Where is their hideaway? How many mages are there? Blah, blah, blah. Andy's answer was always the same. "I don't know." Which was mostly true. It wouldn't have mattered if he did know more details; he had never been a squealer and he was determined not to be one now.

"Maybe he really doesn't know," Andy heard Maude say. "That, or he's an idiot."

"He knows," Mark assured her. "He knows." His communicator beeped. With a flick of the wrist he read and acknowledged it.

"We need to try something else."

"Up the voltage?"

"No," Maude sighed. "We're not getting anywhere by hurting him."

"We just haven't hurt him enough," Mark replied. "Maybe if we remove a limb or two he'll see things our way."

"That's not what I mean."

"Well, we haven't gotten anywhere with your little good cop, bad cop routine."

"Maybe we don't know what would really hurt him?" Maude suggested.

"You know I'm right here, right? I can hear you discussing me." Andy, annoyed, spun in his chamber. "You've been working pretty hard. Maybe you'd like to go outside or take a break or something."

"Shut up," scolded Mark. "I will break you! It's just a matter of time."

"Mmmhmmm, you do that, Sparky," Andy retorted. Mark's eyes were filled with hatred as he shook a clenched fist at Andy.

"Stop!" Maude grabbed Mark's arm. "Think! We need him to find Vaughn."

"I'm not so sure anymore," Mark admitted. "We're not getting anywhere questioning him. Maybe he really doesn't know anything. If that's true, he's worthless to us. I'm going to recommend we liquidate him when I speak to Leo."

"Aw, and we were just getting to know each other," Andy cooed sarcastically.

"That would be a mistake," Maude said before Mark could take another shot at Andy.

"You're not in command here. I am. We've wasted enough time on him already." Mark's rage was freely flowing now. "You were wrong about this one. Stay if you like. I have criminals to catch." He stalked off.

"Nice guy," Andy taunted after Mark left, "if you ignore everything about him."

Exasperated, Maude rounded on him. "Why do you push his buttons? You're just making it harder on yourself."

"I doubt it. I've known lots of guys just like him at school. They all have only one speed—moron. " Andy maneuvered himself so he was directly facing Maude. "It doesn't matter what I say. He'll always have it in for me."

Andy watched her fume silently. He was right of course. "Do all mages have a death wish?" she asked.

"Perhaps this place is getting to me," he conceded. "It's the purple light, it's making me unbalanced."

"Perhaps I could arrange for a little fresh air, if you agree to be of some assistance to us?"

"Will there be blue sky?"

"Certainly."

"And green trees?"

"Of course."

"And flowers and a little stream?"

"That can be arranged."

"That sounds nice."

"You'll help us then?"

"No."

Furious, Maude closed her eyes and counted to ten. Her face was hot. Doubtlessly it was turning bright red. With any luck, that would be the only visible sign that Andy had gotten to her.

"Mark is right," she said at last. "All of you should be exterminated."

"Do you really believe that?"

"Leo says so. That's enough for me."

"You believe this Leo guy? He seems a bit sketchy to me."

"About what?"

"You mean, besides wanting to wipe out everyone who can use magic because of some accident thousands of years ago? Talk about holding a grudge."

"Leo is a great man. He knows what he's doing." Her voice cracked. Somehow, hearing Terra Protectra's mission summed up like that knocked a lot of the nobility out of it.

"I've never killed anyone," Andy went on. "I would never hurt anyone." He stared at her solemnly.

"I... It doesn't matter." Maude sounded unsure. Her voice wavered. "You're one of them, you can't help it."

"Do you really want to be enemies?"

The bluntness of his statement shocked her. She stared at the young man, as if seeing him for the first time. *Who is this guy?* "That's not really a choice is it?"

"Are you sure?" he asked softly.

"I... I'll be back later," she managed to squeak out before marching out of the cell.

***

The air was stifling in the assembly hall as Maude entered. Leo was already on stage. She quickly slipped into an open seat and listened. Everyone knew what was coming, still, the formalities had to be observed. Not one officer fidgeted, except Maude. Hearing the news for the first time with the other officers had seemed surreal. Leo had made his choice. She thought she could respect that, but now, hearing Leo's pomp and pageantry, she wasn't so sure. Leo's words faded into the background as she mulled over what was to come.

"For capturing an enemy, it is with great pride that I hereby name Mark to be my official successor and second in command of Terra Protectra. From now on, he and I speak as one voice. His orders are my orders. And now, I give you your new vice-general, Mark Trowlinger."

The officers clapped enthusiastically as Mark took the stage and shook hands with Leo. Maude followed along mechanically, mindful of those around her. He was her brother after all. She should be proud of him as well. Yet she wasn't. Her last conversation with Andy popped into her head. Maude shook her head to clear it and focus on what Mark was saying.

"Thank-you, Leo," Mark began. "Thank-you for the faith and trust you have placed in me. I vow to devote every fiber of my being towards serving Terra Protectra and towards ensuring those who defy Terra Protectra are punished." He paused as more applause thundered from the audience.

"Today marks a new era for Terra Protectra. Today we are stronger, sharper and more capable than ever before. It is only a matter of time before we hunt down the rest of those who court magic. Soon, we will be victorious and secure our way of life forever!"

Arms raised, Mark hollered as the audience continued to clap and cheer. As the officers rose to give Mark a standing ovation, Maude had had enough. She stood quickly. Her body felt strange, stretched, out of shape—like cooling taffy ready to be cut into pieces. Carefully, trying not to be seen, Maude made her way out of the hall.

Chapter 21

Here We Come

The wind howled as the group materialized in central Tanzania amidst a field of cotton plants. Their hooded heads bowed together as dust swirled around them. With Pheliador's help, Vaughn's robe had been located in an area that was once a prosperous mining hub, but was now thought to be mined out and deserted. Natalie pulled out a map and a GPS unit to confirm their location. It was still about five kilometers to the actual mine site from their current location. Knowing their enemy, teleporting in any closer would certainly risk detection. After getting their bearings, they set out across the field. The plants were heavy with cotton ready to be picked. Looking around, the fields seemed to stretch on for kilometers, with only sparse trees and shrubs dotting the edges of each field to protect against the wind. The odd puff of smoke could be seen in the sky, marking the homes of the fields' farmers.

The price for Pheliador's help had been steep. The Foundation Stone was more than a sparkly piece of rock. It was the largest mana repository Vaughn had. It had been salvaged by Alana right after the accident, and was the only focus for powerful magic they had in their possession. Using the stone meant certain discovery unless thorough precautions were taken to mask the energy discharged during its operation. Even utilizing Pheliador's heavily warded lair the full power of the stone would be easily detected. After much debate, Pheliador convinced them that even with the improved protection runes, he could only use a fraction of its magical energy without being detected. They all had crossed their fingers, hoping it would be enough to find Andy safely. The precautions slowed the search, but ultimately it was still successful.

Vaughn led them at a brisk pace. Where possible, they stuck to the trees and larger bushes on the edges of the fields to cover their approach. Uncertain of what to expect, everyone was alert for Terra Protectra patrols.

Suddenly, Vaughn froze and dove into the bush. Behind him he could hear Alana, Jack, Nat, and Kaida scatter as well. Nestled beside a broken tree trunk stood one of Terra Protectra's monitoring stations. Instinctively, Vaughn sent a bolt of silver light towards the automated device. It exploded in a white flash, leaving only a tiny pile of charred ruins behind.

"All clear," Vaughn called out. The others cautiously drew closer to him. They took turns examining the remains of the automated station guarding the path, thankful Vaughn had detected it and raised the alarm.

"I've neutralized it, hopefully before it sensed us. It won't be sending anything back to warn Terra Protectra now though." There was a collective sigh of relief. *Hopefully this trip won't be for nothing,* thought Vaughn. Stealthily they continued towards the mine.

***

Activity at the mine confirmed their suspicions that the Terra Protectra headquarters was at hand. Vaughn pointed out the black uniforms that could be seen moving around the offices, machine shops, and gates to the others. A large Victorian house stood on a small hilltop above the main camp. A single dirt road led to the mine site. They stopped two hundred meters from the main gate, crouching behind a small stand of mahogany trees. Vaughn scanned the compound, familiarizing himself with the buildings, looking for a way in. He pointed out the guards and another automated sentry to everyone, as well as the main mechanical building, mine services building and barracks. The lair was well-guarded, physically and mystically.

"Alana, take everyone east and use the air shaft to enter the mine. I'll search the house," Vaughn instructed.

"Alone?" Natalie didn't like the sound of that. "Shouldn't we stick together here? Major bad guys around, yes?"

"I want to assume Andy will be somewhere in the mine, but I can't," continued Vaughn. "That's probably where he'll be since it's the most defensible part of the compound, along with most of the guards, which is why you're all going there."

"But you also think he could be in the house?" asked Kaida.

"It's a possibility."

"Someone should go with you." Alana and Vaughn shared an apprehensive look.

"I will stand a better chance of being undetected if I'm alone," Vaughn explained. "Quickly now, we don't want to lose the element of surprise. You know what to do. Get in, find Andy, and get out. Time is not on our side. The longer we are here, the more likely we'll be seen, and the more danger we'll put ourselves in."

Their plans made, Vaughn disappeared first. The others cloaked themselves as Vaughn had done and moved in the opposite direction. Alana led them around to the chain link fence on the east side of the compound, far away from the sentry at the gate. Seconds later an entire section of fence vanished. Guards stationed nearby didn't question the disappearance; to them it had always been that way. Quickly, the four cloaked figures moved from building to building, relying on speed and their robes to mask their magical powers.

***

The ventilation building was quiet as Alana led them inside. Its steel walls sheltered a pair of large fans for circulating air through the mine.

"They must have consolidated the generators in another building," Jack observed as his eyes followed a bundle of thick electrical cables running across the floor and through a makeshift hole in the wall.

"Yay, for them," Nat muttered under her breath.

"Let's go." Alana was already loosening the cowling on one of the fans. Her hair billowed around her head with each puff of air.

"Do you feel that?" asked Nat. "That prickly feeling?" The others shrugged and continued examining the room.

Alana paused and studied the duct carefully. "The cover seems to be coated with something, Misorbium probably. We'll need to remove it by hand. Jack, help me."

Alana deftly slid her hand over the surface of the duct. It glowed purple at her touch. Jack studied it carefully before violently, wrenching it open. A sharp screech of metal scraping on metal filled the room. They froze in their spots, anxiously listening for someone to come and check out the sound.

***

Nigel, mug in hand, was crossing the courtyard with Brian, a new acquaintance who shared his passion for a good cupp'a joe. They were just returning from picking some of the choicest beans Nigel had ever seen. He was showing his harvest to a passing technician when a loud screech stopped them in their tracks.

"You hear that?" asked Brian.

"Reckon I did," replied Nigel. "Ghastly sound. Sounded like it came from the ventilation shed."

"Figure we should check it out?"

"I'm on duty in 15 minutes," replied Nigel, "and I still have to wash and shine myself up a bit. It's probably nothing. Maintenance probably forgot to lube one of the fans most likely. You can never trust those maintenance chaps, mark my words. This one time…"

Nigel's voice trailed off as he disappeared into the barracks. Those nearby resumed whatever it was they had been doing a moment ago, the noise forgotten.

***

"That should do it." Jack flexed his hands attempting to shake the dust and dirt off them from the ventilation cover. His companions let out a collective sigh of relief at not being discovered.

"I still have this strange feeling," insisted Natalie.

"Scaredy cat," teased Jack.

"Kaida, help me," Alana instructed. Together they checked the shaft again.

"Nothing is showing, but stay alert people."

Carefully they slipped by the fan and into the extensive duct system feeding the mine.

***

Nigel had just settled down at his station when an alert signal flashed. "Just my luck," he said under his breath. Setting his coffee cup down, he thumbed the switch for the intercom. "Find Mark. Get him up here right away."

Satisfied his job was done for the moment, he leaned back in his chair and reached for his mug. The alert sounded.

"Again?" He called up the information on his monitor. It wasn't coming from inside the base. It was from Banaras of all places.

"What the..." *Are there security tests going on today?* He couldn't remember. Actually, in the months he had been with Terra Protectra he couldn't remember a single test. *What could be happening there?* He hadn't the foggiest idea.

"What's going on?" Mark demanded as he entered the control room.

"Sir, we've had a priority communication from an operative in Banaras," explained Nigel. "And sir, you better take a look at this."

Mark strode across the command center and inspected the monitor. His brows furrowed at the displayed information.

"Put every officer on alert. Quietly. And you are to personally notify me if anything out of the ordinary happens. I don't care how trivial it may seem."

"Yes, sir."

"I'll inform Leo." Mark was already leaving the control room.

"Yes, sir."

"And step on it!"

"Yes, sir!" Nigel barked Marks orders into the phone.

***

Vaughn closed the glass patio door behind him. He was troubled. Security seemed too light in this part of the compound. At least, his security would have been tighter. He scanned the area with magic. Misorbium hampered his efforts, flashing along the walls as his magic probed the area. If they did have security here, it would surely pick up his efforts but he didn't have a choice. Time wasn't on his side.

A faint prickly sensation on his neck annoyed him. *Interesting.* He scanned again. *Nothing.* Vaughn walked briskly across the room to the double doors on the other side. His robe alerted him to someone coming. Footfalls reached his ears from the other side of the door. He waited until they receded before opening the door and proceeding in the opposite direction.

The hall was sparsely decorated. Vaughn's shoes clicked softly on the bare hardwood floor. He pushed past the mahogany double doors at the end of the hall and found himself in a library. Dark paneled shelves lined the walls up to the ceiling. It was a small library, but the rows of shelves were packed with books. Large skylights lifted the cavernous feel from the space. A single armchair and writing desk were in the middle of the room.

Vaughn scanned again and faintly detected something. He crossed the room and tried again. Something magical was definitely behind the wall. Vaughn froze. His robe alerted him to someone's presence, but he could detect no one in the room. Ignoring the alarm, he set to work finding his prize. It was difficult to find the null mana triggers but he succeeded. A section of shelving slid back into the wall before moving to one side, clearing the way for Vaughn to proceed.

The open tunnel sloped down towards the mine. Bare boards gave way to raw earth and stone. Vaughn's journey ended in a small cavity bored out of the rock. The floor was covered in machines and contraptions in various stages of repair. The magical residue was strong here. Slowly he made his way through the junk and debris. The Oracle was here, somewhere before him, he could feel it. Vaughn bent down and let his hands wander through the cast-off items until they closed around something extremely smooth. *Found it.*

Vaughn held up the remains of the Oracle of Y'alan. He almost didn't recognize it. The clear crystal bust was now blackened at its core, as if burned from the inside out. Pits and grooves covered its once flawless surface, yet an awesome feeling of power still radiated from it.

Still functional? Must be my lucky day. He drew the Oracle close to him, cradling it like a long lost child. Something had changed though. It felt different somehow, yet Vaughn couldn't quite place it. *It has been a long time,* he thought, *and it is much more damaged than I thought possible.*

"I knew you'd come."

Vaughn turned to greet the interloper, making no attempt to hide his prize. He had recognized the voice at once. Before him stood Leo, his uniform prim and proper, with an amused look on his face.

"Still getting Maude to do your laundry?"

"She does an excellent job," Leo confirmed, "but nothing compared to the clock cleaning I'm going to give you." He grinned.

Vaughn grinned back at him. "You've always been obsessive-compulsive. Isn't there a twelve step program for that now?"

Light flared around Vaughn as the symbols on his robe blazed, countering Leo's attempt to drain him. Streaks of silver encircled Vaughn, enclosing the bubbles streaming from him. The shimmering silver field burst the bubbles on contact, absorbing their stolen mana, and strengthening the field in the process.

"You can't win, Vaughn. Surely you can feel your powers draining as we speak. Even if you beat me, you wouldn't make it out of here alive." As he spoke, a bubble of energy erupted from the silver shield around Vaughn and whizzed towards the ceiling.

Vaughn looked around again. A faint purplish glow emanated from various walls around him. *Misorbium.*

"First things first, Leo. Remember what I taught you? You're forgetting the one critical aspect in my favor."

"What's that?"

"This," Vaughn raised the Oracle of Y'alan over his head, and activated it.

Light radiated from Vaughn's hand and a booming voice filled the room as the Oracle came to life.

Chapter 22

Rescuing Rescuers

"This way," Kaida whispered as Alana and Jack hid the unconscious guard in a small storage locker. They had followed the air duct as far as they could, deep into the mine. A ribbon of fluorescent light overhead lit their way as they searched. This was the second guard they had encountered; both had been disposed of without a fuss.

Alana sensed a magical aura early in their foray into the mine, but reaching it had proven challenging. The tunnels twisted and turned, making a direct route hard to find. To Alana's relief, Kaida was able to tap into the security cameras, giving them an excellent view of the labyrinth-like tunnels. Under her guidance they were closing rapidly in on their target, hoping it was Andy.

Kaida's hand shot into the air, stopping Alana. She froze, straining to hear whatever Kaida had noticed. Voices could be heard around the corner. Silently they listened, preparing to strike.

"Tell me where your friends are." The voice was definitely female and very familiar. "When Mark gets back I doubt he'll be in a very good mood. Tell us what we want to know and make things easier for yourself. We're going to find out anyway. There's no reason for you to suffer."

A soft gurgling sound was the only response.

"You're right about that," Natalie yelled. Unable to restrain herself, she charged towards Maude. "Here we are!"

Maude spun towards the door, cursing herself for being too preoccupied with Andy to notice anyone approaching. Purple light crackled in her hands, ready to strike, but she didn't get a chance. Nat was too quick, teleporting a large rock directly at her head. Maude collapsed, unconscious before even reaching the ground.

"Ask and you shall receive," mocked Nat as she stepped over Maude's prone body. The others followed her into the room.

"Andy!" Kaida cried as she drew within sight of him.

He floated limp and lifeless in the middle of the room. Andy's body clearly displayed the torments he had endured at Mark's hands. Alana turned away, unable to acknowledge the consequences of Vaughn's plan. Steeling herself, she slowly turned back. Red, cracked skin was visible through Andy's burnt, torn clothes. His hair was matted. Sweat beaded on his pale face. His eyes remained blank, clearly not registering that they were there.

"Andy, it's us!" Nat yelled, horrified at what she saw.

"Get him out of there," ordered Alana.

Jack ran forward to catch Andy as Kaida examined the machinery holding him in place. Embedded in the floor, it glowed with buttons and symbols she had never seen before. Concentrating, she eliminated them one by one. The purple bubble surrounding Andy shuddered and winked out of existence, dropping Andy into Jack's waiting arms.

"I'll heal him," offered Jack as he slowly lowered him to the ground.

"No," Alana protested. "That might attract attention."

"A bit late for that, isn't it?" Jack jerked his thumb in Maude's direction.

"Fine, make sure he's conscious and stable, but that's it. We need to hurry." Alana sighed.

"Roger."

***

Jack held him close with one arm and put his free hand over Andy's forehead. He formed the healing symbols in his mind and concentrated. Andy blinked and drew a deep breath. Wearily, Jack smiled at his friend.

"Welcome back."

"What kept you?" asked Andy, weakly.

"Well, Nat keeps upping her rates and..."

"Shut yer pie hole," Nat cut him off.

Andy grinned as Jack helped him to his feet. He leaned heavily on Jack, still groggy from his interrogation.

"What about her?" Natalie gestured towards Maude.

Alana considered what to do. "A hostage might be advantageous, at least until we get out of here. Kaida can you..."

"Not while I'm monitoring the security cameras."

"Very well, I'll carry her." A soft glow of energy picked Maude off the floor and carried her over to Alana.

"Oh sure... don't ask me," Nat rolled her eyes.

"Nat... not now."

"Fine," pouted Natalie.

"Kaida, can you find, Vaughn?" asked Alana.

Kaida reached out and touched the wall. Sparks from her hand shot upwards and ran along it down the hallway. A moment later she replied, "I don't see him on any camera."

"Hmm," Alana looked worried.

Natalie pulled out her Waystone and adjusted a knob. "I have him, I think," she said as she banged the instrument against her hip.

"Right, teleport us Nat," Alana instructed.

"Roger."

Jack watched as Natalie closed her eyes, focusing her mind on the task at hand. A familiar glow enveloped her body. "Ahhh!" Nat screamed and doubled over. "I can't, I can't do it. The pain, the prickles... too much."

"I see now," observed Alana. "This place is shielded from teleporters. Of all of us you're the most sensitive to that kind of magical energy."

"We go the old fashioned way then?" Jack suggested.

"What other choice do we have?" Kaida said. "Nat, are you able to walk?"

Natalie found her second wind and stood up, wiping her face with her sleeve. "I'm fine."

"Okay, let's move," barked Alana. "Nat lead us, Kaida, keep an eye on the cameras."

***

The light dimmed as the Oracle became silent once more. Vaughn slowly lowered the Oracle, cradling it to his breast. He watched Leo across from him, his mouth hanging open, shocked by what he had heard and seen.

"Now we know," Vaughn said calmly.

"It's a lie!" screamed Leo. "You did something to it."

"I have done nothing except call up the account of what happened that day. What we both witnessed was exactly what Y'alan saw. It is beyond my power to influence it in any way."

"But, it can't be."

"Now that we both know how Baurum'tatus was destroyed, the question is: are we still enemies?"

"We will always be enemies!" yelled Mark.

He stood in a doorway to Vaughn's left. Purple energy radiated from him. A thick magenta beam shot from his Misorbium covered hands towards Vaughn, who easily deflected it, sending dust and debris flying.

"Foolish child." Vaughn raged. He brandished the Oracle before him, launching a protective silver sphere. Mark fired again, trying to steal Vaughn's energy. The sphere rippled as it absorbed the attack. Again Mark fired. The sentinel glittered as it bobbed and weaved, intercepting every attack as before. Again, and again. The sphere continued its vigil, becoming more radiant with every blow.

"No!" Leo cried. "Stop before you..."

Vaughn unleashed his globe. It stretched, then distorted, and burst, hurling thousands of tiny silver orbs around the room. The orbs scattered the light, covering the room in slivers of illumination and shadow as they hurled towards their victims. Leo and Mark ducked for cover, avoiding most of the deadly spheres. Their uniforms sizzled and popped where contact had been made. Mark's left leg was bleeding.

"I've so had it with this duck and cover nonsense!" Mark yelled and attacked again.

***

The sound of battle echoed throughout the mine. Guards rushed towards the source of the commotion, leaving the tunnels empty.

"Vaughn must have been discovered," Jack noted. He stopped and adjusted his grip on Andy.

"He'll need help," Kaida added.

"Hurry!" Alana ordered, her robes alight in magical symbols. "No need to play it safe anymore."

"About time!" said Nat. "Let's rock these dunderheads!" Kaida took the lead, allowing Natalie to deal with the guards they came across. She led them at a brisk pace. Jack, straining to keep up, had resorted to magic to keep Andy on his feet. They no longer avoided Terra Protectra members. The guards were easy prey as they scrambled blindly to their commander's aid. They fell in heaps along the tunnel walls wherever Andy's rescuers met them.

"Please don't let us be too late," Alana whispered.

***

Seven more Terra Protectra Officers had joined Mark, only two of which were still standing, Vaughn noticed. The room was alive with swirling colors and fiery energies as both sides parried and riposted, trying to find a weakness to exploit. None of the furnishings were intact, most were barely recognizable as anything more than smoldering heaps.

Vaughn still controlled the center of the room but his enemies were trying new strategies—two shielding while the other two attacked. Their combined powers were proving to be a challenge. Too late did Vaughn realize what the strange prickly feeling meant. *So much for a quick getaway,* he thought. They were attempting to flank him. Sweat beaded on Vaughn's brow as he pivoted to keep his attackers in view. He was holding his own, but a sustained fight was something he couldn't win. It was only a matter of time before his energy stores ran out and they would have him.

Vaughn looked back at Leo. He was covering Mark as they huddled in a doorway. Out of the corner of his eye he could see more purple bolts flying. Instinctively, he tensed; his shield shimmered as he reinforced it with his mind. No impact came.

— 172 —

Out of the tunnel behind him he sensed more people entering the room.

"Yes, yes, I know, we're saving the day," Natalie hollered, grinning maniacally.

Two Terra Protectra officers slumped on the floor beside her. "What would you do without us, Vaughny-poo?"

Dumbfounded at this turn of events, Vaughn allowed himself to relax. "You have my deepest gratitude," he said, inclining his head slightly towards his rescuers.

Realizing their fortunes were turning for the worse, Leo and Mark blasted Vaughn together. "For Terra!" they cried. Vaughn's shield absorbed most of the bombardment but enough force breached it to knock him off his feet. He hit the ground hard, winding himself. Streaks of pain shot through his body. Kaida rushed to his aid, slipping him a few full batteries in the process to strengthen his shield.

"That's quite enough out of you," scolded Alana. She stepped forward, parading her cargo for all to see. Maude's limp body hung in the air before her, suspended by Alana's magic. "Call off your goons, Leo. Don't make me get nasty."

"Cowards!" shouted Mark. "How dare you take hostages. Release my sister!"

"Oh?" said Jack. He squared himself to Mark, making sure he could see Andy. "Have you forgotten Andy? That wasn't exactly a tanning salon we found him in."

"You'll never get out of here!" screamed Mark.

"Quiet, you," Nat chastised him with her best school teacher impersonation.

"I propose a trade. We return your niece, you let us go," Alana offered.

"Not with that statue," Leo rebutted. "We trade person for person."

"We already have the person we came for and the Oracle," Kaida interjected. "I'm sure we could fight our way out but that would take time and energy. Perhaps you could stop us, but you'd risk injuring Maude as well. It would be 'convenient' for both parties if you permitted us to leave. Allow this, and we'll return Maude to you."

Leo considered her words, trying to find a hole in her logic.

"Very well," Leo agreed. "Return Maude and we'll lower the field."

"You can't!" Mark was furious. "We've sworn to kill these monsters."

"We've sworn to protect the people of Earth," Leo corrected. "That includes Maude."

"But..." Mark was flabbergasted. "You can't!"

"You first," commanded Alana.

"Very well," Leo acquiesced. He pulled a communicator out and thumbed it open. "Duty Officer, lower the Mobius shield surrounding the base."

"Sir?" replied a questioning voice through heavy static.

"Do it now," Leo commanded.

"Yes, sir."

"It's gone," Natalie confirmed a moment later.

"Very well," Alana said. Maude floated towards Leo and Mark, gently coming to rest on the ground. The paralyzing glow around her vanished and her eyes flew open.

"They're here! Sound the alarm!"

"Yes, child," Leo shushed her. "We know."

Maude looked around and unsteadily got to her feet, trying to get her bearings. She blushed crimson as she realized the full scope of the situation.

"Thank you," said Alana sincerely. "We'll be going now."

"See ya," Nat quipped. She began to focus the energies she needed to teleport them to safety. Light flared around her and engulfed the group.

"Damn you all!" Mark's rage exploded. He unleashed a torrent of energy on the intruders. It ricocheted off Vaughn's sturdy shield and struck the ceiling directly above the spot where Leo and Maude were standing. Chunks of rock rained down on them.

"Watch out!" Leo yelled. He dove at Maude, knocking her away just as a large boulder crashed to the floor where she had been standing. Rocks continued to pile up on Leo's prone body. The impact knocked Maude off her feet and into the teleportation field. An instant later she was gone.

Mark shrieked in anguish, "No!"

Chapter 23

An Unexpected Companion

"What do we do with her?" asked Jack.

The first order of business once they materialized on the sandy beach, not too far from their underground lair, was figuring out what to do with Maude.

"Will she live?" Vaughn asked.

"She's banged-up and unconscious, but otherwise healthy," said Alana.

"Nat, go to the work room and bring back a detention cuff," Vaughn said as he knelt next to Maude.

"Aye, aye." She disappeared and quickly returned with a large bronze ring-shaped device that looked like a bracelet. Nat handed it to Vaughn who slipped it onto Maude's delicate wrist. Immediately, it began to shrink in circumference until it fit snuggly, then it unrolled and stretched to cover Maude's entire forearm. As it locked in place, bright purple symbols appeared on it.

"It's working," confirmed Vaughn. He touched the device with his finger. The symbols changed as he examined the device. "She shouldn't be able to use her powers now. Of course she's still free to run, but powerless, she won't get very far."

"Shall we wake her up?" Jack inquired gleefully. A gallon bucket full of water appeared in his hands. He grinned. "I volunteer to do the honors."

"I think it's best if we all follow Andy's example and get

some rest," replied Vaughn, motioning towards Andy who was already sleeping on the sand. "We'll have lots of time to deal with our new friend tomorrow. Nat, Kaida, take Andy with you, I want to have a word with Alana before we turn in."

"Booooo!" Jack hissed as he emptied the pail into the sand.

"Since you're so full of energy you can watch the prisoner tonight." Vaughn managed to smoothly reproach Jack without cracking a smile.

Jack replied with his obvious, I-know-I'm-being-screwed-over look but merely said, "Fine."

***

As the apprentices left, Vaughn motioned for Alana to walk with him. The breeze was chilly as it rolled in from the sea. The sounds of the waves hitting the shore acted as their guide as they strolled down the dark beach. Alana bent for a moment and removed her shoes, happily squishing the wet sand between her toes as she walked. Vaughn said nothing as he savored the night air.

"So..." Alana began. She was hesitant to break his revelry.

"What I found tonight," Vaughn began, "I had not dared to hope for. I had relinquished the Oracle of Y'alan to the annals of history forever. Needless to say I was pleasantly surprised to be proven wrong." He pulled the Oracle out of his robes and held it lovingly before passing it to Alana. "The cataclysm has drained much from it, and I fear triggering it with Leo took the last of its power."

"Is Leo our ally once more?" she asked.

"Perhaps," he replied, "but it remains to be seen whether

his followers will convert as well. It's too soon to be certain of anyone's intentions."

"Then we must still be cautious."

"Indeed, I fear we may have imprudently wasted a great deal of our strength tonight." Vaughn sighed, idly thinking of everything they had endured in recent days. "We will need the foundation stone to make the Oracle operational again. Our batteries may be able to trigger its last recordings, but its full power, that to predict the future, will require the stone. Of that I am certain. We've come so far, Alana, could the means to bring down the barrier finally be within our grasp?"

"Vaughn…"

"I only hope Pheliador will be in a giving mood when we ask to use it."

Grinning, Alana replied, "Is he ever in a giving mood?" Uncle and niece shared a quiet chuckle. Too soon Alana's mirth gave way to more serious matters. "If we can convince the girl, Maude, maybe she can persuade the others? They certainly won't listen to us."

"It's the only chance we have of resolving matters peacefully. Time is growing short and we're running out of options."

"And Andy?"

"What about him?"

"What if he asks… questions?"

Vaughn thought a moment before responding. *Truthfully, I never expected him to survive*, he thought.

"He doesn't need to know any more than we've told the others."

Alana considered her words carefully. Today had been a great success. Their gamble had paid off extremely well. But, that didn't mean tomorrow would be any easier.

"Very well," she said at last.

They walked along the beach until Alana's curiosity got the better of her again.

"What did the Oracle say?"

"You'll know soon enough. I doubt I could do it justice anyway." They continued their walk in thoughtful silence.

The others were sound asleep when they arrived home. Even Jack had passed out at his post while guarding the prison cell.

Are we in the clear? Vaughn wondered. *Or is this simply the calm before the storm?*

***

The next morning Vaughn had everyone up early to break camp and resume their journey. He didn't trust their foes to give up easily. They teleported to a small woodsy retreat surrounded by thick firs, spruce trees and rolling hills. The traditional log cabin had a small living area, with kitchen and laundry, and an open loft with a few modern touches including a large skylight and a gas fireplace instead of wood-burning. One of the four bedrooms was given to Andy while he recovered. The other rooms, and sofa, were split amongst the remaining mages. Alana wasted no time in sending the younger team members to fetch food from the nearest store, leaving herself and Vaughn to watch over Maude.

Vaughn and Alana sat with Maude in the little living room on an over-stuffed plaid sofa.

"Are you comfortable?" Alana asked.

"Take this thing off of me!" Maude hollered defiantly. She thrust her restrained arm into Vaughn's face.

"There's something I want you to see," Vaughn began, ignoring her tantrum. "Perhaps it will convince you that we are telling the truth."

"I doubt it," Maude grunted. She turned up her nose and looked away from them.

From inside his robe, Vaughn pulled out a soft blue bag and set it down between them. He undid the drawstring and gently pulled out the Oracle of Y'alan. Maude eyed the artifact warily.

"Don't worry, it won't harm you," Vaughn reassured her as Maude frowned. "As Leo probably told you, the Oracle was used in the ceremony that caused the great cataclysm, erecting the barrier around this planet. Because the Oracle was involved in such a work of high magic it is forever linked to that event. I want you to know that we plan on using the Oracle to find a way to reverse the damage done all those years ago. This is something Leo could never dream of doing, but we plan to right the wrongs caused long ago."

"Yeah, right," Maude sneered testily. "You're trying to trick me. You're not pursuing some higher noble purpose. Nothing excuses all the lives you've taken, starting with the mana-wielding citizens of your own destroyed city. You just want more power so you can do us all in once and for all."

Vaughn considered her words a moment before proceeding. "That may be, but there is something else you should know. The Oracle is not just an artifact of great power, it contains the essence of our first ruler. Because the Oracle was present during the cataclysm, we can ask it to show us those final events so that we can see exactly what occurred. We can learn what truly destroyed Baurum'tatus. Watch."

Maude blinked in disbelief as Vaughn brought the Oracle to life. A small hologram of a room was projected onto the ground before her. She stared as the people rushing into the chamber, mesmerized by the chaos and the overwhelmingly bright red light that ended the recording. Shivering, Maude hugged her knees against her chest, trying her best to disappear into a little ball, away from the images she had just seen.

"Would you like to see it again?" asked Alana, studying her intently.

"Go away!" Maude yelled, her mind reeling.

"Of course," Vaughn politely conceded. "We'll talk again tomorrow." He placed the Oracle back in its case before he and Alana left.

It can't be true, Maude thought as she rocked back and forth. A tear slowly ran down her cheek. *It can't be...*

The next day, Vaughn and Maude spoke at length, trying to overcome the long years of mistrust between them. The Oracle's recording was played again and again but afterwards, neither side could claim victory.

"The truth is before you, Maude," he said. "You just need the strength to believe it."

Chapter 24

The Right Thing

Mark paced alongside Leo's bed in the recovery room. Leo slept soundly through the beeps and blips of the life-support machines around him. The prognosis was not good. Terra Protectra Medics had been working continually on Leo since the jailbreak, trying to repair his shattered body. They had managed to stabilize his life signs, but whether he would ever walk again was another matter. The years of procedures to prevent aging had finally caught up to him. Leo knew the costs associated with prolonging his life; that the treatments to slow his cell metabolism and reduce his aging to a crawl would also reduce his regenerative abilities. It was a price he had accepted. Though his body was still stronger and more robust than most, its ability to repair itself was negligible at best, taking weeks to repair even the smallest cuts and bruises. While he was alive, his body would continue to repair itself, if given enough time.

Time was at a premium. Mark repeatedly mulled-over recent events. The doctors' reports had only confirmed what he already knew—it would take years for Leo's body to be able to sustain itself, and much longer to regain full use of his legs. *If he can't walk, can he still lead? We need a leader now, more than ever. From the doctors' reports, his brain is as fit as ever but does that matter?* Mark stopped pacing and walked to Leo's bedside. He studied the face of the man he respected and admired more than anyone he had ever known.

"I will avenge this," he said quietly to himself, adding this latest disgrace to the long tally Vaughn had racked up. He reached out and held his uncle's hand. Outrage at the people who caused this desecration to his family churned in his mind. The faces of his enemies swirled in his head as he sifted through the events leading up to Leo's injuries. Anger expelled all rational and pleasant thoughts from his mind except those of Maude. *What's happening to her? Leo is weak. He let Vaughn go. It is his own fault he was injured. It is his fault she has been captured. He deserves this!*

"Sir," said a uniformed officer in the doorway. "We've analyzed the data from the break-in and have concluded that the intruders did not return to the location of the disturbance recorded just prior to the incursion. We suspect it was a diversion on their part to confuse us." Carefully, Mark listened to the report. Everything presented made sense.

"Has our agent in Banaras sent any more information?" inquired Mark.

"We received this from her twenty minutes ago. It was coded for Leo only…"

"I'll take that!" snapped Mark. He snatched the paper from the officer's hand before he could respond. Leo had painstakingly drilled every code he used into Mark and Maude. Mark hungrily scanned the page, devouring its secrets.

When he was finished reading the report the officer asked, "What are your orders, Sir?"

"Prepare a search team. We will investigate the site first hand," said Mark.

"Sir?"

"I heard your report," continued Mark, "but the fact is, it's the only lead we have right now, aside from… See that the men are ready to go at once."

"Should we wait for Leo to…"

"No," Mark sighed with regret. "We don't know when Leo will be conscious and the longer we wait the more chances we give Vaughn to carry out his devious plans. We've given him enough of a head start already. As of this minute, I am assuming command of Terra Protectra. Do you have a problem with that, Officer?"

"No, Sir!"

"Good, you have your orders."

The officer saluted and left the room. Mark was once again alone with Leo. He squeezed Leo's hand and made a solemn pledge, "I swear I will do everything you couldn't do and make you proud."

Chapter 25

The Road to Recovery

Nothing beats sleeping in on a weekday, thought Andy. He rolled over in his bed, curling the sheets around him so he wouldn't see his bedside clock displaying the time in garish red numbers. The last few days had been rough. Alana healed Andy's remaining injuries the morning after the dramatic escape. But, instead of returning to his chores, he was instructed by Alana to get some rest. He'd been glad to hear it. Natalie, however, was not, as she was assigned to look after him. She was proficient in her duties: every meal served, every item fetched, and every chore done promptly, skillfully, and begrudgingly—scowling and griping the entire time.

The one comfort Natalie did have was that Jack's situation was no better than her own. He had been appointed master custodian of their blonde captive, a duty that was boring him to tears. The restraining cuff on Maude's arm was doing its job exceptionally well, leaving Jack to be more servant than jailor, serving meals and escorting Maude around the retreat, for her 'safety'.

With Andy's other two friends either occupied or not speaking to him, Kaida was his only company. Andy found her steady diet of magic tips and video games to be the perfect way to pass the time. Their time together had allowed them to grow closer and dissolved the air of mystery that had surrounded Queen Kaida. Andy almost felt like he was back in Westbrook relaxing with his school friends, something he missed dearly. Life on a tropical island was everything Andy thought it would be, but at times he still felt like an outsider around his companions.

Rolling onto his back, Andy pulled the sheets up to his chin. He flicked his feet to gather the sheets around them tightly and prevent cold air from touching his toes. Something seemed off today. Nat should have been here with breakfast by now. Andy made a mental note to reprimand her when she showed up.

Andy was surprised when someone knocked at his door. Nat never knocked. Her philosophy was that knocking reduced her efficiency and therefore impeded her already hectic schedule. Andy was pleasantly surprised when the door opened.

"Hello, there," Vaughn said, standing in the doorway. "How are you feeling?"

"I'm better, a little bit at least," Andy lied. After being stuck with his chores, Nat would be furious if he was suddenly in the pink of health. He faked a cough but wasn't sure if Vaughn bought it. He hadn't seen much of Vaughn, or Alana, since the rescue. A strange feeling came over him when he did though, something he couldn't quite explain, but he chalked it up to residual torture residue.

The stories Mark and Leo had told him during his capture rattled around in his head whenever he saw Vaughn and Alana. *Had they really killed people so that they could continue living? Were they responsible for destroying entire cities?* Andy didn't believe any of it. Vaughn and Alana had shown nothing like the vile tendencies Leo and Mark spoke of. *Those creeps just tried to rattle my cage, and they failed.*

"Oh dear, I had hoped you were feeling better. There are lessons you should be learning and how to abuse room service is not one of them."

Andy blushed. *Busted.*

"I suppose I could get in a little practice," he said reluctantly. "What did you have in mind?"

"Your training has been swifter than I expected, but recent events have exposed its shortcomings." Vaughn paused. "I'm sorry, Andy. I feel that your capture is partly my fault. Events are moving much faster than I have foreseen. You've been progressing so quickly, keeping up with you has been challenging. I fear I have neglected a very important part of your studies, something you would have learned easily on your own long ago. Perhaps if we hadn't kept Jack and Natalie so busy you would have stumbled upon it."

Andy continued to stare at Vaughn blankly, not comprehending a word he said. Realizing he was losing his audience, Vaughn shifted to a more direct approach.

"I'm talking about dueling, Andy. How mages fight. It's not very different than what you were doing with Alana, however, it's much more diverse, and much more deadly. If things continue on their present course, more dangerous situations may present themselves. That is why I want Jack and Natalie to work with you on your fighting skills. I know Alana has shown you some basics during your training sessions, but you will need many more skills if we run into Terra Protectra again."

"Oh yeah?" said Andy quietly. "So… What are these duels like?"

"Well," Vaughn said sternly, "you should consider this real combat training. What you learn will certainly be harmful to your opponents."

Andy thought carefully before responding. "Do… can people die in these duels?"

"I see you're not one to beat around the bush," replied Vaughn. "Yes, Andy. If you put enough force behind your magic, it is quite possible to kill someone, should you wish to do so."

"Then no, I don't want to learn how to kill people."

"Andy, you know better than most of us what Terra Protectra is capable of. They certainly won't hesitate to kill you next time. I'm sure of it."

"That doesn't mean we have to do what they do. That would make us just like them, right?"

Vaughn flinched at hearing Andy's words. Silently he remembered the faces of some of those he had killed over the years. The images rattled in his mind, begging for retribution. It was some time before he spoke again.

"That is entirely up to you, but certainly you can see the necessity of knowing how to defend yourself? One of our great philosophers once said, 'The best lesson a warrior can learn is how to avoid a fight.' Sadly, that's not always an option."

"That makes sense, I guess. It's no fun being a prisoner. But, I'm just interested in learning how to defend myself. That's all."

"Very well, it's settled then. I'm proud of you Andy; you're very mature for your age. The courage you showed while in captivity speaks much about your growing character. Yes, I'm very proud of you, and grateful for your refusal to help them find the rest of us. I'm certain you'll be able to handle the difficult choices ahead." Vaughn patted him on the back. Andy couldn't help blushing a bit.

"Jack," called Vaughn. "I have a new sparring partner for you."

Jack ran in looking startled. "What's up?"

"I'd like you to show Andy how to duel. We've discussed it and he's looking forward to his new lessons."

"Mmmm, fresh meat," said Jack grinning.

Andy couldn't help but return the smile. "When do you want us to start?"

"Is now too soon?" asked Vaughn. "Don't worry; I need to talk with Maude anyway. Why don't you find Natalie and the three of you use this time to practice?"

"Nat too, eh?" Jack ran a critical eye over Andy. "I hope your Will is in order, Andy, 'cause Nat's really got it in for you."

"I can handle her."

"Good. That means I don't have to go easy on you either. Just try not to cry too much when I kick your butt, okay?"

"Don't be too sure about that," replied Andy defensively. "Nat doesn't see you as much of a threat, so I doubt I will either."

"Oh really?" Jack's face darkened. "You won't be smiling for long. Trust me, Squirt."

"YEAH, really," Andy taunted. "I'll probably be too busy laughing."

Jack shot Andy another dark look before breaking into a grin and yelling, "Hey Nat, come help me teach this newbie some manners."

Natalie poked her head around the corner and glared at them, irritated at being disturbed from her surrogate chores. Her mood changed entirely as Jack explained their assignment. She stood straighter and threw back her shoulders before exclaiming, "This is going to be the best day ever!"

The three of them ventured off into the woods around the lodge. The trees were old and very tall, with gnarled trunks. Thick mossy patches covered the ground on either side of the dirt trail they followed. Andy deeply breathed in the fresh forest air. A short ways in, Jack spotted a small grassy clearing off to one side of the trail, perfect for their needs. Together they left the trail behind and ventured towards it.

"Take a crack at Nat first, Andy," said Jack. "Her moves will probably be easier for you to detect."

"Chicken, Jack?" Behind him, Andy could hear Natalie making clucking sounds. Curious, he turned to find Nat flapping her arms and strutting like an overstuffed chicken.

"Hardly," replied Jack, mocking Nat's childish display. "One of the keys to dueling, Andy, as I'm sure you noticed with Alana, is that the further your opponents send their magic, the more time you have to recognize them. My powers enhance my own body. Since my powers are mostly directed towards myself, and not projected towards you, it'll be much more difficult for you to detect them. Nat should be more your speed for now."

"All right," agreed Andy.

"His speed? You're mine, scrub," taunted Natalie. She stretched quickly before taking a position in the middle of the clearing. Not knowing what else to do, Andy activated one of the batteries he was carrying, letting the energy course through his body, while trying to read what Nat was doing. Twenty feet separated them as they circled each other. After a few minutes he got impatient.

"What now?" he asked just as he detected a flash of mana from Nat. Instantly he found himself suspended upside-down in front of her. His chest exploded in pain as she landed a roundhouse kick in his solar plexus. Coughing and wheezing, he dropped to the ground.

"And another one bites the dust," yelled Natalie, throwing her hands in the air, revelling in her victory.

Jack walked over to Andy and helped him up. "You all right, man?"

"Maybe, I should watch you guys for a bit first?" said Andy, holding his chest.

"There's an idea, if you're up for it, farm boy."

"Bring it," said Jack, goading her on. "I've been waiting a long time for this."

Andy stumbled to the edge of the clearing and took a seat as the two of them prepared to duke it out. As he sat, Kaida appeared between the trees. Spying Andy, she walked over and sat next to him.

"Come to watch the show?" asked Andy. "I bet you're pretty good at this too." An amused look spread across her face.

"No, I'm not really the fighting type," admitted Kaida. "My abilities are more suited for information retrieval and analysis."

"Ah, so you're a spy!" Andy said.

"You could say that I guess," agreed Kaida. "Knowing how to deflect another person's attacks is always good though. Even if you're not eager to fight, someone else usually is." She winked and nodded towards Jack and Nat as she spoke. "And I like the way Jack pouts when he gets his butt kicked."

Andy smiled and nodded in agreement. He remembered encountering his share of bullies back home. A flash of movement caught his eyes. He turned to watch as Nat narrowly evaded Jack's attack.

Even though they had very different styles, they were evenly matched. Jack's magic gave him the speed and agility to get close to Natalie, but she deftly teleported away from him again and again. It was obvious that Jack could read what Natalie was doing, allowing him to avoid the worst of her attacks, but capitalizing on it was a different matter. *Jack was right*, thought Andy as he watched them. *It's easier to see Natalie's moves.* Jack was very hard to read. Andy could see parts of Jack's body glow with mana as he directed his arcane energy over his body for each attack. The shifts were slight and swift, making it almost impossible to determine what he was doing.

As Andy continued to watch, he became much more aware of what Nat was doing. He was able to make sense of her energy patterns to the point that they telegraphed her intentions perfectly. The match ended when Nat teleported a rope from their quarters around Jacks legs, effectively immobilizing him.

"Cheater!" barked Jack furiously.

"Sticks and stones, sweetie. You ready for another round, Squirt?"

"Sure!"

Andy's next match with Natalie went much differently than the first one. The shock on Natalie's face said it all as Andy mimicked her teleport and blinked behind her before unleashing an energy blast. Natalie flew across the clearing, landing in a heap of leaves. Jack just grinned as he watched Natalie pluck leaves and twigs from her hair.

"He learns fast, doesn't he?" teased Jack.

"We'll see," Nat replied and prepared to go another round with Andy.

***

By the end of the week Andy was wondering if imprisonment wasn't such a bad thing after all. Fresh welts and bruises covered his body. Of course, his opponents were sporting a few of their own as well, and he couldn't help feeling a bit proud.

However, the biggest surprise this week was Andy's ability to copy Natalie's teleportion maneuver over short distances. His lessons copying Alana's shifts and feints were really paying off.

Bouts between Andy and Natalie lasted for hours as both of them blinked around the clearing looking for openings to exploit in their opponent's defenses. As his head touched his pillow each evening, Andy silently welcomed its soft caress as a deep sleep claimed him.

***

A loud thump on his door awoke Andy the next morning. A fortnight had passed since his sparring lessons had started. Before he could wipe the sleep from his eyes, Vaughn stuck his head inside. Andy was surprised to see him. Vaughn had not come to see him since initiating his lessons with Jack and Natalie.

"Hello there!" Vaughn smiled cheerfully as he entered. Andy simply sighed and let himself fall back onto his bed. "I hope your lessons are going well?"

"Oh yeah, just lovely," said Andy. He tried to stifle a yawn but failed miserably.

"We're leaving on an important errand today. If you're feeling well enough to come along, we would certainly appreciate it, but we wouldn't want to put undo stress on you if you're not up for it." How Vaughn said all that with a straight face Andy wasn't sure.

"A break from being pummeled all day would be great. What's this all about?" He was skeptical. Vaughn's track record, leading to his capture and subsequent sparring practice, clearly correlated importance with pain.

"It's very special, very important, Andy," said Vaughn. "Today could change many things for us. New possibilities are presenting themselves and we must strike while we can."

"Sounds exciting," he replied. "I guess I could tag along."

"Excellent. We'll be waiting in the common room and we'll leave when you're ready."

"Okay."

Vaughn turned to leave, letting Andy get ready for the journey.

"Vaughn?" Andy asked cautiously.

"Yes?"

"Does where we're going today have anything to do with sleepers?" Vaughn looked startled at the question.

"Did Leo mention them?"

"Yeah." Andy studied his breakfast tray as he spoke.

"I suppose you have a right to know." Vaughn walked back towards Andy and sat on the corner of the bed. "After the accident, the few remaining mages realized what was coming. Some decided to live out their lives quietly, without magic. Most, decided to sleep through the dry years, hoping the world would correct itself in time. They hoped to resume their lives once everything was restored. They made chambers deep in the Earth where they wouldn't be disturbed and used their remaining mana to place themselves in an ageless sleep. A few were elected to remain behind, tending to the chambers."

"So… you and Alana are looking after them!" Insight flashed though Andy's head.

"Exactly. And no, we're not going to one of the chambers today."

Andy shut his mouth at Vaughn's last words. He had been sure that's where they were going.

Vaughn smiled at his student.

"Eat up; we have much to do today." Vaughn stood and left Andy to his thoughts, closing the door behind him.

Great, another adventure with Vaughn, thought Andy as he dressed. *I wonder who won't be coming back this time.* He ran his fingers through his hair and went to join the others.

***

Everyone was already present in the common room,

including Maude, someone Andy hadn't expected to see. She was looking quite well, certainly better than Jack who sat opposite her on the sofa. Maude no longer wore her uniform. Thanks to Kaida, she was clothed in blue jeans, a burnt orange T-shirt, and a bright green fish barrette adorned her hair. The restraining cuff blazed with arcane purple energy on her right arm. Alana and Vaughn were both wearing their most formal robes, of light blue silk with golden highlights and trim. Vaughn was carrying a matching small leather case, something Andy had never seen before.

"Glad you could join us, Squirt." Jack smiled, obviously relieved by Andy's presence. Maude's reaction was the exact opposite. Her body tightened as he approached and she refused to look at him.

"My, how the tables have turned," Andy commented, trying to provoke a response, but Maude silently stood and walked over to Vaughn.

"What's with her?" whispered Andy.

"Dunno," replied Jack. "Vaughn and Alana have been talking to her alone a lot since she got here. Not that I'm complaining. Gives me time to go to the bathroom at least."

"Form up, people," Alana ordered. "We're leaving."

Everyone gathered in the middle of the room. Jack held Maude by her arm. Andy shuffled close to Jack and asked, "Where are we going?"

"Dude, you're in for a treat," Jack replied with a wink. Stymied, Andy turned back to Vaughn and noticed out of the corner of his eye that Maude was looking at him quizzically. Vaughn cleared his throat.

"Very well. Natalie, if you please."

"Hey, do we really have to take Betty Birkenstocks here with us?" Jack waved his hand in Maude's face as he spoke.

"If you're volunteering to stay here and watch her, then by all means, she can stay behind," Alana teased, a small smile crept onto her face. She may as well have been asking a vegetarian for a steak. The look of horror on Jack's face said it all. "No thanks."

"Besides," added Vaughn, "there are some things I think she should see." Finding herself the center of attention, Maude's face turned bright cherry red, which infuriated her even more, causing her face to grow even redder.

***

The group of seven materialized on a small ledge at the mouth of a large cave. Its walls absorbed the late afternoon sunlight, preventing anyone from seeing more than a few meters inside. Andy took a deep breath, letting the mountain air refresh his lungs.

"Where are we?" asked Andy.

"Just north of Banaras," Alana said. "Get moving."

The other side of the ledge dropped at least a kilometer down to a rugged valley. The scrub vegetation below cast long shadows on the dusty valley floor. A small stream wound its way through the rocky valley terrain. Andy took another minute to enjoy himself before venturing inside the cave.

"Pssst, Jack," whispered Andy. "Why are we here anyway?"

"We're off to see the wizard, my friend," Jack whispered back, "although this time the wizard is really a dragon."

"Really?" Andy was amazed.

He tried to remember everything he had ever heard about dragons. Most stories made them out to be giant lizards, bigger than entire houses, with scaly wings and giant claws. Some even breathed fire or lightning but all were known to have very bad tempers. *That's about it,* he thought. *Oh, and they were very smart.* "Are we asking the dragon for help?"

Jack cocked an eyebrow at Andy. "Something like that. Dragons usually have very different perspectives about things than we do. Vaughn is hoping he'll be able to shed new light on a few things I guess—maybe even solve them too."

Andy laughed. "Is that all? What's the problem? I'll take a crack at it."

"You numbskull," Natalie butted in. "It's the Oracle. Only very powerful magicians can activate it. And because it's in such rough condition, Vaughn is hoping the dragon will be able to help him. Dragon's are very connected to the magical energies around us—more than we ever will be."

"That doesn't sound too tough," said Andy. "Besides, didn't Vaughn activate it when you guys where rescuing me?"

"Yeah, sort'a," Jack replied. "The way I understand it, when Vaughn activated the Oracle of Y'alan, he asked it to speak of the past. That's relatively easy to do. But, when you want to ask it about the future, it's much harder to do. Also, the Oracle always speaks in riddles when it talks about the future. That's why we're recruiting the dragon to help us out."

Understanding clicked for Andy. "Vaughn's going to ask how to remove the barrier, isn't he?"

"Well he sure isn't going to ask what's for dinner tonight," Natalie said.

"I'm starved. What IS for dinner tonight?" inquired Jack, unleashing a round of laughter from his friends. "What?" he said innocently, eliciting strained sighs and smiles from everyone as they continued their hike.

The rocks lining the cavern were dry and dusty. The walls shrank and swelled around them as they descended deep into the ground far from the sunlight above. They weren't in the dark for long. Vaughn snapped his fingers and an orb of light appeared over his right shoulder. Alana did the same at the rear of the group so that everyone could see in the inky blackness as they continued their descent. The sounds of the outside world were lost. Only the echoing sounds of their footsteps kept them company. As Andy walked, he noticed the tunnel became wider than the range illuminated by the glowing orbs. With no walls to guide them, Vaughn relied on his inner sense of direction to keep them on course. Andy studied the floor but could find no trace of a trail. He assumed Vaughn must have walked this path many times before, alone and with Alana. After an hour straight of marching, Andy's mind registered the presence of magical wards protecting the cave. He knew their destination was close at hand.

As they walked, Andy kept trying to look at Maude. She was walking next to Alana at the end of their line. For some reason, every time Andy looked in her direction she tried to hide behind Kaida or Natalie. *One more riddle to solve,* he thought.

Finally the ground leveled off. Andy could see granite walls up ahead. Stalactites and stalagmites were appearing more frequently and the smell of damp earth hung in the air. Vaughn stopped to remove his coat. The temperature had steadily risen on their journey. As they approached the wall, Andy spied a thin slit in the rock. It ran straight from the floor to the ceiling of the cave. Beyond the slit, a narrow passage continued on at length and a light was visible in the distant darkness. Steadily it grew brighter as they approached. Ancient candelabras, dotted the passageway, lit by glowing orbs like Vaughn's.

At the end of the long corridor they came to a small brightly lit room. Old rugs littered the floor and rich tapestries hung along the walls. Epic pictures showing valiant battles in far off lands were scattered around the chamber. Vaughn led them across the room and stopped before an ornate sliding door in the far wall. Scrolling shapes and intricate drawings of animals were etched in gold on its surface. Sounds of muffled movement trickled through from the other side of the great door. Cautiously they slid the barrier aside and stepped through.

Chapter 26

Underground Secrets

It was impossible to see the middle of the next room. The light was dim, like an overcast sky at dusk. Curtains and screens cluttered the floor and walls creating a mini maze of furnishings. Magical energy flooded Andy's senses, making him feel lightheaded. Looking around, he could tell the others were experiencing similar feelings, everyone except for Maude. Her shoulders were hunched and her arms were wrapped around her body protectively.

One side of the room was completely covered with plants and flowers, a living rainbow in the bowels of the earth. Vaughn stopped in the center of the room. There, sprawled on a large pile of mismatched pillows, lounged a huge dragon. Lights reflected off its copper body as the dragon lay majestically with its muscled legs, ending in large sharp claws, curled beneath its body. Large leathery wings draped its back, rising and falling in time with its breathing.

The sight was impressive, yet Andy couldn't help thinking something was odd. The large thick scales covering the body were dull and its body seemed gaunt and frail for such a large beast. What scared Andy the most was not the dragon's teeth or claws, but its large eyes that took in everything around it. Andy felt transparent under the dragon's penetrating gaze, sending shivers down his spine.

Interlaced amongst the pillows were hundreds, if not

thousands, of gems and jewels. One in particular caught Andy's eye. It was as big as an ostrich egg, and glowed a brilliant yellow. Sensing Andy's curiosity, the dragon wrapped a powerful paw around it protectively. Andy gaped in awe at the dragon as, even sitting, it towered over Vaughn.

"Hail, Pheliador, Keeper of the Auri. I apologize for the intrusion," began Vaughn, "but I carry grave news."

The large head pitched to one side upon hearing Vaughn's voice as the dragon raised his head from his pillowed bed. Pheliador flicked his tail in amusement and eyed his visitors.

"Auri?" whispered Andy.

"Archives," murmured Nat impatiently. "Don't interrupt."

"I see you, Vaughn Stormbaur. Hail and well met," replied the dragon, finishing the traditional salutation.

"I sense... new people with you. Who have you brought here?"

"We've had two additions since our last meeting. Please welcome Andy," Vaughn extended his arm towards him.

A shaky "Hi," was all Andy could utter.

Pheliador's giant head swiveled to face Andy.

"Your blood calls to me. It is strong, closer to me than any in a long time, but.."

"... and Maude," finished Vaughn.

Pheliador growled as he stared at Maude. His tail thrashed vigorously side to side.

"You are not of our kind. Why, are you here?"

Maude glanced anxiously at Vaughn, unconsciously taking a step away from the angry dragon.

"She has been a great help to us. Her presence here..."

"She is not welcome!" roared the dragon, raising himself off his pillowy perch.

"I, on my honor, personally vouch for her character and integrity. May her transgressions be my own. May her punishments be my own."

These words seemed to calm Pheliador somewhat. He settled down onto the pillows again and stared directly at Vaughn.

"I will hold you to your oath. Have no beliefs that your position will save you. If anything happens, both your lives will be forfeit." Pheliador sat again, directly in front of Vaughn.

"I understand. Shall we get down to business?"

"Very well, show me the Oracle,"

It seemed dragons were not ones to waste time. From the bag he was carrying, Vaughn carefully extracted the blackened crystal bust. Andy watched as Pheliador stared at the Oracle intently.

"Before we begin, I want to see what happened, that day." Pheliador spoke without shifting his gaze from the Oracle.

"That is entirely understandable. Please proceed," replied Vaughn.

Before Andy could wonder what the dragon meant, the room disappeared in a wash of silver and grey, leaving only emptiness surrounding him. Out of nothing appeared a marble room, slightly oval in shape and gleaming white. Arched windows lined the walls, except for the wall with a single door on the far side, revealing a majestic sunset. Above him, globes of light hovered, illuminating every inch of the room.

Andy looked left, then right, trying to guess where he actually was, and realized he was sitting in the middle of a giant diagram inscribed with ancient runes. It covered the floor, extending all the way to the door across from him. Two lines sprang forth from where he was sitting, connecting him to two other objects, and them to each other, forming a triangle in the middle of the floor.

A little further out, he could see another ring of seven lines, again with objects at the corners. Andy made out some gems at one corner and some feathers at another, but the rest were a mystery to him. At the very edge he counted eleven sides in all, with strange bowls, plates, and hangings of things he had never seen before.

Glyphs and runes of various sizes were etched everywhere between the lines, some running along them, others grouped together occupying the empty spaces between the lines. Studying the pattern, he recognized some runes in the same sequence found circling the mana gems Vaughn had given him. Most of them were a mystery, however, beyond his hasty education. Lines, runes, mana.

Suddenly he heard himself speaking, but not in his own voice. This voice was much deeper than his own, gravelly and dark. He spoke low, slowly, deliberately, as if for his benefit alone, trying to order the thoughts flowing through his head. The language was foreign to Andy but its effects were easily observed. As he spoke the lines connecting the magical trophies glowed and the runes surrounding them flared to life.

He kept talking, chanting the same mantra over and over. Andy was transfixed by the transformation around him. The glyphs were rising from the floor, creating a jungle of floating shapes. He could feel the magical intensity of the rite increasing. Specks of pure energy flashed high overhead.

The windows were dark now. Time seemed irrelevant as Andy continued chanting, alone in the room, surrounded by mana. His perception was transformed as well. The white marble walls had taken on a distinctive champaign tinge and the entire ceiling was awash in sparkling lights.

Outside, time continued, the sky once again crimson and

golden, followed by azure dotted with puffy white clouds. As the sun streaked high in the sky, Andy hovered amid the floating runes and spell components. The air around him was thick like honey, golden, saturated with energy. He felt his pulse racing with new life, pumping adrenaline throughout his body. The moment was almost here, the spell was almost complete.

A knock.

Again, louder than before.

A dull thud seeming almost a world away reverberated through the room. Sharp words, from the other side of the door, fought their way into the room. Andy strained to hear them through the liquid energy pervading the room. It was the same language as before, incomprehensible, yet Andy instinctively sensed the meaning of the words.

"Rolimus, by order of the High Council, you are ordered to cease all magical activities and surrender yourself to the will of the council."

Andy laughed, or was it Rolimus—he couldn't tell anymore. Sound waves rippled towards the door, as he spoke again.

"You are too late. I no longer answer to the Council. The heavens are mine alone to command. Within moments my divinity will be realized. Enter if you dare. You may have the honor of being the first to bow before me."

The door burst open. Two dozen Peacekeepers wearing green and platinum robes with black trim, stopped on the threshold, their mouths agape in disbelief. Andy doubted they had ever seen such highly concentrated pure mana before. They remained clustered there, unsure what to do.

He watched as the officer in front, their leader he assumed, mustered all his courage and stepped into the room. The mana reacted immediately, like upturned Jello—the Peacekeeper's inborn ability to absorb mana shifted the overwhelming yet delicate balance of power. Behind him, another Peacekeeper squeezed into the room, furthering the imbalance. As he walked past his leader, his thigh brushed a floating decanter, spilling its contents of Ura ink, the magical liquid used in rune writing. Free of its container, the ink glowed blue with energy. As it flowed, sections of the surrounding diagram blurred and melted away, leaving gaping holes in the design. Runes and glyphs where the ink spilt immediately morphed into meaningless gibberish or worse, unknown glyphs instigating a chaotic chain reaction. The condensed mana around the Peacekeepers darkened from purest honey to deepest crimson. The magical stain worked its way around the room, consuming everything.

A low moan escaped Andy's lips as his masterwork came undone. The air vanished from his body as crimson energy overwhelmed his vision. Finally, crimson gave way to grey, and his senses returned to Pheliador's lair.

***

"Now we know, what happened the day the barrier came to be," said Pheliador, seemingly for his benefit alone. "I only wish we could have known sooner. Much could have been averted."

"What's done is done," replied Vaughn, "but we still never know what tomorrow may bring."

Pheliador nodded in agreement. "I too am curious about what other surprises may be in store. Are you ready to proceed?"

"I am."

"Very well."

"Where is..." began Vaughn, but Pheliador had already procured the Foundation Stone and held it before him. The opaque yellow stone glowed like a tiny sun. With little ceremony,

Vaughn placed the Oracle of Y'alan on top of the Foundation Stone. Sparks flew as they locked together.

Pheliador stooped, studying the crystal statue with a critical eye. He grunted in dismay as he examined the blackened crystal core of the Oracle, trying to comprehend the power necessary to create such destruction.

"This is the Oracle?" Pheliador looked skeptical. He too sensed something odd about the crystal bust before him.

"It is," assured Alana. "Vaughn recovered it from Leo himself. We've all seen its recording of the final moments of Baurum'tatus."

Satisfied, Pheliador gracefully shifted his stance, stretched, and beat his grand wings resolutely.

"Are you prepared, Vaughn?" asked Pheliador.

"Yes, I am ready." Vaughn threw back his shoulders, composing himself. "Everyone, stand back."

Andy and the others joined Jack who was already seated on a pile of pillows. They formed a crude semi-circle around the Oracle and waited.

Pheliador spoke, "We gather here today to pay homage to our past, to what was and what was lost. We come seeking wisdom and guidance and ask our ancestors for their help. We ask the speaker of Y'alan to hear our plea."

The great dragon bowed low to the statue in deep concentration. The gleaming Foundation Stone flared wildly, sending beams of light dancing across the faces of all present. Andy held his breath as a pool of pure white mana was forming just below the Oracle and glowing ribbons of white could be seen entering the statue itself. The charred blackness at the centre of the Oracle seemed to combat the white light, stubbornly refusing to yield. Everyone watched anxiously and waited as the mana slowly filled the statue of Y'alan, the remains of the greatest mage who had ever lived.

Vaughn flung his arms toward the heavens and began his plea, "Hear me, Kalridge Eldoran Y'alan! I seek your council. Hear me, Oracle of Baurum'tatus!"

The mana inside the Oracle changed instantly from bright white to thick, lustrous silver that consumed the blackened core. Andy swore he saw the jaw of the statue start to move. He blinked to clear his vision, *Statues don't move.* Yet in one fluid motion, the Oracle stretched upwards, as if Y'alan himself was growing out of the silvery bust bearing his name. A ghostly specter of gleaming translucent silver emerged from the shell of the statue. The Oracle had returned.

"Rolimus!" Alana cried. This was not the Oracle at all. "It can't be!"

"Who has summoned me?" the apparition demanded, its gruff voice echoing loudly in the room.

"I have. I, Vaughinlus Stormbaur the VIII, High Chancellor of Baurum'tatus. Who are you? What trickery is this?" demanded Vaughn. The image before him was unmistakably Rolimus, yet that was certainly impossible.

"Ah, so it is." Rolimus seemed to recognize the man standing before him. "It is good to see you again, Vaughn. Certainly you must recognize me? How fares beloved Baurum'tatus?"

"Alas, it is no more," replied Vaughn. "But you haven't answered my question.

"Your eyes don't deceive you. I am Rolimus, at least what's left of him."

"How did you become this way?"

"That I have no answer for except the knowledge that Y'alan before me met a similar fate while performing powerful magic of his own. It seems I have fared no better."

"Where is the real Oracle?" asked Alana.

"That voice… " Rolimus turned and studied Alana. "Is this the princess before me? You have matured well, though I remember a younger you. How long has it been? I suppose it matters not. To answer your question though, I can not say. Whether the Oracle survived or not is beyond my knowing. Is that what you thought I was? Perhaps I still can be of assistance. What is the knowledge you seek? What do you ask of me, Vaughinlus?"

"Are you aware of the barrier that now surrounds this planet?" asked Vaughn. "I ask you to remember the last day your powers were used in this world, the day you unleashed your powerful magic and changed the world. I ask how to undo the damage done that day. I ask how to restore this world to the way it once was."

A palpable silence filled the room as everyone waited for Rolimus's response.

"Time forges onward: forever building forever changing, forever healing and forever destroying. Those of us locked beyond time's grasp are left endlessly pondering what will be and forever questioning what has been done."

The spirit stood silently for a long time. Slowly, almost reluctantly, he spoke again:

'As the jungle king swings,
hand rises over hand.
To see what was again,
look from the outside in,
or tremble unwilling to stand,
for destruction hastily springs.'

Upon finishing his reply, the new-found Oracle dissolved into a silvery mist that swirled back into the small statue.

The bright light winked out of the bust, its mana spent. The foundation stone beneath also grew dark and lifeless, depleted of all energy. Everyone looked at one another with puzzled faces.

"What the heck was that?" Natalie raged, her hair whipping around her face as she jumped to her feet. "I've gotten better advice from bubble gum wrappers!"

"Pheliador," asked Alana, "do you understand what was said?"

The dragon swished his tail excitedly while his front paws splayed against the stone floor. Pheliador looked directly at Maude.

"Is Leo dead?" he asked.

"Not yet, and surely not by the likes of you!" Half a dozen purple beams struck Pheliador simultaneously. The force knocked him off his feet, sending him flying into the pile of pillows. The smell of charred flesh filled the room. Everyone scrambled for cover as uniformed men swarmed the perimeter of the room, ablaze in shades of purple. Their right hands and wrists were encased in what looked like Misorbium tubes, the source of the blasts. One of them seemed to be carrying a large rug slung over his left shoulder.

"Mark, no!" Maude screamed.

"Nice of you to waste most of your mana on that little light show," said Mark victoriously. "I knew you were too soft for this, Maude. Leo was a fool to think you were suited for this job."

"How did..." started Natalie, befuddlement clear on her face as she attempted to rationalize meeting Mark here. "Back in the museum... where exactly did you get that new rug, Maude?"

Before Maude could answer, an officer behind Mark threw the rolled up rug he was carrying onto the ground between the combatants. A sharp cry emanated from it as the rug hit the ground. Between the layers of rug, Juana's head was barely visible.

"We've had your little rug shop under surveillance for some time now," Mark continued. "Leo used it as one of the few reliable ways we could keep track of you. That's changed. After today there won't be anything to keep track of."

"Sabrina?" Alana asked, her words barely more than a whisper.

"She's been taken care of, I assure you," replied Mark.

"Mark, listen to me," pleaded Maude. "You're wrong; these people are trying to save…"

"Enough! What sorcery have you done to brainwash my sister?"

"The strongest magic we know," replied Alana. "The power of truth."

"Rubbish. You've been spreading your lies."

"They have not," Maude countered firmly. "Ask Leo yourself. He heard what the Oracle said the day they broke into our headquarters. He's the one not being truthful…"

"Traitor! You can die with your friends!" screamed Mark, raising his hands to unleash another blow as a deep roar shook the room.

The dragon was on the attack. Andy shook as Pheliador roared with rage, savagely pounced on the nearest officer, and sank his teeth deep into his flesh. Chaos ensued as everyone began firing at once. Streams of silver and gold were met with Terra Protectra's beams of mauve and violet. Jack followed Pheliador's lead and charged the nearest Terra Protectra soldier, tackling him to the ground.

In the middle of the melee, Andy stood motionless, stunned at the turn of events. *How can these people do this to each other?* he thought. He watched the unfolding battle in a trance, not knowing what to do until a firm hand grabbed him and hauled him down behind a pile of cushions.

"What are you doing?" shouted Alana, shaking him by the shoulders. "It's them or us. We must fight!"

A blinding bolt of energy struck her from behind, throwing her against Andy. He held Alana in his arms as she writhed in pain. The last of her mana drained, Alana began to age before Andy's eyes. Her long dark hair grew white; her skin wrinkled and cracked showing veins clearly beneath its almost transparent surface. The only things that didn't change were her eyes. They retained their fiery blue intensity even in her advanced age.

"Kaida! The Oracle!" Vaughn's voice cut through the din. A steady barrage had him seeking refuge behind an old folding screen. Its decoratively engraved surface was immediately pock-marked with holes and craters, forcing Vaughn to keep moving.

A wild shot from one of the officers loosened a huge chunk of rock from the ceiling, sending it crashing into the melee. Clouds of dust threatened to choke the combatants. Vaughn desperately raced towards the pile of rocks, hoping for some semblance of cover.

Kaida swung her head towards Vaughn as she fired. She looked from him to the crystal bust still attached to the foundation stone in the middle of the floor and dove for them. Rolling to absorb the impact, her hands snaked out and grabbed the powerful artifacts, clutching them closely to her chest as she raced to where Vaughn was hiding. Behind her, Pheliador breathed fire, engulfing several officers in billowing flames. Kaida passed the Oracle and the foundation stone to Vaughn who quickly secured them in protective bags.

"We have to get out of here quickly," Vaughn barked. In

the background Pheliador's roars continued to rock the cavern. Two officers were trying to contain him, a third lay next to them covered in blood. Vaughn glimpsed Jack moving to help the dragon, his previous opponent lay unmoving on the ground. Surveying the scene, his eyes fixed on a small doorway on the far side of the room. A smoking screen covered most of the entrance, but Vaughn could faintly make out steps behind it. He put two fingers in his mouth, whistled as hard as he could, and frantically waved his arm towards the doorway.

"Natalie! Get Juana!" Vaughn ordered, pointing instinctively at the rug rolling on the floor. Nat ducked an incoming blast and teleported next to the rug. The next instant she was at the steps, frantically freeing the prisoner from within.

Seeing Vaughn, arms waving, Andy understood his meaning at once. He wrapped his arms around Alana and dragged her to her feet. She slumped against him as he half carried, half dragged her towards their destination. After only a few meters, a Terra Protectra Officer barred their way, eager to take the fight to them anew.

"Keep going, Andy," Alana muttered weakly. "Straight through!"

***

Andy wasn't the only one with problems. Mark intercepted Maude in her flight to safety.

"You are betraying everything Leo taught us," Mark bellowed, gripping his twin's arm mercilessly.

"No, you are with your wild vendetta! I've seen what the Oracle has witnessed," Maude said, frantically trying to shake free of Mark's hold. The others were already in the doorway and Jack waved for her to join them. Andy's eyes were glassy as he stared at the twins. Mark's face twisted in rage, his eyes venomous.

"And you believe those lies? The Oracle is a magical device. It can't be trusted." Mark shook his head, seething with every word.

"Let me go, Mark. I'm your sister. You can trust me..."

"I have no sister!" Mark yelled and struck her across the face with his free hand.

Before Maude registered the shock of the impact, a blazing fireball struck Mark square in the chest, sending him flying and knocking Maude to the ground.

"C'mon!" Maude could faintly hear Jack's shouting, her ears still ringing from the blast and the battle around her. Shakily, with Jack's help, she got to her feet and ran. Over her shoulder she spotted Andy watching them. Their eye's locked and she couldn't help thinking, *Why did he save me?* Bolts of violet energy chased her towards the door, barely missing her as she flung herself through.

***

Andy gritted his teeth. Bearing Alana wasn't an easy task. They moved forward, steadily towards the door. An officer charged at them, unwilling to let his quarries escape, his arms ready for a mortal blow. As they collided and fell to the floor, Andy lost his grip on Alana and rolled clear of the desperate struggle between predator and prey. Seeking an opening, Alana seized the officer's face in her hands. "Yes, you'll do nicely," she said.

A reddish glow enveloped her hands as she gripped her combatant. The officer screamed in agony as tendrils of steam gushed forth from his body. The officer's flesh seemed to deflate and shrivel while Alana's rapidly regained its youthful appearance. As his flesh withered, a pale cloud rose from his body, only to be absorbed by Alana. A moment later a charred corpse, its mouth still frozen in a silent scream, was all that remained. Alana clenched and unclenched her hands, testing them, gauging how much strength had returned to her. Satisfied with her borrowed youth, she looked for Andy. She spotted him a few meters away. He seemed groggy and was stubbornly crawling through the wrecked furnishings as if looking for something.

"Andy!" she cried.

"Alana!" Andy turned towards her voice.

As if on cue, a volley of light scorched the air between them. Alana ducked out of the way, Andy cried in pain. One of the beams had hit him. Alana rose to save him only to see Pheliador standing over Andy, guarding him with his body. The dragon bent his head low, inspecting his charge before confiding:

"You must survive. We are alike, Andy. Trust not those who seek to share power. Remember that!"

Andy was puzzled by Pheliador's words, but before he could ponder them, he felt the familiar sensation of being teleported away.

***

Horrified, Alana screamed. She couldn't think. *What just happened?*

"Pheliador!" Natalie yelled from the staircase. She could see the dragon across the room fighting fiercely.

"GO!" roared Pheliador as he swiped at another officer. Globes of mana streamed from him again and again as Terra Protectra concentrated their attacks on him.

Alana wasted no time. She sprinted through the door as Vaughn hauled Natalie away, and ordered the others to follow. Together, they ran up the stairs in long strides. Vaughn glanced behind to see a pair of zealous Terra Protectra officers pursuing them.

"Alana!" Vaughn yelled. "If you wouldn't mind…"

Looking around, Alana spied their pursuers. Balls of flame appeared above her head and streaked down the stairs, hitting the rock stairs directly in front of the officers. The rain of rock and dirt shook the passageway and it began to crumble, filling the stairway behind them with stone and debris. They surged up the endless stairs for what felt like an eternity until a heavy curtain blocked their progress. Vaughn stumbled as he brushed it aside, colliding with a desk in the open room, sending it crashing across the floor as they all tumbled out of the staircase.

Vaughn recognized the room at once. The piles of rugs and tapestries were guarded by a lone Terra Protectra officer sitting next to a bound Gnome. Jack charged him at once. With Natalie's help, they quickly over-powered the guard. Kaida untied Sabrina.

"Juana!" Sabrina gasped between sobs. "I couldn't do anything. They…"

"We know," Vaughn said calmly. "Mark brought her along to gloat."

"I'm here, Sabrina," Juana rushed to her mentor's side, engulfing her in a heartfelt embrace.

"Pheliador?" Sabrina asked, panic gripping at her voice.

Vaughn shook his head sadly. "Not likely," was his only reply.

"I'll fix them!" she cried, and ran off past another hanging tapestry.

"What will she…" began Maude.

"Gnomes are very protective of their friends and pets," Alana answered. "She'll likely cause a rip-roaring ruckus before she's through. Probably calling in reinforcements as I speak."

"In any case," Vaughn said. "We can't stay here. Nat, can you…"

"Negative," she cut in, "I'm out of juice. And there's too many of us."

"Maude, I assume you're coming with us?" Alana asked.

"I don't have much of a choice now, do I?" Maude replied.

"Welcome to the team." Jack grinned sarcastically.

"Wait. What about Andy?" Kaida asked. "We should go after him."

"I'll go. Alone I should be able to…" Nat trailed off.

"No…" Vaughn said wearily. "Let him go, for now. Wherever Pheliador sent him, I'm sure he's safe. At least for the moment anyway."

Stunned at Andy's disappearance, Natalie nodded absently, lost in thought.

"We should to be off, as well. I'd prefer to make our way through the city on foot," said Vaughn. "It's slower, but the crowds will hide us. Hopefully most of Mark's goons are too busy digging their way out to cause us any more trouble."

"I can lead you out of the city," volunteered Juana. "It's the least I can do."

Vaughn nodded in agreement.

"Very well." He stepped aside and let Juana lead them out.

***

Together they ran through the rug shop and into the busy street. The crowd of people slowed them down and they hoped their enemies were still safely occupied. The smell of rain was in the air as they wound their way southwards along the river, passing endless ghats and boatmen. As they reached the edge of the city it started to pour, soaking their robes in moments.

"I must return, Sabrina..." Juana looked worried. "Where will you head to now?"

"Leave that to us. I'm sure Sabrina will need your help. You did a great job," replied Alana, trying to ease her fears. "We can carry on from here."

"Thank you. I..." Juana looked disappointed, as if trying to decide something important, and knowing neither option open to her was welcoming. She stopped and managed a slight bow before running back into the city's throng of people and disappearing from sight.

Vaughn led them down the road, into the wilderness surrounding the city. Seeing no signs of pursuit allowed them to relax, just a little, but they kept moving, desperate to put as much distance between themselves and their hunters as possible. Dusk soon arrived as they continued south, staying to either side of the ancient cobblestone road.

After hours of walking, Vaughn recognized where they were and signalled them to halt about twenty kilometers from town. They took shelter in a small shrine along the road. The simple wooden walls housed a small Buddha statue, grinning serenely in the cold night. They sat huddled together in one corner of the building, weary and wary. Cool air sent shivers rippling through them as their damp clothes clung to their skin.

"We're not far now." Vaughn's voice melted into the darkness.

"From what?" Jack asked. "Catching pneumonia?" His testy response echoed the frustration they all felt.

"Wait here," Vaughn said as he stood and left the building. Exhausted from their terrifying battle and the subsequent journey through the night, one by one the mages, and Maude, nodded-off, lulled by the sound of rain rapping against the roof.

Chapter 27

Short Work

The morning light shone through the open window, directly onto Maude's face. She struggled to free an arm from her twisted blanket to cover her eyes in hopes of savoring a few more minutes of sleep. *Wait, when did I get a blanket?*

Maude sat up and hit her head on the low wooden ceiling. She cursed softly to herself and rubbed her forehead. Opening her eyes confirmed that she was lying on a stone floor next to Natalie. No one else was in sight. The wooden walls were covered with thick lignified roots. A few holes in the planks, makeshift windows, were spaced around the room but a door was not readily apparent.

"Wake up," she said softly as she nudged Natalie's shoulder. Nat batted her hand away.

"Five more minutes," she murmured sleepily and rolled over.

"Get up, Nat!" Maude said more forcefully.

"All right, all right... OW!" Natalie rubbed her head where she too had hit the ceiling. "What's the big idea?"

"Ah, you're awake," a gruff voice interrupted her whining.

Both girls spied a large red hat before them. Lowering her gaze, Nat saw a tiny face with a long white beard, rosy cheeks and twinkling brown eyes. His height identified the man as a gnome.

"Eric's my name," he said. "I suppose you're curious about the 'whats' and the 'wheres', but come and have some breakfast before we start all that bother."

Maude looked at Natalie, silently questioning the intentions of their new host.

"I am a bit hungry," Nat said and shrugged.

"Well, then," continued the gnome, "come and get it while it's hot." He turned and walked out of the building, which was rather large by gnome standards.

Not knowing what else to do, they followed Eric, crawling on their stomachs until they cleared the entryway he had opened. Once outside, they found themselves in a heavily wooded area. Large Banyan trees twined together, preventing them from seeing very far. Gnomes hurried past them as they walked, some moving so fast it was hard to keep track of them as they scurried over the damp ground. Across the camp they saw Vaughn sitting next to a campfire, smoking his pipe, and talking to a somber looking gnome.

As they approached, Vaughn turned and waved, beckoning them closer. They recognized his companion as they drew near; it was Sabrina. Her clothes were dirty and her face was tear-streaked.

"… was Otiltis," Sabrina finished, distress and heartbreak apparent in her tone.

Vaughn nodded in acknowledgement, sympathizing with Sabrina, before looking up and greeting the new arrivals.

"Good morning," he said. "Did both of you sleep well? There's some oatmeal on the fire if you're hungry."

The fire before them was smouldering, but enough to keep the morning meal warm. Maude sat next to Vaughn and rubbed her arms in the cool morning air. Nat helped herself to a bowl of oatmeal before sitting next to her. Holding a small hankie Sabrina wiped her eyes and smiled weakly at them.

"Sabrina and I were just discussing yesterday's events," explained Vaughn.

"Yeah? Have you figured out how those goons found us?" asked Nat, clearly holding a grudge for being forced to run away.

"I'm afraid so," began Sabrina. She intently studied her feet before gathering the courage to continue. "I hate to say it. I still don't want to believe it, but I think it was Juana who led them to Pheliador's lair. I saw her helping one of the officers out of the rubble. He was skinny, with bond hair and blue eyes. They talked for a long time and then left the chamber together."

"I see..." was Vaughn's only response except for a deep crease on his forehead.

"Why that little..." Nat was anything but reserved. "And she led us out of—she just wanted to keep tabs on us. No wonder she looked reluctant to leave."

"Sabrina, you need to get your people away from here. There's a good chance we were followed or that Juana told Terra Protectra about this place. We're not safe here."

"I agree," replied Sabrina meekly. "I'm speaking with the clan elders shortly. I should go and prepare. Enjoy the fire."

With that, she stood and darted off, leaving the others in silence. The three of them sat together quietly, luxuriating in the warm fire before them. Their mood was subdued as they reflected on the previous night's events.

At last Vaughn spoke, "Pheliador is dead."

"... And Mark?" Maude asked reflexively. "Was he the one Juana was talking to?"

"She doesn't know," replied Vaughn. "There were a few bodies on the ground but Sabrina didn't stop to check."

"Poor thing," Nat sympathized. "She seems so

heartbroken."

"Gnomes can get quite attached to the animals they care for. It's in their nature, not that a dragon is just any animal," replied Vaughn, blowing smoke rings into the fire, an old habit of his that helped to calm his nerves. "In the old days, right after the accident, there was a bargain struck between the surviving mages and the gnomes to look after Pheliador. The gnomes delight in taking care of creatures and protecting the forests. Unfortunately, due to the state of the modern world, they've been driven out of most places."

"Why did they help us then?" asked Maude.

"Well," Vaughn explained sagely, "I was able to convince them that helping us would be beneficial to them. They agreed to aid us in return for some favors from us."

"What type of favors?" Maude insisted.

"He means mana batteries," blurted Natalie. "Filled ones probably."

"I see," said Maude knowingly. Vaughn looked like he had been caught with his hand in the cookie jar. "I never realized they were such valuable assets. The order never realized that non-humans could use storage gems as well."

"Mana is a precious commodity these days," explained Vaughn. "While other creatures can certainly tap into the mana stored in these devices, only we are able to fill them, giving us a certain amount of leverage."

"Convenient, for you." Maude looked at Vaughn with an accusing eye. "Very convenient."

Vaughn answered her with a quick half grin, as he stuck his pipe between his lips again and drew in deeply. The sun was rising quickly, chasing away the clouds from the night before and burning away the dew on the ground.

"Maude," Vaughn said seriously, "by bringing you along,

I assumed you now supported our cause. If that's not the case, I can make arrangements for you to.."

"You know darn well what I think. That doesn't mean I have to agree with every little thing you do though."

They stared at each other, neither moving, sizing each other up to see whose will would preside.

"What is Otiltis?" Natalie asked, anxiously changing the subject between spoonfuls of oatmeal. She was watching Vaughn closely as he examined the bowl of his pipe. "It sounded like…"

"It was a prison," replied Maude. Natalie looked at the blonde girl in surprise, her spoon still in her mouth. "It was an ancient prison where magical people and creatures were sent."

"Oh, then why did…"

"Maude is mostly correct," Vaughn interrupted. "Otiltis was more than just a prison. It was also our main observatory and science outpost in the old days. It was built as a fortress to keep things in, as well as out." He examined his pipe again, realized its tobacco was exhausted, and knocked it against the log he was sitting on to clean it.

"That's neat and everything," Nat managed between mouthfuls in a dismissive tone. "What's that got to do with us? Star gazing isn't going to help us. I'd check my horoscope more often if it did."

"Do you remember what the Oracle said, about 'looking from the outside in'?" asked Vaughn knowingly.

"Sure," Nat replied. She spied Jack, Alana, and Kaida stretching as they stumbled out of their sleeping quarters and waved to them. Jack was rubbing his head sleepily as they walked over.

"Well, Otiltis may allow us to do just that," Vaughn explained.

"What do you mean?"

"But," Maude ignored Natalie's question, "how would we get there?"

Vaughn was silent as their companions joined them.

"Any news?" Alana asked Vaughn as she took a seat on the log next to him. Kaida joined Natalie, hugging here knees against her chest. Her hair fell forward, hiding her face, as she rested her chin on her knees.

"Yo," Jack greeted them half-heartedly, still massaging his forehead. His eyes closed as he stifled a yawn. Under his hand, covered with bits of dirt and vegetation, Vaughn noticed a large circular bruise was forming. Jack, stumbling and bumbling, stopped before the pot of oatmeal as if guided by some divine hand and helped himself to a heaping bowl.

Vaughn spoke quickly as he brought them up to speed. The news of Pheliador's death weighed heavily on all of them.

"I say we thump those TP goons good and hard," Jack suggested. "There can't be many of them left. Let's wipe them out and end it. They've been monkeys on our backs for long enough."

"No." Maude's expression soured. "They don't deserve that."

"Listen, lady." Jack was beside himself. "That wasn't exactly a tea party they threw for us down there. They're trying to kill us! We should get to them before they can regroup and BAM!, crush'em."

"You can't!" shrieked Maude.

"Better them than me!" Jack slammed his spoon into his oatmeal, spraying it everywhere.

"Enough!" said Alana, "We are not attacking anyone. Period. Yes, we have killed, but only out of necessity, not pleasure."

"I think this is very necessary!"

"Jack, please. By attacking them we'll be no better than they are."

"Humph," Jack glowered. "I should pull an Andy and leave while I can." His final words hung in the air, defiantly.

"You most certainly will not!" Natalie shook her spoon at him.

"Oh, ya?"

"Yeah!"

"Get out! You all go now," a gruff voice broke in, disrupting the argument. A band of gnomes had gathered in front of them. Their loud bickering had drawn more attention than they realized. An elderly gnome, almost a head taller than his companions, was standing on a log across from them looking very cross. His cheeks were enflamed and his eyes bore into them like daggers as he unleashed a scolding.

"You have disturbed us long enough. Old one, our deal was for one night's shelter yet you are still lounging in our home and eating our food. Take your loud tongues and go."

"Master Celdwic, I humbly apologize," Vaughn began. "It appears last night's events have distressed us mentally more than physically. We will respect your wishes and leave immediately." Vaughn shot Jack and Natalie stern looks as he rose, making sure they realized this was not the time or place for further discussion, and motioned for them to follow him. "Once again we beg your pardon and thank you for your kind hospitality. You are most generous."

Celdwic looked disappointed that Vaughn wasn't going to fight him. He glared one final time at the mages before jumping down and rejoining the group of gnomes behind him. As the gnomes returned to their tree dwellings, Vaughn guided his friends to the edge of the clearing and into the woods.

After a few moments, Maude broke the silence. "So,

where are we going?"

"To see what was again, look from the outside in," Vaughn quoted. Seeing Maude's confusing, he added, "Why, the moon of course."

Chapter 28

Dangerous Confessions

The hum of his life-support equipment droned constantly in the background as Leo peered out the window. The sun was setting, casting muted red-gold tones onto the cloudy sky. His body was wrapped in a thick blanket and yet he still felt bone-chillingly cold. Although he was still frail and unable to walk, Leo's condition had stabilized to the point where he could sit up and move his head, albeit slowly. Leo's physicians had modified his favorite chair to hold the medical equipment his body desperately needed, giving him back a minor amount of the mobility he once enjoyed. Its sturdy oak arms wrapped around him cocoon-like, holding his body in place.

The door opened with a bang. Mark stood on the threshold covered in dirt. Streaks of blood covered his face and his uniform was torn and ragged. An orderly tried to guide him into another room so he could have his injuries tended to, but Mark shook him off. His intense gaze focused on Leo.

"What happened?" Leo asked, confused.

"They're gone," was all Mark said.

"Who?"

"We were ambushed. They're all gone." He walked over to his mentor, clearly agitated.

"Vaughn's gone? The others...? Mark, what happened?"

"We went to investigate a large surge in magical energy, hoping to find Vaughn and his accomplices. And we did find them, along with this huge... with wings. We tried to fight but it was... they were... then the roof..."

"So, you rushed in and got more than you bargained for," Leo sighed, exasperated. "What's the matter with you, Mark? I'm sure I explained to you many times how dangerous the dragons of old were. Were there any casualties?"

"Yesss....." Mark's face went slack, the fires in his eyes extinguished. Leo looked at him soberly and waited for a reply. When Mark offered none, Leo continued grimly.

"You are the only survivor? Was Maude..."

"We were betrayed!" Mark howled, regaining his fury. "Vaughn has turned her against us. I would never have believed it if I hadn't seen it with my own eyes."

"Your sister chose to stay with them?"

"I have no sister."

"She must know," Leo said, shaking his head sadly.

"She knows nothing," Mark ranted. "She's a traitor to our cause."

"No, Mark. We're the traitors," he said simply, without emotion.

"You're still unwell, Leo. You should rest," Mark snapped critically, unwilling to listen to any notion that he'd done something wrong. He turned to leave.

"Mark, I saw the true cause of the catastrophe as it occurred all those years ago. Vaughn showed me through the Oracle."

"And you believed him?" Mark was incredulous. "Everything that murderer says is a lie."

"The Oracle does not lie," Leo said. "Not even Vaughn can make it do that."

"How do you know?"

"We are responsible, Mark. We peacekeepers caused the

catastrophe," Leo spoke slowly, choosing his words carefully. "The Oracle showed me the magical rite being performed by Rolimus, Vaughn's research partner. I remember that day, having been sent to arrest Vaughn, myself. We knew the oracle was missing but we never dreamed… We were determined to retrieve it at all costs. I can't tell you what Rolimus was trying to do, but, through the oracle, I saw how the peacekeepers disturbed the warding runes around the ceremonial casting when they stormed in to arrest him. The peacekeepers upset the delicate balance of mana in the room and the wave of red…" Leo stopped, unable to continue.

Mark stared at Leo, absorbing everything. "It doesn't change anything.'

"It changes everything!" said Leo, feebly trying to argue his point. "And you damn well know it. Vaughn is not a liar. What he has been doing, what he's doing now, is not to destroy the world but to save it."

"Nonsense, what could possibly…?"

"The shield is failing. The barrier isolating us from the rest of the magical universe is crumbling. That's why mana pools are becoming more common. Cracks are forming high above us that are allowing mana to trickle back into the earth's domain. And it won't always be a trickle. When enough cracks form, it will collapse altogether. When that happens…"

"It won't happen. I won't let Vaughn do it."

"Mark, you're not listening to me. The end is coming. We need Vaughn to…"

"Vaughn is insane. You've said so yourself. He doesn't want to save the world. He wants to destroy it."

"Mark, I know this is hard for you to hear, but I was wrong."

Mark turned and stared out the window. The last rays of the sun were barely visible over the horizon.

"No, Leo… you're wrong."

"What?"

"It's all your fault." Spinning on his heel to face Leo, Mark screamed. "You betrayed us! You let Vaughn escape! You allowed Maude to turn against us!"

"Nonsense, what are you talking about?"

"You are right about one thing, though, the end is coming: Vaughn's end and yours." Abruptly calm, Mark circled Leo slowly as he spoke.

"What? What are you talking about?"

"I promised to protect this world from Vaughn, no matter the cost. I intend to keep that promise, even if you do not."

"Mark, listen to me…" Leo stopped cold as an unmistakable click came from the back of his chair, followed by silence. Horror gripped Leo as his mind registered what had happened. His life support equipment had been turned off. Leo gasped as his breathing became shallow and erratic. The rhythmic beat of his heart slowed and his eyes clouded over as he stared helplessly at Mark.

"You were correct, the end is coming soon." Mark turned and strode out of the room. "Good bye, Leo." He didn't look back.

Chapter 29

Sea Treasures

Dark clouds loomed over the stormy seas off the Caribbean coast. Far from land, a small wooden raft rose and fell with the surging swells. Yet despite the sea's fury, the crudely constructed raft of logs and twine remained anchored to one spot, defiantly. Without captain or passengers, it bobbed leisurely on the waves marking the location of the ancient ruins buried beneath.

Jack was exhausted. Silently he cursed Andy for not being here to help him as he checked the mana battery holding his breathing bubble in place. His physical talents made him capable of surviving the ocean depths for any length of time—provided his batteries held out. Satisfied its power was holding, Jack wished that the grumblings in his tummy were as easily rectified.

Upon reaching the ocean floor, he had been surprised by how accurate Vaughn's description had been, and he knew precisely where to dig. Sand and debris had long ago claimed the sunken rubble as their own. Clearing it away was strenuous due to the sheer volume of it. Despite Jack's best efforts to stir-up as little sand as possible, the deep blue haze of water around him was slowly muddied with dregs from the sea floor. It was tedious work but worth the effort.

In the middle of the excavation site, Jack uncovered a giant arch—just as Vaughn had promised. Its once white marble surface was now stained and covered with coral and other marine jetsam. Large glyphs were still visible across the top, although faded and lifeless. *I can't believe it's still in once piece,* Jack thought as he swam towards it, signaling to the others that the arch was ready for transport. Fragments of two other arches he had discovered during his excavations lay scattered amongst the ruins of other once great buildings. Jack ran his hand over the arch's surface, silently communing with it. A large school of fish swam by, inspecting what had happened to their tidy sea floor home. Something tapped him on the shoulder. Startled, Jack turned to find Natalie flailing wildly beside him. He reached out and grabbed her arm, steadying her, and pulled her closer. Jack waited for her to calm down before leaning forward, letting his breathing bubble merge with hers.

"That was quick," he said.

"I hate teleporting underwater. It's so disorienting. Is this it?"

"It better be. I'm beat."

"I'll say. This thing is huge! Vaughn is freaking out from all the waiting," Nat explained, rolling her eyes. "You ready? It's freezing down here."

"Let's go." Jack reached out with his free hand to grasp the side of the arch.

Natalie moved to touch the arch as well, separating their breathing bubbles. A brief flash of light enveloped them and a great roar of seawater rushed to fill the vacancy left by the disappearing arch and its rescuers.

Chapter 30

Into the Unknown

The sand was pleasantly warm under the noon day sun, yet Andy shivered uncontrollably, trying to cope with the realization that he was alone. Pheliador's last words kept running through his head. *What could I possibly have in common with a dragon?*

He had never been alone before, not like this anyway. Being home while his mother worked, he knew she was always just a phone call away. Here, on this secluded beach, somewhere—he had absolutely no clue where—a phone was a luxury he would have gladly accepted. A seagull soared overhead, a tiny blur at the edge of his vision. Its shrill cry waking him from his reverie of recent events and prompted him to action.

What do I do now? Vaughn could be anywhere, if he's even still alive. And what did Pheliador mean by not trusting those who share power?

These questions kept resurfacing in his thoughts. After a week of wrestling with them, he still had no answers. Daily life on his little island was much simpler. Andy had to admit that camping out on the island, under a lean-to of palm fronds he had constructed, was relaxing. Fishing with magic was like shooting ducks in a barrel, ensuring he'd never go hungry. Jack would use a hook Andy thought to himself and smiled. Even if he WAS starving. A cloud passed overhead, casting him into shadow as the water lapped at his feet. The tide was coming in. Time to go.

But, go where? If Vaughn and the others had been captured or worse, their headquarters would probably have been found by now. Only one place came to mind.

He teleported home to Westbrook.

Andy materialized in his former bedroom amidst his old hockey posters, plastic model cars, and comic books. He held his breath as he strained to hear if anyone was home. Silence. He forced himself to relax; his mind still unsure if he was ready to see his mother again. How do you explain that one minute you're just a normal kid and the next, Bam: Mage!

He didn't know. As Andy looked around his room, he was surprised to see how little everything had changed. The bed was made (okay that had changed), the carpet looked cleaner (another change), but all his toys and books were where he had left them. It felt a little odd standing there, almost as if he didn't belong there anymore. All this reminiscing didn't change the fact that he was still soaking wet, and a puddle was forming on the carpet around him. Quickly he changed out of his clothes and threw on an old bath robe before heading to the bathroom for a shower. A long hot shower was just the thing he needed. The hot water and steam soothed his body and eased his mind. Andy leaned against the shower wall and let the water do its magic.

THUD! THUD!

"Who's in there? I can hear the water running! Come out this instant before I call the police!" THUD! THUD! THUD!

His mother's voice was laced with alarm and excitement as she called through the bathroom door, rousing Andy from his showery stupor. He hesitantly shut off the water and wrapped a towel around himself before opening the bathroom door.

"Andy?" His mom stared at him in disbelief, lowering the wooden rolling pin she had been using to bang on the door. She held it awkwardly, unsure of what to do next.

"Hi, Mom," Andy replied, suddenly uncomfortable under her astonished gaze. This wasn't how he pictured their reunion at all. He cinched his towel tighter. Water dripped freely off his back and legs. "I didn't think you were home."

"I just got back from work. What are you doing here? Are you okay? Shouldn't you be in school?" Her voice was steady once again, but Andy could tell she was still trying to grasp what was going on.

"Err... I'm on a break."

"Really? It's not time for summer vacation yet?"

"Well, we really don't follow the same schedule as..."

"Oh, of course, silly me," she said, seemingly grateful things made sense once again. "It is a private school after all. I wish they had given me a timetable though. They must do everything a little differently."

"You have no idea."

"Put some clothes on, Andy, and we'll talk. Are you hungry? There are some fresh apples. I just picked them up on my way home."

Andy merely nodded as he stepped out of the newly formed puddle and headed to his room. He quickly rummaged through his closet and pulled on an old pair of dark green cargo pants and a purple hoodie before setting off for the kitchen. Nothing had changed there either. The same pictures hung on the walls, the same table and chairs, even the same fruit bowl lay on the table. He sat at the table and helped himself to an apple.

"So..." his mother began. She set a cup of coffee on the table and sat across from him. "Tell me about your studies. Do they give you lots of work? Are they strict? I don't want you goofing off. This school is a great opportunity for you. It's tough out there, Andy, you have to make the most out of every opportunity you get."

"I know, Mom," replied Andy, taking a bite of apple. He looked down, studying the bitten fruit in his hand. "Everything's fine. Really."

"Hmm, that good, huh?" A knowing smile crossed his mother's lips. "Of course I don't expect you to study all the time. Have they any sports teams? Meet anyone interesting there?"

"I did a little fishing, but mostly we play volleyball. Oh, I guess playing cards is popular too."

"I don't want you gambling, Andrew," she said sternly, her mood switching from inquisitive to judicious in a heartbeat, and back again. "I'm surprised they don't have a hockey team."

"Yeah, so was I," blurted Andy. "Volleyball is fun though, I guess. It's hard to play hockey on the beach anyway."

"Mmm, a lot of girls play volleyball, too?" asked his mother.

"Yeah, they're pretty good, but—hey, what has that got to do with anything?"

"Nothing," she said absently, dismissing his question. "You seem preoccupied, Andy. What's on your mind?"

"What makes you say that?"

"Because I'm your mother and I'd be a pretty poor one if I couldn't tell when something was bothering my son. Now spill."

Andy sat quietly for a moment before answering, trying to decide what to say. Finally he sighed and said, "Mom, how do you know what the right thing to do is?"

"Well, that's not easy to answer…" she said, taken back a little. "Is there something specific on your mind?"

"Just, well… say someone you know does something really bad but they think it's in everyone's best interests. Does that still make what they did wrong?"

"This wouldn't happen to be anyone I know, would it?"

replied Andy's mom. A wry smile crossed her lips as she studied her son.

"Mom…"

"Okay, okay. Son, sometimes things may appear to be bad but they're really not, like going to the dentist. Hardly anyone likes having someone poke around inside their mouth but they still go because it's good for them."

"I don't think that's quite what I had in mind."

"This friend, he did something really bad, did he?"

"Some think so, but a few don't. They think that what happened was necessary."

"Did someone get hurt?"

"Well…"

"Andy, many people have tried to justify questionable acts by saying their interests serve the common good. Most of the time though, they don't; they're just short-cuts. Getting what you want without hurting someone else may be tricky at times, but it's the best way to go and the right way to go. Taking short-cuts may seem like a good idea but when you do, you usually miss out on something important too. And when you look back you'll realize what you thought was a short-cut really wasn't. It's okay to think big and have high expectations. I encourage you to follow your dreams. Just make sure you don't lose yourself in the process. The only way to do that is by taking the long way and carefully considering everything along the way. It may seem hard or even impossible at the time, but it's worth it in the end."

"I'm not sure I understand."

"How about this…What you're asking is really not black and white, okay? I gave you my opinion but the answer you're seeking, the one that will mean the most to you, is the one that only you can come up with. That's probably the best advice I can give you. As your mother, my view my not be the same as yours, but, hopefully it's pretty close." She winked at him. "Ultimately though, you will have to decide for yourself if the course of action was justified. Does that make sense?"

"I guess," Andy admitted. "It doesn't really help me though."

"Chin up, dear. I know you'll figure it out. And be sure to tell me all about it when you do," she added. She stood and walked over to him. Andy squirmed as she kissed him on the cheek. "I'm glad you're here, Andy. Now, set the table while I fix supper."

Andy sighed. *Looks like I'll have to work this out on my own time.*

It was easy to fall back into his old routines. His mother even encouraged this by giving Andy all his old chores to do again. Gradually, as the days stretched on, Andy's sense of self returned, allowing him to distance himself from his memories of Pheliador's lair, almost as if he was watching everything happen through someone else. Andy knew what had happened was still very real, but the distance between himself and his magical comrades gave him a sense of freedom and relief from not having to deal with it any more.

In fact, Andy had stopped using magic altogether. Partially because he couldn't use it when his mom was around, or when he was with his school friends. He feared having to explain for days how he had developed such powers and what his friends would say if they found out. But mostly Andy didn't use magic because he simply didn't feel the need to do so. His chores were easy enough. Finishing his chores early meant finding something else to do, which wasn't always easy in a small town.

Almost a week past before Andy actually did try to finish his chores early. He had made plans to meet Bret and Ryan after school at Uggabuga's. Getting there early meant getting his pick of booths to sit in and maybe enough time for a snack before his friends showed up. The sun was shining brightly as he left the house. Puddles of melted snow dotted the sidewalk, evidence of the changing seasons around him. Familiar scents of greasy food welcomed Andy as he entered Uggabuga's Donair Shop.

The seats were more faded than before and a few of the video games in the corner had been swapped for newer ones, but everything else was as he remembered it. A few customers sat scattered around the place, none of whom Andy recognized. His hard work had paid off, allowing him to grab a booth by the window. He ordered a large chocolate malt, his long-time favorite comfort treat, just the thing to indulge in on a fine day like today. As he ate he stared out the window, watching the shadows cast by the buildings lengthen.

"Hey, Andy."

Shocked, Andy looked around. He didn't remember hearing the door open. The familiar shapes of Josh and Bret were standing next to his table.

"Hey, guys," Andy nodded in recognition. They took his greeting as an invitation to sit and did so.

"Last we heard you were sent off to some high-brow school," said Bret.

"Without saying goodbye," said Josh. "Very sub par. Bret was heartbroken."

"You seem to have gotten over it," cracked Andy straight-faced.

"I have, thanks for asking. Are you on a break or something?"

"You could say that," said Andy trying to evade further questions. He glanced out the window, wondering if Ryan would arrive. "How have things been?"

"Pretty good, we won regionals again." Josh and Bret

filled him in on everything that had happened in their home town. It felt good to talk about normal teenage things, even though they seemed inconsequential compared to what he had been through.

"Oh, and Lance gave up computer games," Bret added.

"What? Why's that?"

Josh shrugged.

"He kept getting destroyed in his favorite role-playing game. What's it called?" continued Bret. Josh just gave Bret a blank look. "Anyway, this big dragon started following him around and killing him every time he logged in to play. It was hilarious. That dragon is pure champion."

"Computer games are for kids anyway." Josh cynically studied the window sill. "We're men, aren't we? We have manly pursuits. Like, check out what's coming."

"Ouch," exclaimed Bret. "Hotties at twelve o'clock."

Reluctantly, Andy turned to see who was causing the commotion. *These guys never change. What a bunch of...* He froze, a spoonful of malt halfway to his mouth, as he recognized Maude and Natalie heading towards the restaurant. Strangely, Maude wasn't wearing the tell tale restraining cuff Vaughn had placed on her arm. They entered and walked directly to Andy's booth. Nat flashed him a knowing smile.

"How did you find me?" he asked quietly.

"Hello? Magic!" Nat replied, rolling her eyes. "Some genius you are." Maude hung back, uncertain as to how to act.

"Hey, beautiful," Josh said with a wink. "Looking for some company?"

Nat eyed them critically before replying with a curt, "Beat it, scrub."

"We want to talk to Andy. Alone," added Maude.

"Well, well, well, been holding out on us, eh, Andy?"

Bret cooed.

"It's not like that," stammered Andy, embarrassed.

"Oh, really?" said Josh. "Then maybe…"

"No. And, no," Natalie stated coldly. "Now get lost before I lose my temper."

"Oooo, we're sooo scared," Bret and Josh laughed mockingly in unison as they rose from the booth.

"Later, Andy. Give us the details, 'kay?"

Andy smiled sullenly as the guys headed onto the street. As they walked by the window, he noticed the backs of Bret's and Josh's hockey jackets suddenly had "Team Loser" written on them in block letters.

"Nice," Andy said as Maude and Natalie sat down. "Very subtle."

"They're morons," Nat said, "but they do have good taste."

Andy sat in silence for some time, wondering what to say. Both sides steeled themselves for that they knew was coming.

"Vaughn wants me to come back I take it," said Andy.

"He does," Nat said simply.

"Mmm hmm. Why didn't he come himself? Why are you here?" he said, looking at Maude.

"He's busy, I guess. Since I've chosen to help him, he hopes I can convince you to do the same."

"Why did you decide to stay?"

"Because the Oracle, or Rolimus rather, showed me what really happened."

"Huh?

Maude explained what she had seen when the Oracle was activated. She had accepted the truth and realized that Leo and Mark were perpetrating lies.

"In the end, saving the world comes first. If we don't do

anything…"

"That's it? Do what Vaughn wants or people will die?" Andy felt anger rise in his chest.

"Andy," Maude tried to clarify her viewpoint, "what matters is that you need people to help you learn how to control your powers if you want to continue using magic. Ultimately, you can choose to use those powers for good, but at your age that's not something you can do without guidance."

"You mean Vaughn's guidance? So I can be just like him? That doesn't sound very appealing."

Maude eyed him critically. "It's strange. I never thought about it much, being restrained and everything, but… you really are different than Vaughn. Sitting here I can sense you quite well and it's not at all like the feeling I get from Vaughn."

"I'm flattered."

"But, when we ambushed you, you really felt like Vaughn, not like *you*."

"I was wearing one of Vaughn's old robes. That's probably why."

"I guess," conceded Maude, "That must have been a really large crystal you were filling. We didn't know what Vaughn was doing with so much energy. We thought he was flying a whale or something."

"Actually, refilling crystals makes you harder to detect since you're basically sucking mana out of the air," Natalie added. Her words hung between them as they all realized what had happened. No one could deny the implications. If Andy had been detected so easily, the only logical reason was not a pleasant one.

"Vaughn set me up? Now you're asking me to trust him? I don't think so," Andy was livid. He turned on Maude.

"We don't know for sure…" said Natalie, however,

her words lacked her previous conviction, "if that's what really happened. I'm sure there is a reasonable, less scandalous explanation."

"Yeah? Well let me know when you find one." Andy turned to go, rising from the booth.

"You're throwing your future away! Think about what Vaughn and Alana have shown you—what they still CAN show you." Nat was furious.

"At what price? So I can learn how to betray people too?"

"You can't judge them. They did what was necessary to survive, so we would all survive. Someone had to look for a cure. Someone had to stand guard while the others slept."

"Is that supposed to justify everything they've done?"

"I know it doesn't make them infallible, but you have to look at it from their point of view. What else could they do? Neither wanted to be violent; they don't enjoy killing people. They had no alternative."

"There has to be another way," Andy said defiantly.

"Right now we have a chance to end this feud once and for all, AND return the Earth to the way it was before the great catastrophe. Isn't that something worth fighting for?" asked Natalie

"Come with you and restore mana to the world? Is that it? Is that your best pitch?"

"It's the truth," said Maude defensively. "Give it a chance; give Vaughn a chance to explain."

Andy considered carefully before deciding. His newfound optimism fleeing, he wasn't sure where he belonged anymore. *Should I go and help those fighting hard to save magic, or stay here, hiding in exile from the people who need me and from the part of myself that loves doing magic?* Finally he realized there wasn't a choice at all.

"Fine, I'll come," Andy stated grimly. His choice made. His path clear. "But I won't like it."

Chapter 31

Up and Away

The world shimmered briefly as Andy, Maude and Natalie teleported to meet the others. They appeared next to the giant arch Jack had recovered and erected in the middle of a small clearing. Its gleaming white surface surprised Andy as he examined the large structure.

"What's that?" Andy asked, anger receding.

"That, my inquisitive friend, is our ticket off this rock."

Looking up, Andy spied Jack perched on top of the arch. He was clad in only a pair of dark shorts in the hot sun. A bucket stood next to him and a dirty rag was in his hand. Jack saw Andy looking at the bucket.

"Don't start. It feels good to get your hands dirty sometimes. Yours truly was solely responsible for recovering and cleaning this masterpiece because you weren't around to help me."

"You missed a spot." Andy pointed close to where Jack was sitting. In the short time he had been away, Andy hadn't realized how much he had missed his companions. Grinning inwardly, he walked around the massive arch. Attached to the base of one of the legs, Andy spotted the Foundation Stone, the largest mana battery in existence. A dozen glowing runes hovered above the battery, ready to activate the archway upon command.

"C'mon, I'll take you up to Otiltis," offered Jack. "The others are already there."

Andy let out a deep sigh. *Vaughn's not even here.* The energy he had mustered for their meeting felt wasted. He was uneasy about their reunion, and the prospect of meeting Vaughn someplace unknown wasn't remotely appealing. Andy was still lost in thought when the arch flashed and they were teleported to the moon.

The walls of a cavernous room spun before Andy's eyes and he was hit with a wave of nausea. Stunned, he crumbled to the ground. A burning sensation coursed through his body. *Is this Vaughn's doing?* Out of the corner of his eye, he spotted Natalie and Maude on the ground as well. Jack alone was still standing but he was wobbling slightly. *What's going on?*

Andy's nausea was quickly replaced by an all-encompassing warmth that he'd experienced once before… Understanding burst upon him. *It's mana! This place has heaps of it floating free.* Andy relaxed and let the raw mana flow through him. It was like floating in a hot tub that was just the right temperature. He felt light and strong and invincible.

"Hey, you just gonna lie there all day or what?" Jack nudged Andy with his foot. "I know it takes a little getting used to, but seriously…"

Andy blushed as he realized a stream of drool had been leaking out of his mouth. He wiped his chin on his sleeve and forced himself to stand. His body still felt buoyant. Without realizing it, Andy was hovering, giving in to a sense of adventure as he explored his surroundings. Jack chuckled softly to himself as he watched Andy float around the room.

The room they'd materialized in was more window than wall upon closer inspection. Three walls and the roof displayed the vast lunar landscape. Its barren, rocky terrain acquired a rosy hue from the crystalline walls surrounding them, protecting them from the airless void outside. In the center of the room stood another arch, identical to the one they had come through. The dusky grey floor was littered with geometric designs and runes. The far wall was made from the same white marble as the arch, and centered on it was a heavy iron door

"Vaughn believes Otiltis is beyond the barrier."

"So," began Andy, "is this what it was like before?"

"I guess so," Jack surmised. "C'mon, there's lots to see."

Nat was on her feet but Maude was not fairing well. Her teeth were bared as she struggled against the physical effects of the mana. Her breathing was shallow and raspy.

"Maude?" Nat said with concern. "Are you going to be okay?"

"Give me time to..." Maude croaked as she curled into a ball. Jack and Andy could plainly see the pain on her face as she tried to adjust to her new environment. *That's what happens to people who aren't magical,* Andy thought. *How many people won't be strong enough to survive if the barrier breaks?* They waited patiently. Minutes passed before Maude's breathing resumed its regular rhythm. Slowly she uncurled herself and shakily got to her feet.

"Let's go," Maude instructed, eager to get on with matters.

Andy followed the others as they walked toward the door. It slid open silently as they approached, opening into a maze of white marble corridors. Mounds of crushed marble dotted the halls in places, and giant holes in the walls above the piles explained where the rubble had come from. Age appeared to be ravaging the building despite its magical foundation. Lines of various colors marked different walls, guiding those walking the halls towards different parts of the complex.

Jack touched the nearest surface and a streak of orange lit up along the length of the wall. They followed it past a myriad of different rooms and passageways. Andy couldn't get over how big the place was. *To construct something of this size on the MOON, is truly incredible.*

The orange stripe stopped at a large door, much like the one they had entered through, except that this one was covered with glyphs. Jack continued forward and the door opened, revealing an assortment of consoles and displays. More holes and scorch marks lined the walls. Kaida was sitting at one of the consoles, trying to coax some life out of it.

"Hey, Kaida," Andy said warmly. She smiled and waved at Andy and the others.

"Vaughn said this place used to be an observatory and a penitentiary back in the old days," Jack explained. "A lot of the stuff doesn't work, some does though. We found some old music boxes and even a couple space suits, we think. But best of all, we found some more Foundation Stones. Vaughn was pretty pleased to find them. Kaida's trying to sort out what works and what doesn't. Maybe she'll even dig up a record or two. Come check this out."

Jack motioned to another door and ran towards it eagerly. Andy, Maude and Natalie followed him inside. The room was octagonal and roofless. In the center of the floor was a huge telescope unlike anything Andy had ever seen. Crystals of every color protruded from the marble tube that made up the bulk of its body. Brass and copper gears provided the mechanisms for pointing the telescope. Starlight twinkled down on them. Andy marveled at the faint blue glow coming from the runes around the top of the walls. *There is no barrier above us,* Andy thought. *Only magic is keeping us alive.*

"Humph hum," Natalie cleared her throat. Andy looked over in her direction and spotted Vaughn and Alana coming towards them from another entrance on the side of the room.

Instantly Andy's gaze hardened and all hints of a smile vanished from his lips.

"Welcome back, Andy. It's good to see again." Vaughn smiled and spread his arms wide,

"Back off, grandpa," Andy snarled, avoiding Vaughn's embrace. "I'm just here to do what I can. You can keep your touchy feely garbage to yourself."

"I'm hurt. After all I've done for you…"

"Oh, save it!" Andy yelled. "I know about your little trick with your robe, the day we went to fill the crystals, the day I was captured. You never had any intention of protecting me."

Vaughn studied Andy silently. "Andy, if you would let me explain, what I put you through was a necessary evil."

"Oh, 'a necessary evil,' eh?" Andy mocked. "The great, all powerful High Chancellor sends a boy to do a man's job. I understand completely. You're a coward. I can't believe I looked up to you."

"Now see here," Vaughn boomed, "what I did was necessary for the good of us all. Don't forget it was me who took you in and taught you how to control your abilities."

"Spare me your self-righteous lecture. I'm here because you need me. Period. That's why you were so eager to train me, not because you wanted to help me. I don't need you. I was doing just fine 'til you came along. I'll never need you."

"Your insolence is wearing thin. You forget your place. I caution you before I…"

"Before what? You going to make me sit in a corner, or give me a spanking?"

"A spanking hardly covers what you deserve for speaking to me like this."

"Yeah? Bring it, Old Man. Show me what you've got." As he spoke Andy opened himself to the energy around him.

Here, unrestrained by fragile mana batteries, he could taste what magical feats he was capable of, what real power felt like. His body blazed with a new found vigor as he watched Vaughn in anticipation.

"Fine." Vaughn returned Andy's gaze unwaveringly. He too let his body absorb the energy it craved.

"Vaughn, don't," Alana begged. "We don't… You don't have time to find a…"

"I'm fairly certain only one of us will be standing once this is settled. He will know his place. But, just so there's no question who the better man is, I will relinquish my robe to you during this fight. I doubt I'll need it against someone of his skill."

"We don't have time…"

"We're making time, Alana. Then we can finish what needs to be done. Are you ready, Andrew? When you once again call me master, I will spare you. "

"That's never going to happen," Andy shouted.

"So you say."

"Whatever."

The fight had begun. Both instinctively locked eyes. Muscles tensed. Knees bent. They circled like tigers, looking for an opening, keenly aware of the shifts and twists of the other's aura.

***

Vaughn, the aged veteran, knew the tricks and intricacies of dueling. *Let the young pup come, I'll show him.* He checked himself, concealing his advantage, intent on allowing Andy the first move. Confident in his superiority, he performed a feint and prepared for an attack.

***

Andy used every iota of control he could muster. His skills were refined from weeks in incarceration. Masking his intended movements from Vaughn, while sensing what his opponent was planning to do, had become second nature to him. *I can't match his experience but he can't match my youth. My only chance is to make him expend his energy and wear him out.* He began with a series of simple jabs that Alana had once tormented him with on a daily basis, testing his adversary and quickly learning to read him better.

"Is that all you've got, my young friend?" Vaughn laughed openly at his opponent, taunting him. He countered Andy's digs easily. "Let me show you what dueling is all about." With that, Vaughn unleashed a deadly beam of silvery light.

Unprepared to counter, Andy blinked out of existence as he teleported out of the way, causing the beam to explode against the wall where he had been standing. Vaughn fired as soon as Andy materialized. Andy gained a better look at Vaughn's glyph's as Vaughn fired again. Andy dodged, blinking directly in front of Vaughn. He grabbed Vaughn, reading everything he could as the blast wave from Vaughn's second beam impacted another wall, reducing it to rubble. A split second was all Andy needed. He copied Vaughn's own attack, forming a thick beam inches from Vaughn's chest. Vaughn reacted instantly, reading Andy's clumsily copied glyphs and forming a shield to ward off the attack. The impact of beam on shield sent the two combatants flying apart. Andy was blown across the room, landing hard on his back. Vaughn checked himself against the far wall and attacked with another beam of magical energy. Andy formed the shield Vaughn had shown him, protecting himself head to toe with silvery energy, before renewing his assault with the information gleamed from their brief contact.

Breathing hard, Andy assessed his opponent. So far he'd been able to react to Vaughn's attacks in time. But how long could he keep it up? *He knows how to shield himself from my attacks,* Andy thought. *I need something he'd never expect, something...* He knew what he had to do.

Lying on the ground, Andy now launched a beam of energy at Vaughn to keep him off balance. With his remaining strength, Andy attacked Vaughn's mind.

Vaughn stopped in mid-step as Andy's attack hit its mark. Spastically, he threw his head back and screamed, falling to his knees and tearing at his hair. That moment was all Andy needed; he summoned his remaining strength and blasted Vaughn with all his might. Defenseless, Vaughn was lifted like a limp rag doll and smashed into the wall. He crumpled to the ground, his mind and body unable to channel another bit of energy. Tendrils of steam rose from his battered body. Vaughn's chest heaved in despair as he caught sight of his hands. They were wrinkled and old. Instinctively he knew what that meant. The last soul he had consumed was spent. The last of his powers had been drained by Andy's attacks. He had lost.

"Vaughn!" Alana rushed to his side and held him. Her eyes welled with tears.

"It's okay, don't cry." Vaughn's gravelly voice was little more than a strained whisper. "My time is past and only one thing remains. You must put our plan in motion, the sooner the better."

"I've had enough of his plans," Andy said as he towered over Vaughn and Alana, adrenalin from the match still freely flowing through his body. His eyes watched them mercilessly.

"Idiot," Alana's voice dripped venom as she spoke. "Why do you think we've come here?"

"Hmmph," Andy turned and strode out of the chamber, memories of his treatment at the hands of his captors fresh in his mind—treatment that Vaughn was responsible for.

Jack and the others watched him go, unsure whether to follow or not. The door slid shut behind him before they could make up their minds.

Quietly, Alana said to herself, "He has to know." Tears streamed down her face.

Chapter 32

The Sad Truth

Kaida watched Andy storm through the command center and into the hallway beyond. He stopped just outside the door. *What am I doing? I'm acting like a child. Think, man.* He stood there, fuming.

Finally Kaida opened the door. "You should see this," she said.

"What? You find something?"

"Some of the final recordings. I think you should see them." Andy followed her meekly as she led him to the working terminal. When he had settled himself, she started the recording.

Gzzzt. The face of a middle-aged man appeared above the controls. His hair was short and well kept. Wrinkles surrounded his dark-ringed eyes.

"It's been over a week and we still have not been able to contact the capital. My junior officers have led several teams down to the surface but none have returned. We have been studying the barrier but, as yet, all attempts to destroy it have failed. Any energy we direct at it is absorbed. We were hoping data from the planet would help solve the problem but ..."

Gzzzt. "Seven months have passed since the incident and we still have had neither contact from the surface, nor any success removing the barrier. Our most immediate problem is our inmates. Because no one has returned from the earth expeditions, security is short-staffed. We still haven't been able to explain to anyone's satisfaction how the barrier formed. Worse, we don't know what to do with those whose prison terms have been served—and their anger is mounting. Do we let them out? I don't see how we can send them to the surface..."

Gzzzt. "We can't control them! They've taken control of cell units nine through fourteen and are moving fast. They don't believe we are cut-off from the Earth. They're demanding freedom even though we have no place to send them. What am I going to do?"

Gzzzt. The speaker's face appeared, but this time it was bruised and bloody. A long scar ran down the left side of his face and his speech was slow and forced.

"Most of my men are dead. The few of us who survived don't have much time left. The medical wing was destroyed in the fighting. All of the inmates have passed through the arch to reach the Earth's surface. Good riddance. Maybe we should follow them. After all, we're dead either way...."

Andy continued to stare at the console as the image faded away. Those poor people. They deserve... For the first time, he realized just how many people had already been affected by the catastrophe long ago. The pain and suffering was immense, and who knew how many people had ultimately died in the aftermath of the accident. They deserve to be remembered. If Vaughn and Alana hadn't... The scope of the ordeal made his head-spin. I can't let all those deaths be for nothing. And what of the sleepers? Will they die too if... I must find a way to...

As Andy thought to himself, Jack, Maude, and Natalie

joined him in the control room.

"Whatever we do, we have to do it quickly," Kaida warned.

"Why's that?" asked Jack.

"Look at this." Kaida tapped a few controls and a giant holograph of the Earth appeared before them. Surrounding the planet was a thin ruby light, the barrier. It was blemished and faded in places, cracks readily apparent. Kaida pointed to two large, neighboring holes that were significantly different than the others. Their edges were convex, pointing outwards, instead of concave.

"See this one, and that one? They were made when we came here, by our punching through the barrier to reach the moon. Obviously the barrier has weakened enough to allow Arch travel through it. But these new openings are destabilizing. Cracks are already appearing here and…"

Everyone looked at Kaida as if she was speaking Greek. Their blank expressions only frustrated her. Sighing, she tried dumbing down her explanation.

"We caused these holes. They are going to collapse. We need to stop it from collapsing." This seemed to work. Vacant expressions turned instantly to shock and disbelief.

"Seriously?" Nat looked at the hologram. "Wait, two holes? Why are they in different spots if we used the same Arch?"

"We used the same Arches on Earth and the Moon," explained Kaida. "But the moon is not stationary. As it orbits the Earth, the path between these two points changes. The barrier seems to revolve geosynchronously with the Earth. Therefore we passed through the barrier in two different places. Once when Vaughn, Alana, Jack, and I came up, and another when you all arrived."

"But I went back down, where's the third hole?"

"Jack, you didn't stay here long enough for the moon's position to change. If you look at the hole here, you can tell it's slightly bigger than the second one. That's probably due to your return trip."

"Can we repair them?" Andy asked.

"That's crazy talk," Jack balked. "We want the barrier to collapse."

"But not like this," explained Kaida. "We need to stop the free energy around us from hitting the Earth all at once. A slow, controlled collapse of the barrier is the only option. Too much energy hitting the planet would be like…"

"It'll be like our containment vortex hitting the entire planet at once," finished Maude. "Remember Andy? The only reason you survived was because the batteries you had with you cushioned the blow."

"I remember…"

"But that was different," argued Jack. "You're negative energy…"

"Jack," pleaded Natalie, "remember how we all collapsed the first time we came up here? What do you think is going to happen to all the normal people on the planet when this much mana hits them? It'll be like going from the surface of the ocean to a thousand feet below it in a matter of seconds. No one will survive that."

The room grew unnaturally quiet.

"How long do we have?" asked Andy.

Kaida tapped a few more buttons. "I can't be certain. These instruments were never designed to study something like this. It could be days, weeks at the most."

They eyed each other, each hoping someone would volunteer a plan to stop a second catastrophe. There was one question on everyone's mind: *What would Vaughn do?* Andy looked to the back of the room where Vaughn lay motionless, barely breathing. His head was propped up on a small cushion and an old blanket covered his body. He probably would know what to do, Andy admitted reluctantly. *I'm the one responsible for the condition he's in, so I guess, I'm going to have to rectify the situation.*

"Okay," said Andy firmly. He made eye contract with each person in turn as he spoke. "This is what we're going to do."

Chapter 33

Nothing to Lose

Papers and other oddities littered the floor around the antique wooden desk. Drained from his endeavors, Mark slumped in the high-backed chair. His revelation of Leo's treason instigated a frenzied search for any evidence of collusion with their arch enemies. After rigorously searching Leo's office, Mark had found none.

An alarm rang in the hall. Mark ignored it; one of the other officers would check it. *Wait… there are no other officers.* His spirits sank. The news of Leo's death had swept like wildfire through the ranks. He dutifully recounted how Leo heroically fought to the end. His presence in the infirmary when Leo past away bolstered his story's credibility. Few questioned his words or asked for more details. Mark recalled the grieving looks he had received walking down the halls, marshalling the troops as Leo would have done.

One stood out in particular, a lowly system's operative, Nigel or something. Mark had never liked him. Nigel had convinced the others that he was crazy and out of control! *Absurd.* When Mark had tried to demonstrate his wisdom by killing some of the mutineers, the rest had scattered like dust in the wind.

Cowards, the lot of them.

Sighing, Mark dragged himself out of the chair as the alarm sounded again. The listening posts scattered around the globe were still operational even though no one was monitoring them.

What could it be now? He bitterly recalled the last alarms from Banaras as he made his way to the command center. His uniform hung unbuttoned from his shoulders. Misorbium bands, Mark's trophies plundered from the gloves of the unfaithful, had been crudely sewn onto his uniform. They swung loosely as he walked to the control room. The instruments chirped again before he could turn the alarm off. The display echoed the readings as he tried to understand what was going on. *Two readings of this magnitude, in the same place? Vaughn must be extremely over-confident.* Mark tapped the screen as he transmitted the coordinates to his atlas. *Something big is coming. There's only one thing to do.*

He strode purposefully from the room.

Chapter 34

Final Preparations

Jack wiped his face with a handkerchief. They had just finished gathering up all the Foundation Stones that Otiltis could spare and were placing them around the Travel Arch. *Hopefully it'll be enough*, he thought.

They had spent the past two days planning and scavenging equipment for their mission. Andy felt this was as long as they could wait. The hope was that the energy in the stones would cushion the flood of mana pouring through the holes in the barrier. Even Vaughn had agreed it was the most plausible means of saving the planet. He had regained most of his strength, thanks to the mana-rich environment of the station which bolstered his natural defenses, making short work of his injuries.

Vaughn and Alana entered the Arch room followed quietly by Natalie and Kaida.

"Everything is ready," Jack confirmed.

"I trust your judgment," replied Vaughn, "Remember, there won't be any second chances." He eyed the collection of stones and sighed. Jack knew exactly what Vaughn was thinking—the pile seemed perilously meager for the task they were undertaking.

The door slid open again as Andy and Maude entered. Andy checked the preparations. Everything seemed ready. Timing would be critical if their plan was to succeed. Kaida calculated that two groups would need to beam down between the two holes they had previously created, combining them into one huge hole. Hopefully they would be able to control the flow, allowing enough mana to reach the surface, creating a cushion to absorb the rest before the entire barrier collapsed.

"I'm still not sure how this is going to work," Jack mumbled.

"Think of it like rain," replied Kaida, sighing. "When it rains lightly what happens?"

"We get wet?"

"Besides that."

"Not much I guess."

"Now think what happens when it rains really hard, or even hails," asked Kaida.

"Things get damaged, even broken"

"Exactly," Kaida said with pride, seeing progress being made. "Now, what happens when it rains really hard into a puddle?"

"Mmm, I dunno." replied Jack.

"That's probably because not much happens," replied Kaida, losing confidence in her pupil. "Think of it this way. The magical energy is like rain and the cushion we're trying to make is the puddle that will protect the Earth from when the real storm hits. Got it?"

"Ya… err…. no."

Kaida sighed again. "Just go, goat boy."

***

Across the room Andy and Vaughn sat together. Gone was Vaughn's earlier confidence, replaced by a newfound humility and deep respect for the young man sitting across from him.

"Vaughn, I…" Andy said.

"I know, Andy. I can only blame myself for what happened," Vaughn said. "I probably would have done the same thing had our positions been reversed."

Andy bowed his head in silence. Vaughn's words had relieved some of the guilt he felt since their fight and proved how precarious the line was between right and revenge. A line Andy was determined never to cross again.

"Come," continued Vaughn. "We have work to do. Give the rest of us a few minutes before you and Maude follow. That way we can move the stones out of the way."

"Vaughn, if anything…"

"It will be as it shall be. We will see you soon."

Andy nodded in agreement. The Arch flashed leaving Andy and Maude alone.

"Do you really think this will work?" Maude asked nervously.

"It has to," he replied. Together they walked toward the Arch and got into position. Andy pressed the activation runes. The Archway flickered briefly then died.

"What happened?"

"I… I don't know." He frantically pounded on the runes again. They remained dark and lifeless.

"C'mon," Andy ran to the door and down the hall to the command room. The holograph of the Earth was still visible. He inspected the image. Sure enough, one giant scar on the barrier was visible. The edges of it were slowly turning downward, prying the barrier from its secure loft high about the Earth.

"It worked. It's collapsing!" exclaimed Maude.

"Yes, but why won't the Arch work?" Andy's hands flew over the controls, searching for an answer. "The others must have gotten through since the holes have merged into one giant tear in the barrier. I can't locate the Travel Arch on the planet. It's as though it… vanished."

"What do we do, Andy?"

"We need to get back to Earth. There's not much we can do way out here."

The plan was working, so far, but… If something happened to the Arch, could something have happened to the others as well? Andy's mind sifted through possible contingency plans. *What now?*

"But how are we supposed to get back? Can you teleport us?" Maude voiced the thoughts racing through Andy's head. The distance involved was far greater than he had tried before, and there were two of them… true he was far stronger than ever before thanks to the abundance of raw mana engulfing the moon but would it be enough? If the teleport worked, would he have the strength to deal with whatever had gone wrong once he got there? There was only one option he could think of.

"We're going out there!"

***

The Earth shimmered into existence just as the Travel Arch exploded. Chunks of white marble were strewn everywhere as the mages scrambled along the ground seeking cover from the wreckage.

"Protect the batteries!" Vaughn yelled as he covered his head with his arms. Alana spotted a large hunk hurling towards Vaughn and instinctively dove to his side, knocking him out of the way. Kaida spotted a Foundation Stone rolling away from the Arch and ran after it. She reached out to grab the stone just as a violet bolt of energy struck it. The explosion shattered the stone and sent her flying through the air. She landed with a dull thump, blood streaming from a nasty gash in her head, unmoving.

"Kaida!" Natalie screamed and ran towards her. Another

bolt flew past and struck the remains of the Travel Arch as she dove to reach her friend.

"Kaida! Kaida! Can you hear me?"

Jack recovered quickly from the initial explosion and began scanning the tree lined perimeter of the clearing for their adversary. A flurry of violet bolts flew overhead, forcing him to the ground. Mocking laughter filled the air.

"Mark?" Nat's question hung in the air, answered by a volley of violet energy bolts.

"Finally, I'll destroy you for all of the suffering you've caused. You arrogant thugs! Did you really think I wouldn't notice the mana pouring in around this place?" Mark cackled again, clearly savoring the moment.

"Jack! Nat! Deal with him!" ordered Vaughn through the din. "We don't have any time to lose. Alana and I will manage the mana."

"Deal with me? Sending your lackeys to play with me? I'm hurt, Vaughn, really. Won't you play with me, too?" Mark fired a bolt at Vaughn, but it was intercepted by Jack.

"Let's do this!" Jack roared as he charged Mark. Alana wasted no time. She opened the remaining Foundation Stones with a wave of her hand. The mana they contained shimmered and sparked as it was released and eagerly soaked up by the land around them.

Vaughn scrambled to his feet and searched the sky for any sign of the hole they had created. He didn't have to look far before he spotted it. A shiver ran down his spine as he prepared himself.

***

"This way!" Andy yelled as he dragged Maude behind him through the halls.

"What do you mean, 'go out there'?" she asked.

"We're too far away from the hole here," he explained between strained breaths. "Magic takes more energy to perform the farther away you are from your target, and I'm going to need every bit of energy I can muster to pull this off. I need to be closer." They turned a corner and came to a dead end. A row of lockers lined the wall in front of them. Andy hurriedly opened the first locker and began rummaging through it.

"That's great for you! You may be able to conjure up some space survival bubble or something but I can't," Maude argued emphatically.

"Don't worry about it," he said as he pulled a white one piece suit with a thick blue collar and cuffs out of the locker and threw it to Maude before pulling out one for himself. "The suit will keep you alive. We found them when we were looking for batteries."

"You... you can't be serious?"

"Put it on. We don't have time to argue," Andy stated, careful not to upset her further. Maude's skepticism was plain on her face.

"And then what? We're just going to take a leisurely stroll towards the Earth? Do you know how long that will take?"

"The Travel Arch on this end still works. We won't be able to aim it as accurately as before but I think I can still use it to get us back or at least close enough for me to teleport us safely where we need to be."

"But..."

"Maude, I need you out there." Andy stared deep into her eyes as he spoke.

"Okay." Maude lowered her gaze. "Andy, I trust you."

Andy let out a small sigh. "Let's go." They dressed swiftly in silence before heading back to the arch room. The Travel Arch loomed quietly over them as Andy added a rune here and modified a rune there on its smooth white surface. Finally, Andy motioned for Maude to stand next to him. He adjusted the collar on her suit and activated its runes before activating his own suit.

"Let's go," he said.

Maude nodded in acknowledgement. Andy gripped Maude's hand tightly and waved his hand at the arch. A flash of light swallowed them, sending them towards the Earth.

Holy! was all Andy could think as they floated in space. Before him loomed the gaping hole in the barrier. Maude held onto him with both hands. He remembered how Otiltis's instruments had dutifully relayed the data on the hole to him. Seeing it in person though was something else entirely. As the awe wore off, Andy realized that the hole was still rapidly increasing in size. It had almost doubled in area since their companions had left.

"Maude, we have to work fast. I'll try and stop it from expanding. You need to try and slow the magical energy from entering. Absorb it or block it or something."

Her face was a sickly white as she still hadn't become completely comfortable in the mana-rich environment. She stared down at the planet below them, unblinking.

"Maude! Stay with me."

"Okay, I'll try." She breathed deeply as she extended one hand towards the hole and gripped Andy firmly with the other.

"Hopefully we can buy them some time before everything breaks loose." Andy focused deeply on the mana surrounding him and formed a giant ring around the opening, trying to brace the crumbling edges of the barrier. The strain was incredible. *Please don't let us be too late.*

***

Energy bolts flew erratically as the battle raged. Vaughn was thankful that Jack and Natalie were keeping Mark busy.

He and Alana were fixated on the expanding hole above them. Enough energy was flowing through it now to be seen and felt by any living being. The energy was a tangible entity plummeting down from the heavens. Vaughn swore it looked like honey dripping down towards them.

"Here it comes," Alana yelled above the raucous combat. She and Vaughn knew what to do. They opened themselves to the energy, acting as sponges, drawing it towards them and into them. Vaughn coughed as mana saturated the air around him. Never before had he tried to direct so much energy at once. Alana too, staggered, unprepared for the onslaught of energy they faced. The ground rumbled beneath their feet.

The sudden surge in magical energy affected everyone, empowering Jack and Natalie. Mark stumbled as the wave of energy washed over them. His Misorbium garments glowed brighter than ever, straining to absorb the energy around him.

"Impossible!" Mark said furiously. "I…"

Jack tackled him before he could finish, knocking the wind out of Mark as they sprawled on the ground.

"Believe it!" Jack yelled, his fist raised. Mark's head bounced off the ground as Jack struck him repeatedly. Mark's clothes flared as Misorbium drained the mana from his opponent. Jack slumped forward, unconscious, his body unable to keep up with the surge and ebb of magic coursing through him.

"Nooo!" Natalie screamed.

Laughing, Mark rolled Jack's limp body off him and stood up. His eyes, ablaze with triumph, stared directly at Natalie. "You're next!"

Alana choked back tears as she watched Natalie fall to the ground. Her grief turned to dread as Mark gazed over to where she and Vaughn were engrossed in their work. Mark walked towards them, alight in purple flames as the Misorbium lining his clothes nullified the mana around him. He stopped just beyond the edge of the energy stream surrounding Vaughn and Alana.

"Vaughn!" cried Alana.

"I see him. Don't worry," replied Vaughn, trying to sound convincing.

"So, old man," Mark sneered as he approached, "it appears your luck's finally run out."

"I've never believed in luck," said Vaughn defiantly. "Only those who lack the courage to believe in themselves put themselves in the hands of providence."

"Yadda yadda yadda, DIE!" Mark cried and ripped a huge ball of energy away from Vaughn.

"That tickled," Vaughn said, smiling. "Surely you can do better."

"You can't stop me!" yelled Mark. "Your peons can't save you!"

"Then come here, boy," beckoned Vaughn, "and give it your best shot!"

***

Furious, Mark hurtled himself at Vaughn and Alana. His clothes flared purple as he entered the eye of the storm. The onslaught of energy halted him in his tracks. Mark convulsed, trying to adapt to the swarming energy as a penguin acclimatized to the Antarctic would try to adapt to the Sierra desert. Raw energy crackled around him as he continued to absorb more and more mana. His aura glowed brighter by the second. Vaughn instinctively looked at Alana but her intuition had already told her what to do. Together they released a portion of the energy they were channeling into themselves and directed it towards their assailant. Mark's expression changed from fury to shock to resignation, as his aura shot from lavender to pure white. Overloaded beyond his limits, Mark vanished in one final burst of light.

***

The strain was unbearable. Andy couldn't tell how long they had been out there, but it felt like forever. Floating next to him, Maude shared the same grim expression. Regret crossed his mind for involving her in his hastily conceived plan. Still, he believed his plan was the right one. *Hold on Andy*, he said to himself. *Hold on.*

***

Vaughn and Alana floated in the current of streaming energy. Their bodies shimmered as they struggled to slow its progress. The toll on their bodies was rapidly surpassing any conceivable limits.

"Have you seen my dog!" Vaughn screamed. Strangely, Vaughn didn't know what had come over him until he felt it. His skin boiled grotesquely as ghostly apparitions freed themselves from his body. The torrent of mana was rekindling the stolen souls Vaughn had nourished himself with over the years, allowing them to break free of their earthly confinements. *How fitting*, thought Vaughn. He looked over at Alana and witnessed the same fountain of souls springing from her body.

***

"Andy! Help!"

"Maude!" Andy cried in vain as he saw Maude spasm uncontrollably before him. He felt the surge in pressure as the stream of energy flowing towards her vanished and the full flood of mana bore down on his reinforcements. It was too much for him. The strain on his body was no longer bearable. He feared he might be ripped into millions of tiny slivers if he didn't acquiesce to the forces around him. The walls of the magical shell cracked and shattered. Large pieces around the hole broke free and dissolved into the raging stream of pure mana. Desperately, Andy clung to fragments of the shell, trying to restore what he could, only to be dragged into the stream, sending himself and Maude plummeting towards the planet below.

***

With every soul freed, Vaughn and Alana's bodies became less solid, until they were nearly transparent. Vaughn and Alana locked eyes one final time. *This is it. There's nothing more we can do.* Their bodies hung in the air as the mana consumed them. With a blinding flash of light, they were gone, leaving the mana to mushroom around them, no regulation remained to hinder its progress.

The released mana billowed over the land, bending and distorting everything it passed over, leaving behind a shiny, sparkling landscape in its wake. Grass was greener, lakes were bluer, air was fresher and more satisfying. Buildings creaked as the fabric of space warped and absorbed the rush of turbulent energy. Stores and shopping malls quaked and shuddered, but did not crumble. High rise apartments and offices shook but did not shatter.

***

Jack looked on in awe and horror, realizing the sacrifices Vaughn and Alana had made. Success had come with a heavy price. Vaughn and Alana had bought the time needed for enough mana to reach the surface, seeding the land to cushion the torrent of magic that followed, with their lives. He could still feel the Earth, now oiled with mana, as it bent and flexed with the torrent or magic washing over it. Jack struggled to sit up, knowing that some of his friends still weren't accounted for. He couldn't rest until they were.

Chapter 35

Homecoming

Nigel kicked his feet up onto the coffee table as he settled in to watch television for the night. He had been celebrating his return to London with Colin earlier by blending the last of his hand-picked beans with a choice Columbian roast he really enjoyed. Colin had enjoyed it as well, especially after he had added an ample amount of Irish whiskey from his personal stash to the brew. Colin enjoyed it so much that he was snoring merrily in the next room. Nigel didn't mind. It was through Colin that he had found his latest job, working as a subway transit officer. After the whole Tanzanian affair, he was looking for something nice and quiet to keep him busy. A loud snore interrupted his reverie. Turning his head, he quickly checked on Colin before flipping to the evening news.

"Tonight on World News, our top story, reports of spectacular lights and astounding happenings are pouring in from all across the globe. We take you now live to our news correspondent on the scene, Bona."

"Thanks, Dan. Earlier today, sightings of unexplainable phenomena started pouring in, starting with a spectacular light show that shook the very earth beneath our feet. Since the initial rumblings, reports of people, mostly teenagers, accomplishing incredible feats have swamped our correspondents. One woman reports sending her son to the grocery store some five miles away, and the boy returning instantly with everything she'd asked for. Customers in the upscale department store, AllMart, were astonished to see a girl trying on a dress. While not exactly earth-shattering, witnesses say the dress was changing color and restyling itself around her body, as if by magic. A pig farmer near Letwenshire phoned in to tell us that some of his hogs were escaping their pens even though the fences were six feet high and the gates remained closed and locked. He was quoted as saying, 'It's almost as if they flew over the rails. I can't explain it any other… *zzZzt*."

Static blared on television sets everywhere before the image of a young man with big green eyes and disheveled strawberry blond hair filled the screen.

"Greetings, I'm sure everyone is puzzled by recent events. Please try not to be alarmed. I assure you the world is not ending, in fact, a new beginning is upon us. Something lost to us for thousands of years has returned: magic. Some of you will undoubtedly be more affected than others by this event. Since we have lived without magic for so long there is bound to be confusion about what it can do and how to use it safely. I don't have time to go into the specifics at the moment. I just want to stress that magic is not something to be feared or despised. It can be used for good or bad, but above all, it is a natural part of our universe, and a natural part of us.

"In the coming days I'm sure many of you will recognize your unique abilities. I would like to invite those people to come to me and my fellow mages for training and guidance in using their new talents. More details will come shortly. Until then, be well and don't panic. Farewell."

Zzzzt. Televisions everywhere refocused on their regularly scheduled programming, including the face of a very confused news anchor.

Jack and Andy set the new shelf snugly against the wall. It was a busy time for them. Kaida was still in bed, but was expected to make a full recovery. Her wounds were the most severe of them all. They were all glad that the crisis was over. They were busy blowing off steam in their own ways.

Andy visited Westbrook often to check in with his mother. She had seen his impromptu speech on television and was eager to wring every detail of his adventures out of him. Natalie was having a blast teleporting around the world. So far no one else had been found with her talents and she was relishing the attention she gathered every time she appeared out of thin air. She'd even heard reports that a fan club dedicated to her had sprung up in Japan. She was also busy instructing the few magically inclined she crossed paths with on how to reach their island home, christened New Baurum. Jack was lying low, enjoying some well deserved rest and fishing off the coast of their underground lair on his homemade raft.

Maude had taken the death of her brother hard, but words couldn't express the impact the loss of Leo had on her. She had said goodbye to Andy only yesterday, leaving temporarily to look after funeral arrangements for her uncle, but it felt a lot longer. Leo had always wanted to be buried close to his beloved Baurum'tatus and she was determined for him to get his wish. Andy couldn't help but wonder if Leo's death - Leo the lion, king of the jungle, had been forseen by the oracle. The remains of Terra Protectra were scattered across the globe. Maude vowed to clean up the mess before returning to the island community.

Andy carefully placed the Oracle of Rolimus in the center of the shelf before adding its companions. Jack helped him set the crystallized remains of Vaughn and Alana on either side of the Oracle. Neither had displayed any special abilities, much less talked to anyone, but they weren't taking any chances. Now that magic had come home to the Earth, you never could tell what would happen next.

Epilogue

Violent gusts of wind knocked over a pair of lawn chairs on the beach. The tide was coming in, bringing a storm with it. Ominous clouds rolled over the horizon promising rain.

In a dimly lit chamber far beneath the Earth's surface, an energy meter set off a low wail. The magical energy sinking through the earth had finally reached a concentration level high enough to trigger the device. Lights in a nearby underground alcove flared to life, illuminating a sleek crystal box about seven feet long and three feet wide. Its multifaceted sides caught the light and refracted it into its component colors on the walls surrounding the container. The siren changed from a wail to a rhythmic beeping, and on the fourth beep the top of the container began to rise, releasing a thick vapor into the chamber.

A long slender hand reached up into the open air and flexed its fingers before grasping the edge of the sleeping chamber. Long nails clicked against the crystal surface as the hand gripped the frame tightly, steadying the occupant as he climbed out of the container. Heavily, the sleeper leaned against the wall as his legs re-familiarized themselves with walking. His eyes were half closed, his head cocked to one side, as if listening to a faint melody. A smile played across his lips as he tested his too long idle vocal cords.

"It is time."

About the Author

Born in Edmonton, Alberta, A. A. Powley's life-long love affair with science fiction and fantasy books took root at an early age. But, only after pursuing many alternative occupations ranging from Wal-Mart Department Manager, to Surveyor, to Computer Analyst, did he allow his passion for stories to sway his career path.

He began writing seriously in 2006, resulting in *The Oracle of Y'alan*, a tale of a young boy born special and persecuted for it. Today, A. A. Powley still calls Alberta home and is hard at work on his next project.

ISBN 142514659-7